DAWN OF THE TRADE

PRAISE FOR DAWN OF THE TRADE

"*Dawn of the Trade* grabs you from the first page. A compelling story you shouldn't miss."
—Brian Drake, author of the *Sam Raven* series

"An exhilarating, high-stakes crime story with twists and turns from start to finish."
—January Bain, author of *City of Lies*

"Jarrett Mazza writes in a distinctive style that hits like a punch in the gut and yanks the reader into a vividly realized blend of thrills, excitement, and compelling characters. DAWN OF THE TRADE is a great debut novel, and I look forward to seeing what the author comes up with next!"
—Best-selling author, James Reasoner

"Following in the footsteps of *Roadhouse*, Mazza's *Dawn of the Trade* is all action. It tells the story of a man with a code who makes himself at home with a community of like-minded warriors: the Doormen. The night club setting—NYC's the Conquistador—is so atmospheric that it's a major character all on its own!"
—John Corr, author of *Eight Times Up*

"Jarrett Mazza has written one hell of a good book with *Dawn of the Trade*. His protagonist, Jon Haze, a tough-as-nails former marine, is the kind of guy you'd want next to you when your back's against the wall. This one has it all: excellent writing, fabulous action scenes, intriguing plotting, and best of all, it's the first in a new series. Do yourself a favor and pick up this first Doorman novel. You won't regret it."

–Michael A. Black, author of the *Trackdown* series

DAWN OF THE TRADE

DOORMAN
BOOK 1

JARRETT MAZZA

**ROUGH
EDGES
PRESS**

Rough Edges Press
An Imprint of Wolfpack Publishing
1707 E. Diana Street
Tampa, FL 33610

roughedgespress.com

Paperback ISBN 978-1-68549-729-3
eBook ISBN 978-1-68549-728-6
LCCN 2024937451

For Mom.
Always there, always prepared.

DAWN OF THE TRADE

PROLOGUE

THE LAST SIGHT HE SAW WAS THE FACE OF HIS BEST friend, bleeding and burned. The building was hit by an IED. Commonly known as an *Improvised Explosive Device*, it was buried in a gutter outside. The one who died was more than just a friend to Marine Jon Haze. He was a brother and he was a guardian. He was the same guardian who Jon swore he'd watch out for because it was his job.

Before the building collapsed, Jon was trekking through a broken house. He faced down a blistering desert sun as it warmed his chest and face.

"I wish I had a beer right about now," said James, the other Marine.

"Make that two," replied Jon.

Side-by-side, Jon and James had enlisted at the same time. They joined the same unit, and now, they were both knocking down the same doors in the same country. Another squadron of Marines trailed six steps behind and combed the other nearby streets.

"What do you plan to do once you get back?" Jon asked.

James's M16 was hung across his chest, the same as Jon's. Before Jon kicked in the door, he waited for James to answer.

"Why do you always ask *me* that question?" James asked.

This was not the first time Jon had said this to James. He did so before, but too many days were spent in the sand. Now, the thought of home was what kept Jon going. The thought of him at his house drinking a cold brewski was beyond alluring.

Often it was all he had. It reminded Jon of what was waiting for him *if* he returned.

He just needed more time.

"Gonna do the same as you."

"Same as *me?*" asked Jon. He held his rifle and looked at his friend.

The memories of what they had seen began flooding in. He enjoyed all of them. Jon Haze's vision was fuzzy. For a second, he wasn't all here. He was back to living in simpler times. With his mind constantly forgetting, Jon often lost focus.

All of this was happening again.

"Same as—" Before James said more, a harsh whistling cut through the air.

James froze. Initially, his expression was firm but now a look of absolute awe had washed over. Jon was this way. Then, a second later, he wasn't. Shrapnel pierced James's skull and opened his forehead. Blood sprayed Jon's face while James fell.

"Bombs!" shouted another Marine.

There was no feeling left in Jon's body after this.

When he looked down, he saw James wasn't the only one hit. Part of Jon's right leg was obliterated. All that was left *was* his left.

"Jon, you had the lookout. You didn't see! What the hell? What the hell?"

"No...I..." As his friend lay dying in Jon's arms, his last thought morphed into pricks that poked at his every nerve. Jon was about to explain when this thought ceased. So did the rest of his body. He was at war, but he was gone. He was gone the same as James.

Jon sobbed until everything went silent. Now the war was over and Jon was *home*. It was just like he always wanted it to be. However, now Jon was overwhelmed with thoughts he could not control. He wrestled with nightmares and he woke at the same time every day. He screamed James's name, until it was all he could hear and all he could think of. He continued to scream and didn't care if anyone heard or not. He screamed until he fell asleep and wished for another dream. None would come. Now there were no more dreams.

Now, there were only nightmares.

CHAPTER 1
THE GAME

PRESENT DAY

Jon could have busted this asshole's nose and watched his teeth spill onto the dance floor. The music was blaring. It produced a hard ringing that rattled Jon's eardrums and locked him inside a vibrating shell.

But then again, that was the job: watch, assess, move, *react*.

Being a bouncer is a game of worst-case scenario versus best. Right now, Jon Haze thought only about the situation unfolding at the bar. He recalled his training.

Words are more important than actions, never underestimate any situation, and always use your best judgment.

Jon never denied the logic or the value in this statement.

The tussle started with two boys screaming at each other while two girls squeezed in between. They were trying to keep the boys calm. A group of spectators huddled around the belligerent fools. Jon was there just the same. It started with a shove, only a little contact, but then this is how these things usually began.

After this, someone hits, there's a push, and then a strike. This was the moment whereby the bouncers were supposed to step in and put an end to the *conflict*. This is known as the call, their call as *Doormen*.

Jon was still new to the profession. However, Jon wanted the first fight to happen as fast as possible. He always waited for someone else to make the first move. Looking around, Jon spotted two more of his fellow Doormen.

Danix Slade and Sam Vaughn were both more experienced than Jon. When Jon saw them, he nodded to show he was on the same page. He stomped to make his presence known. His intent was always to deescalate, never to intensify. Still, Jon was, and always would be, a Marine. At the same time, he was learning to control his imposing demeanor.

Now was *not* the time to push. Next to the group of knuckleheads, Jon went in. He heard the voice of his mentor, the legendary cooler, Mr. Addison Krowe.

"Watch the eyes, be ready for anything, and use your words. Always, always be cool."

"Come on, fellas, let's take it easy, yeah?"

"Fuck you!"

The expletives spewed back and forth like ping-pong balls. The two drunk men beaked off just as Jon began to close in. Anything could happen. And so, flexing his fists, Jon considered the moves he was trained to deploy. Wrist grab, headlock, and joint strike were all solid options. Maybe Jon could deliver a hit to the knee. And, *if worst came to worst*, the tackle, and then the chokehold could come later.

Difficult, but Addison's voice continued. *"Use words."*

"Come on, fellas," Jon advised. "Let's take things down a notch, yeah?"

Hand up, Jon slipped it between the boys. And then, about to neutralize and hopefully repair, a loud gunshot sprang up from the background. Jon shuddered as the violent noise forced a quiver. He ducked and fell to one knee.

Now, he wasn't in the club like he once was. Now, all he could see were faces.

Now he was back on the battlefield. He was back at war.

Jon's doctor assured him that PTSD was real. It could lead to some serious changes.

The ground quaked and Jon was back to hearing the thunderous sounds of cannons and grenades. Fist sliding back, an insurgent shouted and stomped. Jon staggered. The man in the club was wielding something. It could be anything! Jon wasn't sure.

What Jon saw...could be a grenade.

No one would bring that in here, to New York's most respectable nightclub.

But then there it was. It was a grenade, at least that's what Jon Haze saw.

In the midst of making his decision, Jon was caught by the strong hands of a friend. He was being held by another bouncer, Danix. A former SEAL and MMA fighter, Danix was one of the oldest bouncers employed. Stepping past Jon, the fight continued. Jon's lack of vision was what allowed him to capture only fragments of the ongoing sight.

What he saw last was Danix's fist. Danix wrapped the first knucklehead in a choke and Jon was thinking about the words he should have used at the time. This was his job, and yet, he did not finish it. Sam was in the middle too. With his arms spread, Sam did his best to keep everyone apart and away, dividing the ones who were the closest, what Jon saw later was nothing more than a bunch of bumping bodies. It was like they were all being tossed in a salad. So long as Jon kept remembering the past, then maybe he wasn't cut out for a trade determined by the present.

He needed to be here. Always here.

Should he not be, then Jon Haze—former Marine and former good guy—would have no choice but to do the same. If he wasn't there, then he might as well not be anywhere.

He might as well be dead.

His world was a powder keg. It was about to light up like the Fourth of fucking July. Jon Haze wanted to stop it before it did.

CHAPTER 2
BACK

TWO MONTHS EARLIER

At home, Jon lay comfortably in his bed. He slept until sunrise and thought he heard his alarm. Instead, it was a yelping as well as a shuffling of footsteps. Initially adverse to meeting people at this time, Jon was being encouraged by his mother to see more friends.

Jon looked at himself in the mirror behind his door. With no shirt, there were scars etched along Jon's chest. Like lashings, broken lines scribbled along the Marine's body. He was also without a leg. While Jon accepted this long ago, it was only now just starting to get easier.

Jon closed his eyes as new thoughts began to emerge. He could hear bombs, screams, and all the other terrifying sounds of war.

Head down, Jon followed the steps outlined by his therapist. This was a service mandated to all vets after they returned home. Jon was to go see his doctor three times a week, which was not much, but it was helpful sometimes. When Jon wasn't in therapy regularly, he was up at four in the morning and training at his local gym. Jon lifted heavy weights and ran several miles. This helped him most. Yet now, as Jon's mother called him from the kitchen, he knew it was because someone was here to see him.

When Jon saw who it was, he was glad.

"Billy?" Jon asked. He was taken aback by his friend's arrival.

"Jon!" A boy with slick hair stampeded into Jon's bedroom while screaming.

Billy was one of Jon's oldest friends. He didn't care whether or not Jon was dressed when he abruptly entered. Then again, that was Billy. There was so little he cared for. There was even less he felt he needed to respect. In this case, it was a person's space, and that person was Jon.

"Jon, Billy's here," Jon's mother stated. Showing a clear lack of enthusiasm, Jon's mom was Betsy. She was a kind, patient, and sweet woman who loved her son, and Jon knew how much she did. It's why he still lived at home, with her. While Jon knew it, he didn't often say it out loud and did nothing to let her know how much he did.

"Yeah, Mom," Jon said, still unimpressed. "I can see him standing right here in front of me."

"Hell yeah, he can," replied Billy. He bounced off Jon's bed and joyfully hopped around. "Thanks a lot, Mrs. Haze, for letting me come in and see my boy here. Know it's been hard, but hey, what are friends for, yeah?"

"Yeah, Billy, I understand." Jon's mother stood in the hallway.

She was polite enough to wait outside because Jon wasn't fully dressed. The same couldn't be said for Billy, however. Falling smack onto Jon's mattress again, he dropped in a loud plop. Then, Billy casually stretched and tucked his hand under Jon's pillow.

"I understand that my boy needs some time away, out in the open, among friends," Billy said.

"Out?" asked Jon.

"Out where?" Betsy joined Jon in questioning.

Jon watched as Billy grinned. His face was so smug and goofy. Always spontaneous and the first to step in to try something new, Jon looked at his friend and considered going with him.

Yet, so far, he hadn't decided.

"Out somewhere good, somewhere new. See, what I'm talkin' about is one of the hottest clubs in this city. It's the most exclusive and the most desirable. It's one of the most intense nightlife destinations of all time. I'm talking about...The Conquistador!"

Billy's syllables were spoken with much joy and laughter. Billy gasped and further expressed his chief and most wanted desire.

"The Conquista...what?" asked Jon.

"What's that?" asked Jon's mom.

"It's a club," said Billy. "But not just any club," he added. "See, The Conquistador is *the* club. My buddy who works at the door hooked me up. He's gonna give us a booth tonight, and I wanna treat my boy over here to a few drinks, a few songs, and maybe even a few ladies too."

Jon's mom's eyes rolled. Jon's did too.

"My way of saying welcome back and thank you for your service." Billy gave a corny salute and Jon sighed. While he hardly believed Billy, he appreciated the gesture. *Sort of.*

Jon was not keen on people giving him thanks. It was so boring and expected. But, if Jon was going to be honest, a night out wasn't the worst idea. It actually made him feel excited to move around and remember where he was.

He was home.

"A booth, huh?"

"A *big* booth," said Billy, arms spread and still bouncing excitedly.

"Cool." Head down, Jon continued to consider the possibility. He really *did* want to go.

"Are you sure going to a club is really the best idea right now, Jon?"

Jon shrugged. Always, his mother was concerned. She cared for Jon's well-being more than ever before. She treated him like he was this fragile little thing that needed to be protected at all times. To be honest, Jon felt like a vase. Even the slightest bump or nudge and he would fall and shatter. Despite his mother's caution and frequent pestering, now was the time for Jon to show her how he was capable. Nightclubs, while not *exactly* Jon's thing, still appealed to the Marine. It did enough to get his ass out of bed.

Looking at Billy with a sly and thrilled expression, Jon provided an answer.

"Sure, I'm in. I'll go."

"Sweet!" Billy sprang off the bed while Jon stood there in his boxer shorts. He stared at himself in the mirror and checked his body again.

"Let's grab a ride for ten then, yeah? Does that work?"

Jon nodded at Billy while continuing to inspect his reflection. Counting the scars on his chest, more memories surged and Jon closed his eyes.

"Yeah," said Jon, clawing at the memories. "I'll go."

"Awesome," said Billy. "See ya then, brother."

"See ya then."

Upon exiting, Jon peripherally monitored Billy's movements. His mother stepped aside, and before Billy left, he turned to give the final word.

"Oh, and make sure you wear somethin' classy, you know?" Billy asked Jon.

"Right." Truthfully, Jon knew this already.

However, he couldn't think of the last time whereby something he wore was considered classy. In spite of this, Jon had a few ideas about the wardrobe he would try tonight.

"Will do."

"Great."

———

Jon skulked out of his house at the recommended time. Deep in thought, Jon looked at his mother as she inched herself closer. "Are you sure about this?"

With no comments left to make, Jon's stoicism remained.

He liked to think he looked the part. Mostly, he felt sort of in good spirits. But the more he stared at himself, the more he noticed. And, the more he noticed, the more Jon could hear his mother both within *and* outside his own mind.

"Are you sure you want to do this?" Jon didn't have much to add.

"Yes," he said. "I need a night out. I need it. I *need* it."

Leaving his house, silence followed Jon like a shadow. With his eyes back to being closed, Jon focused. Why he did, he didn't know. Outside, it was so quiet that Jon could barely hear himself breathe.

CHAPTER 3
NOTICED

ALTHOUGH NOT IN AN EXPENSIVE SUIT, JON OWNED only one. At the club, he stood in a line of fifty people. He and Billy were together, waiting and talking. Among a cascade of lavishly dressed attendees, both boys stood under a glowing sign and stained-glass windows. They were now near the royal entrance to the palace/nightclub known as The Conquistador. While not a clubbing expert by any means, Jon did admire the setting.

What he saw so far, he liked a lot.

Despite being based in New York, Las Vegas did hold the title for being the pinnacle of nightclubs. So far, The Conquistador was living up to its startling image. Jon looked through the windows and heard boisterous sounds echoing from the inside.

Right now, Jon found it to be quite accelerating. He could feel his heart racing. His fingers twitched as the excitement continued to build. Lively and packed with energy, Jon wore a pair of mediocre loafers while Billy lit a cigarette before making his way back inside.

"Bro, you're gonna love it once we get in there. Trust me."

"Yeah," said Jon, not skeptical, except he did have a few questions. "But why aren't we allowed in? Didn't you say we got a booth?"

"Sure," said Billy. "But you think we're the only one who's got a booth? Club's got like fifteen, bro. There all organized differently depending on how much you're willing to pay. And right now, we're at the bottom, sadly."

"Booths have tiers?" asked Jon.

"Here they do," said Billy.

"Right." Jon was feeling slightly self-conscious about his prosthetic. He didn't know why. Whatever anyone could do, Jon could do too. He tried letting this insecurity go. Still waiting, Jon examined all the potential people who were about to make their way inside.

From what Jon could see, the age of the crowd fell between twenty and thirty-five. This was the standard demographic for people frequenting clubs. Right now, there were girls standing in sparkling dresses, wearing short skirts and high heels. They wore sequins-styled outfits and their hair was long and coiffed. Their faces were covered in fat streaks of gleaming makeup. The boys wore suits similar to Jon's, with collared shirts and ties. Donning leather shoes and sneakers, mostly Jordans, the last time Jon saw a crowd this large was days before he enlisted.

Tonight, it was a comfortable evening. The weather was crisp and soothing. After twenty minutes of waiting, the line began to move. Jon closed in on the entrance.

"Yo, yo! We're goin' in!" said Billy. "We're goin' fucking in!"

"Great."

Following the line, Jon stayed close to his friend. Now eyeing a group of girls, Billy winked. He pivoted back before cheerily greeting them as they headed inside. Moving toward the glittering entrance, the passage was arched. For Jon, it felt like he was about to slip into a glorious palace fit for a Pharaoh.

However, that was the intention of this place.

In its regal setting, The Conquistador mimicked the timeless luxuries from a time long past. It was inspired by Pharaohs and Caesars and Jon's gaze twinkled as he entered the golden castle. Almost in, Jon walked up to a towering black man guarding both the doors. Big and broad-shouldered, the man was an easy six-nine and an even easier three-hundred.

"Hold up just one sec."

Jon stopped. He respected boundaries as well as a person's space. He glanced at the name tag and saw the man's name: *Jamal*.

"We'll let you in in just a minute, all right?" Jamal spoke to Jon calmly and with respect.

"Sounds good." Jon stood with this Jamal, the man at the door, while Billy stayed a few steps behind.

Phone out, Jon saw that Jamal was sending a text.

"Hey," said the doorman.

Jon was so focused on the doorway he forgot how close Jamal was standing.

This man's massive body made him impossible to miss. Turning his head, Jon looked at Jamal, whose eyes were down. While Jon was somewhat used to his prosthetic, he knew when someone noticed it, except Jamal smirked when catching a glimpse.

Such a reaction was not always the first, but sometimes it did come later.

"Your leg," Jamal said. "You *wearin'* one?"

Jon squinted almost to a scowl. How this man noticed Jon's leg was either very impressive or very insulting. Frankly, Jon didn't care which was which.

"Why?"

"Sorry," Jamal said. "Didn't mean to offend ya. It's just, I know a war injury when I see one, and I know a former Marine when I see one too."

"Aw yeah?" said Jon, less offended than before. If he was standing in the company of another Marine, then he was not a stranger, not anymore. "And you would know that how?"

"Served too," said Jamal.

"Really?" said Jon. "Where?"

"Two tours. Afghanistan. You?"

Jon heard the gunshots like he was back in the desert, back in the shit. However, now was the time whereby his therapist would tell him to focus and drown out all noises. He needed to remember where he was, and Jon was here, not there.

He was home.

"*Three.*"

"Damn," Jamal said to Jon. "In the shit too, huh?"

"Yeah," Jon replied, thinking about James. He could still hear his screams. "Right in the shit."

Jon expected the Black doorman to ask more about his leg, but Jamal turned back at the door. Jamal gripped the rope and jerked his head to another man. This next man was a bouncer with peppered hair, a pockmarked complexion, and thick eyebrows spread above his eyes like wet paint.

Nodding, Jon waited.

"We good to go on in?" asked Billy. He was speaking to Jamal as well as the other bouncer. He had a name tag too.

His said *Sam*.

"Yeah. Go on in," said Sam.

Billy sauntered and Jon followed closely behind. Before making his way inside, Jamal stopped and offered his hand to Jon.

"Nice to meet you, brother. Have fun, yeah?"

Jon looked up and down. The word *brother* was the right one to use. A brother, Jon most certainly was.

"You too."

"Be safe."

Smiling, Jamal nodded and gave his respect. What Jon gave in return was a salute. It was a way of acknowledging those who served the same as he did. It wasn't forced. For Jon, it was just what he did and all he knew how to do.

Respect was the pillar of the military, and Jon didn't just bring bad memories and trauma home with him. He brought lessons and truths too.

CHAPTER 4
FACELESS AND UNMOVING

SMIRKING ALL THE WAY IN, JON FELT APPRECIATED, and so he felt happy. He was not the only one who could still hear the same thumping beats. Head bouncing to the rhythm, Billy sidled up to Jon, placed his hand on Jon's shoulder, and then leaned in.

"Aw yeah? You ready? You ready?" Billy gave Jon a friendly slap on his arm and he continued to saunter.

The passage they stepped through was a long and sparkling tunnel. It was lit with strobe lights and the floor captured all the invariable light. The entire space was like being in a glow stick. The music exploded. Beyond, Jon could see several silhouettes beginning to take shape. They bounced to the incoming beats from a DJ booth poised on the center stage.

"Here we go! Here we go!" Billy approached a railing that overlooked the dance floor. Jon hopped and stayed close. Flooded with a sea of gyrating bodies, what Jon saw, he liked a lot. People were happy, free, and alive. Now among the cascade of varying shapes and blissful faces, Billy's arms spread. The music continued to produce a resounding boom that touched everything in its wake.

"Welcome to paradise," said Billy.

Jon said nothing. That was not quite how he would describe this, but it was good.

"There's our booth!" Billy nudged Jon, and the Marine stepped down a narrow staircase that led to the next level. Roaming across the dance floor, Jon marched. As he moved around a few of the people, everyone he spotted was absorbed by the immersive and contagious atmosphere.

"This way!" Overcome by the sounds of loud music, Billy's voice was muddled.

What was heard, Jon could barely comprehend. On his way to the booth, Jon gawked at a group of boys standing in a booth next to theirs.

So far, Jon counted five.

Drinking in suits, they glared at Jon as if they knew who he was. Although they were not many, the strength of these boorish fools came in numbers. If Jon had to place these guys, he'd say they looked like hockey players.

How did he know?

Growing up in Bayside, Queens, Jon knew a thing or two about athletes. He knew how they acted, how hockey players dressed, and most importantly, how they behaved while in public. Hockey players travel in packs. They are usually the first to start their own brand of nonsense and horseshit. Also, seeing themselves as tougher than they are, often they're just a bunch of roughhousers. They're thugs who like to hit, punch, push and shove. Without a shred of skill to back any of this up, whatever they did have didn't matter.

There were ten of them. Jon glimpsed in their direction and he sat with Billy. He could hear them over the music, and as he unbuttoned his jacket, Billy flagged down a waitress in a black cocktail dress.

"Hey, can we get a bottle down here, please?"

The waitress was astounding. Jon couldn't take his eyes off her. Slender, she was tight, and the girl's hair was so lusciously black it looked like silk. Jon turned to hide his leer.

"Sure," she said. "I'm Kya."

Although the music was loud, this Kya girl was close. The proximity helped Jon to hear her better. She was a shorter girl, and as she leaned in, Jon thought he caught a hint of allure in her eyes. Hoping she saw him the way he saw her, maybe he—

"Great!" Billy yelled over the music. "Nice to meet you! I'm Billy! This is Jon! We're going to need it ASAP, a'ight?"

A pleasant grin began to show on Kya's face. Jon wasn't sure if Kya was playing nice or if he and Billy were better compared to everyone else. The way Billy had chosen to speak to her, Jon could see, wasn't exactly new to the trade. Even still, Kya smiled. From the corner of her eye, she gave Jon a look. Before, he wasn't sure. Now he was. She *did* see him.

"Absolutely! Just a bottle of Cristal to start!" Kya exclaimed.

"Please!" shouted Billy.

Kya parted from Jon and Billy's booth and a celebratory hoot popped from his thrilled face. Soon after hearing the sound, Jon felt a shove before a drink wet the back of his neck. It spilled onto the collar of Jon's expensive dress shirt.

"Hey!" Billy sprung from his seat and glared at the gathering of boys. He shouted and shuffled closer. Jon was already getting bad vibes. His head was spinning, and he twitched and glowered.

He didn't like these guys, not one bit.

CHAPTER 5
BLACKNESS

Jon looked ahead until he saw the dance floor. With so many there, he couldn't imagine getting up or going in. No, what Jon needed now was the chance to exist without noise. And yet, here he was, locked in a whirlwind of sounds that shocked him to his core. The party was clearly out of hand. Jon felt a tremor shoot through his body. This was something he hadn't felt since the war. Whenever a new conflict surfaces and another threat begins to take shape, a reflex surges inside each and every soldier. As something either passed, acknowledged, or halted altogether, it's not quite adrenaline. No, it's what comes *after* adrenaline. It's that burst of unexplainable, enhanced and pervasive...*power*.

Standing up, Jon stepped off to the side. Peering over his shoulder, he gave his attention to the party that had assembled behind him.

"Hey," said Jon. He wanted to hide his frustration as he leaned over the seat.

First, he tried getting the attention of the guy who

was standing the closest. Jon was careful about his approach. His head was straight and his mind was right too. Jon hoped it would stay that way. Jumping around, this dude was in full swing. Despite where Jon was, he pretended like he wasn't even there.

"Hey, can I just speak with you for a quick sec, man, please?" Seeing a few more chatting, Jon waited for a response.

"What?"

The guy turned while holding a champagne glass. Pivoting, the guy gawked. His lower lip curled up and then down.

"Just..." Jon replied. He was taking a second to choose his words carefully. "You're spilling your drinks all over us. I know it was an accident and all, but we'd appreciate it if you just watched yourself, you know? We paid a lot for this booth. Don't want to get it dirty, know what I mean?"

The guy hissed and looked away to avoid eye contact. There was another response too. It was an obnoxious chortle. While Jon was nice, the answer was a swift pop to the elbow. It was a push done to knock Jon's arm out of the way. After making contact, the man rotated and gave his back to Jon. As more swarmed, the situation escalated. And yet, all Jon had done was ask this band to be watchful of their drinks. He didn't want them to spill. Jon couldn't believe what happened next.

What these boys needed to do was to mind their manners.

"Yo! Let's just get the bouncer, Jon, man. Come on." Billy waved his hand and the goon snickered at the suggestion. It was no use.

"Look, I know you guys are excited," said Jon, "and

having a ball and all, but please...we just want our space, you know. That's all."

"Hey, bro," snapped another jackass. Unlike his bulkier friend, this one was smaller and his collar was popped. "He didn't move into your space. Now stop harassing him, and let us be, all right?"

"All right," said Jon. "Fair." He took his seat.

"Don't bother with 'em," advised Billy. "Let's just go, get our own drinks, and move on."

Jon bit down hard on his lip. The entire exchange left the Marine enraged. However, now choosing to remain nice and calm, Jon was patient. He was looking out for his mind first and foremost. You never know who you're going to encounter at a nightclub.

Jon sat, and from behind, came a splash followed by a hollering of seven gasping fellows.

"Hey!" shouted Billy. "What the hell, dude!"

Jon watched Billy glare. Now, the boys were pushing it. The main guy had crossed the line and Jon didn't want to make it worse, but then it already was.

"Hey! I said knock it off! I said..." Jon raised his voice, and though he did not engage with the boys, he also didn't move a muscle. Jon's head was spinning. He could hear new sounds and saw more flashing lights. Among the incessant blinking, Jon felt dizzy and unbalanced. Leaning back, Jon fell and continued to fall.

"Back up, man!" Billy screamed as Jon went down.

Now on the grimy floor, Jon looked up and saw the same guy who splashed him. Closing his fingers into a fist, Jon had made his intentions clear.

Hell no. This was it.

CHAPTER 6
FIRST THROWDOWN

WITH THE PUNCHES NOW FLYING, JON SNATCHED one of the fists.

Using an old trick he learned back in the Corps, Jon contorted his opponent's arm and brought the fool onto one of the tables.

The dude crashed. After this happened, the entire situation exploded.

"Shit!" Jon heard Billy scream. In the middle of a tussle, a cluster of bums tossed Jon aside like he was nothing.

"Jon!" Billy's reaction was an indication about how he was still trying to protect Jon. Another fist from another arrogant asshole quickly emerged, and he clobbered the friend of the Marine hard in his face.

A straight knockout, Billy was out like a light. Jon looked at Billy's body. He was lying there, so painfully lifeless. The commotion that surfaced made the altercation more visible. With all eyes on the fight now, everyone stopped and stared.

There were ten guys and three girls, and in-between was Jon.

"Shit." Jon watched as the swarm began to expand.

Tempers had been set loose and anything could unfold as a result. Jon scanned the space and did his best to assess. He hoped the bouncers might come and intervene. None did. And in the time between thinking they would and checking on Billy, Jon simplified his plan.

He was just going to stay out of the way.

Jon swerved, cut, and slid himself along the booth.

Jon dodged a hand, and the guy reaching for him fell forward. Having almost tripped over a cushion in the booth, the man was down. Jon checked the other who was trying to punch, and this fool was now head-to-head with the Marine. Whoever this fool was, he was an intoxicated oaf who threw all his weight behind only one punch. He was barely able to stand after each one.

Bad move, Jon thought.

He kicked and somersaulted after pushing one guy into the crowd. So far, not a single punch hit. Still, Jon knew that eventually, one of them *would*. And when it *did*, Jon would not have the time to recover or retaliate.

There were just too many skulls and too many bodies.

Jon continued to rotate and deflected more movements with a few hard cross blocks. Then, flipping back, a pair of hands snagged Jon by the shoulders. However, Jon stayed in motion. Veering and pivoting, Jon bumped into one of the nearby pillars.

"Ah!"

He was facing the largest boy in the pack. The man

crossed and jabbed. Jon leaned into each of the punches and took the blow head-on, literally.

"Ah!" the man snapped. His fist clocked Jon's skull. "Goddamn it."

With more boys standing around, Jon glimpsed and noticed there were three bouncers on the approach. It was too late. By the time they arrived, the club was jammed. Their response time was compromised by the sheer volume of those in their vicinity.

Yet, they saw the fight and did nothing.

Why?

CHAPTER 7
MOVEMENT

THE CONQUISTADOR SUPPOSEDLY HAD THE BEST security in the business, or so Billy said. Based on what Jon had observed, they didn't seem like the best. Then again, he was unsure how bouncers could have handled a similar situation.

Maybe they were better. Maybe they were *the best of the best.*

Jon took another look at the guy standing next to him. Jon had little to use here. His adrenaline was pumping and his heart rate was jacked. His level of frustration had accumulated to level ten, so Jon used it. Thrusting back the dude, instead of going for a punch, Jon recalled another lesson learned in the Marines. A chop to the neck is ten times more effective than a punch to the face.

At least, this was what Jon's staff sergeant claimed.

Not knowing if this was at all true, Jon's hand was straight, and seconds later, he found the neck. After this, Jon sent his hand straight for the fool's jugular. Quick and brutal, Jon clobbered this approaching dude's veiny neck. Deadly and accurate, Jon felt his muscles clash with the man's slick skin and felt the full impact of the blow.

"Yo, Marc! Jesus!"

Marc was the name of the boy Jon karate chopped. Once hit by the Marine, all he could do now was look sullenly at his own body.

More flashbacks surfaced in Jon. Then came the shakes and the *visions*. Glaring at the remaining bunch, there were too many for Jon to fight alone.

Others gawked from farther away.

"You..."

Holding his ground, Jon kept his body tight and contained his fear. Keeping it all stored inside, Jon attempted to bring it all out at once. So long as these guys charged full tilt, then the outcome would continue to be just as unpredictable.

Gazing ahead, five more stampeded. Jon kept rotating. Like a twister in motion, it was impossible to take on so many and Jon couldn't stay. He could run and was also unable to truly see all of his surroundings.

The entire time, Jon was in motion but questioned where they were.

Why weren't they here?

Where were the bloody bouncers?

And yet, in the corner of Jon's eyes, he spotted five. Finally, they were here but still, they weren't bouncing anyone. No, instead, they were siphoning the crowd, watching the fight and all watching Jon.

He rolled yet another table as the same band of fools continued to chase.

Falling down, Jon collided with another who was lurking behind him. Big and brooding, this next man was like a wall. When Jon turned, his hand was cocked back and ready to strike. Jon's reaction was reflexive. It was not as aggressive as the others he delivered so far.

He threw a straight punch. Jon's fist was grabbed by a new towering mammoth positioned behind him. Bald, this man was a cross between an MMA fighter and one of those gridiron maniacs.

Whoever he was, he held onto Jon's hand and glared. "That's enough."

Clutching Jon's wrist, he tried moving it. Although Jon wanted to, the power of this man's grip, combined with his raw strength, made it difficult. Jon couldn't squirm, even if he used his other hand to assist.

The bald man whipped Jon aside. He looked at two other bouncers.

One was Asian, slender and light, while the other looked Italian. He was the same one from the door. With the angular jawline, Jon thought this guy was a total badass. The stoicism of these three bouncers was both terrifying and gratifying.

Keeping their arms crossed, the bouncers studied the scene before they reacted.

While there were five boys out of control, the first bouncer was Danix. He stepped in right away. Using his left foot, Danix kicked one guy in the knee. Then, he used his elbow to deliver a ferocious, clean upper-strike. It sounded like a baseball bat clacking against a tree.

Gobsmacked, the dude fell, and Danix snagged his neck.

Instantly, Danix head-locked the fool and pulled him away. The boys could see their friend taken away like yesterday's trash and decided to move in. They vehemently approached the two-fifty strongman.

"Jesus Christ!" shouted one.

A flashing silhouette zipped past Jon's view. Like an apparition, this new man was conjured only from air and shadow. This Asian bouncer was a master in hand-to-hand. He executed a solid flying kick that sent the boys flying over a set of chairs. And, just like that, they were down, the same as all the rest.

Jon was on his stomach. He was under the impression this was a last resort. However, with every strike and every counter posed against the impending attacks, it seemed placed, almost timed. Jon hit back with his own kick, and the last fools were assaulted by yet another bouncer.

Jon tried to assess the newest bouncer's fighting style.

It was strangely familiar but Jon's best guess was karate. However, what he was seeing seemed more unique and more complicated. This other man didn't strike. Instead, he grabbed joints like the wrists and the fingers. He locked elbows and contorted the guy's arm. Holding his attacker, this new bouncer swung his hip and tossed the guy into Danix's massive hands.

By then, the commotion simmered. Everything was under control.

The knuckleheads who were once with Jon had all separated. They'd been pulled apart like cotton candy.

With everyone backed off and away, Jon stood tall.

Who was this new guy and why did he choose to save Jon?

CHAPTER 8
CONVERSATIONS

Although the bouncers arrived later than anticipated, they still protected the club patrons, even the ones standing too close to the fight. Now that Jon was out of the conflict, he closed his eyes and needed time to catch his breath. While in the midst of doing this, Jon heard the same thumping beats as well as the same cheering voices.

Soon after, Jon was struck again with another cold, brutal sense of déjà vu.

Billy was lying on his back. Jon crawled on top of him. Tapping Billy's cheek, Jon tried to wake his friend. He even shouted and waited for Billy to move. "Billy! Can you hear me?!"

A soft moan emerged and Billy's lashes fluttered. Gradually, he returned, and Jon continued to talk to Billy until he was coherent. However, after a knockout, the person hit usually requires at least fifteen to twelve seconds to come back.

This was more than what Billy needed now.

"Come sit by the booth. Come on."

"Uh…"

When Jon eased Billy into a chair, he was about to turn and get some ice from a champagne bucket. A giant bruise had formed above Billy's left eye. Jon reached for the cubes but then heard a loud voice shout from inside the crowd.

A *what* followed by the phrase *that fucker*. In the end, Jon recognized the tone.

It was not long ago he heard it. Peering back, Jon's adrenaline spiked again. Unlike before, when Jon's intentions were to use his words, the idiot called Marc wasn't going to take *no* for an answer.

At this point, he damn well should have.

Jon summoned whatever energy he still had left and channeled it all into one last kick.

Jon's prosthetic was light. He was mobile because he had adapted to its design. And, in what was a vicious and vapid attack, Jon struck this Marc dead center. He hit him right where he needed to.

"Ah!" Marc was so floored from the strike he instantly collapsed.

Jon's intention was only to knock Marc down.

However, Marc was now holding his side. Evidently, the force almost shattered the boy's ribcage. Feeling the bones crushing under the weight of Jon's foot, Jon didn't want to believe he'd broken Marc's ribs. Based on what he was feeling, Jon didn't know *how* he couldn't have.

Marc fell and his wrath escalated. Still in a hissy fit, Jon stormed after the fallen man. Jon thought about all he had endured so far at The Conquistador. It was supposed to be his day of relaxation and disconnection, and yet, Jon couldn't bear to handle anything else.

He tried talking to Marc, but it didn't work.

He tried being nice, and this didn't work either. He tried to be non-threatening and Jon had made it clear his intentions were *not* to escalate or to fight.

And yet, none of it worked.

After knocking his attacker down again, the gratification and the appeal left Jon Haze reeling. No more invading thoughts. He was satisfied and what Jon experienced afterward was not different than when he succeeded in a rescue or eliminated an enemy target. Although the threat was neutralized, all Jon had to do once it was done was find his way back home.

But now that he was already there, Jon was looking at Billy. His hands, which had once trembled, now felt like they were being slowly stitched back together. A deep breath, Marc began to stand while Jon's fists were clenched. "No, you stay down!"

Marc stomped. Jon's leg was bent like it was about to snap.

Before another strike was delivered, Jon's back leg was caught and contorted. He spun around like a ballerina. He felt someone else next to him. Jon looked at a man in a black suit with a unique fighting style as well as a very soft voice.

"Hold it there, kid. I think you're all done for the night."

The first thought in Jon's mind was leadership. The man here was not like the other security. He was in complete control and possessed a unique set of skills. Jon was happy to see him. "Who are you?"

"Name's Addison. Addison Krowe," replied the man. "I'm the cooler here, head of security. What say you and I go to my office and have ourselves a little chat? I'll show you the way."

CHAPTER 9
AN OFFER

WEARY AND STILL BLEEDING, JON WAS ESCORTED upstairs by this Addison Krowe. He was taken out of the club and brought into an entirely separate part of The Conquistador. On the second floor, both Jon and Addison entered a narrow hallway. It was a space that lay beyond a railing covered with sparkling lights, and the passage was covered by a velvet border.

Two men stood there with their hands crossed. While Jon could have easily asked where he was being taken, his mind was still tossing from the altercation. Moving on, Jon sized up anyone who had the nerve to give him a dirty look. Wherever Addison Krowe was taking him, Jon felt like he was being commanded to keep following. Those who Jon saw were now whispering to each other. The scene Jon had caused was enough to gift him some temporary celebrity status. Although he appreciated the attention, Jon couldn't see how he was not one. When he was halfway through the door, he felt warm air exuding from behind.

"So where exactly are you taking me to, Mr.

Krowe?" In this level, the music proved to have less of an impact. Jon didn't need to shout in order to speak. Addison entered a passcode into a digital box beneath his door handle. He didn't know Jon was watching, but the Marine saw the digits. He saw them all, actually. After Addison entered the code, the door beeped, and opened.

"You'll see soon enough."

This encounter, from Jon's perspective, had all the inner workings of what could be a bad one. Although Jon never backed down from a fight, he did cause a lot of damage. Then again, so did Billy, and so did that band of idiots who challenged Jon.

But they weren't here. It was Jon who was called in.

Addison opened the door and stepped aside to invite the Marine into this room.

Struck with the aroma of vanilla and pine, Addison's office was a sleek gentleman's lair. In the dead center sat a marble desk. Behind it were bookshelves filled with pictures of Addison as well as some seriously famous people. Jon gazed at a set of plaques next to these photos. Each one was a reward commending The Conquistador for all its glorious accommodations and affirming its status as one of the best clubs ever. There were scenes of other people in suits and holding fat bottles of champagne. Lastly, there was one picture of Addison Krowe. Here, he was with a woman.

It was the first one that Jon noticed.

It was a capturing of what he could only assume was his wife.

Jon assumed.

"Please. Come on in. Have a seat," Addison said.

Jon was still in awe of the prestige as well as the power that now surrounded him.

If he ever had an office someday, Jon wanted it to look like this.

"My name is Addison Krowe. As I told you, I'm the head of security here at The Conquistador."

Jon didn't take Addison for a head of any security. His office was too high class for someone in that position, or so Jon assumed. "Funny. I thought you were the owner," said Jon.

"Me?" said Addison. "Owner? Ha!" With his head back, a condescending guffaw squeaked from Addison's clenched jaw. "No. Owner is Larry Thomas." Addison pointed to the corner of his desk.

There was a portrait of an older man with a bald head dressed in a tuxedo. He looked like one of those rich politicians, but this man was apparently Larry Thomas. And with him was Addison as well as the same woman whom Jon spotted in the picture not long ago.

"Father-in-law."

"Father-in-law?" asked Jon.

"Yes," confirmed Addison. "He built this club. It's his baby. Not sure if you knew that, but it is."

"I didn't," said Jon.

"Great."

"Hmm." There was a moment of silence and Jon gawked at Addison. The cooler sat primly behind his desk but had yet to inform Jon about why he was asked to be here now.

"Look, whatever damage I caused," said Jon, "I can help pay for it, but you have to believe me when I say those guys started it. I was only defending myself. I'm sure you can understand."

"Right," said Addison, a grin lingering in the corner of his mouth. "You...want to...pay for the damage, do you?"

"Yeah," said Jon. Addison's head was tilted and he was amused with Jon's pointless offer. "That's why I'm here, is it not?"

Jon leaned in to look closer at Addison.

"No. The reason you're here," said Addison, "is because I was actually impressed with what I saw."

"What you saw?" asked Jon. He had an idea about what Addison was referring to, though he didn't know exactly what it was.

"Could tell you had some experience in high-intensity situations. Besides, with all those phones out, I'd say you're probably all over YouTube and Facebook by now, and you don't even know it yet."

Jon didn't consider whether or not this was true. He liked to think that it was.

"Let me guess, Army Rangers?" Addison asked.

Shaking his head, Jon glared. "*Marines.*"

"Ah. Some of our guys are ex-military too," said Addison. "I believe you've met a few of them already, actually."

"Right." Jon recalled the three men who intervened during the fight.

The big one, whom Jon knew as Danix, the other one was an Asian man who delivered that solid kick. The last one had gray hair. He was the one Jon spotted at the door with Jamal. He believed they fit the ex-military mold, but again, all of this was unclear.

"Did you serve too?" Jon asked Addison.

"Me?" Addison asked. "Nah. Sorry."

"But you're the cooler, though," Jon replied.

Addison snickered. "Sort of, I guess you could say. I prefer the title Head of Security and Operations Manager, but hey, doesn't matter to me. Besides, do all coolers *need* to be ex-military and know how to fight in order to be good at their jobs?"

Jon meditated on this question, then he shook his head.

"Well, no, but—"

"See, a job like this...it's mostly about communication," Addison explained. "Well, communication and planning, I should say. I do have a black belt in Aikido though. Not what you might call *real* fighting experience, except for the odd tussle or two back in the day, but I've been in this game a long time. And I've been in it long enough to know what counts and what doesn't. Club security was part of my upbringing. Dad owned one," said Addison. "He taught me all the ins and outs since before I could remember."

"Cool," said Jon. He was somewhat impressed.

"Got a law degree from NYU," added Addison. "Worked here the whole way through it actually, until I was promoted. And now, I help make this place one of the hottest nightclubs in the country."

"I see," said Jon.

"Not what other people make it out to be," Addison continued. "Tough business. Organized. Structured, and at times very *stressful*. But, once you got the right clients comin' in, and all the methods down, all the right decorations, everything else falls into place, for the most part. The trouble is keeping it *in* place," Addison said. He looked around the office and Jon saw more pictures, more portraits and more plaques. Each one contained its own story. And maybe that's why Jon was here now. He was going to be told a story.

"Keeping our spot comes at a price, I'm afraid," said Addison.

"Is that why I'm here, to pay the price?"

"No, you're here because I want you to work here." Addison sharply turned his head. The offer was now only starting to sound legitimate. *Real*.

"Me? Work *here*?" asked Jon.

"You interested?" Addison asked back.

"Uh..." Jon examined the office again. "Well, I mean, why *me*?"

"What?" This question was one Addison expected.

"Why *me*?" Jon repeated himself.

Addison leaned back and Jon watched as he folded his hands. He was examining his new boss, who was posed to appear dignified, almost powerful. His shoulders were back and his fingers were interlocked. And yet, this entire hiring process made Jon think there was more happening here than he realized.

"Let's just say I know what it's like to come home and not know what you're supposed to do," said Addison. "I saw you worked well under pressure. You were also willing to think things through and actually give people the opportunity to do the right thing. Often, fights in clubs end far worse than they did tonight. I think because of what you did, fewer people suffered."

"Do you really think that?"

Addison gave Jon a humble nod and answered with an assertive grin. "I do."

Addison's gaze was fixed on Jon like he was actually an ex-military operative working behind the scenes.

But, while staring at Jon, Addison Krowe's eyes beamed with focus and intrigue.

"Well, if you're asking me if I'm interested," said Jon, "I mean, shouldn't there be some sort of screening process, so I know what to do?"

Jon only assumed this was true.

"Better than putting a person in the shit and then see how they respond?" Addison's question was rhetorical, so Jon said nothing afterward. "No," said Addison. "But if you do accept, then there's a lot more you'll have to learn, no doubt. Even still, we'd be happy to teach you, if you're willing to join us, that is. Also, I've never seen someone take on three guys and walk away. You know your way in and out. You know egression, safety, and control, and I'd be lying if I said I didn't want to see more of all that going forward."

"More?"

"*A lot* more," Addison confirmed.

"Hmm..." Jon was hesitant. The pain in his head had re-emerged. His hands were shaking, so he secured them under his thighs. Hiding these quaking movements, Jon looked down at his prosthetic and looked back at Addison Krowe. His potential boss was now sitting back and smirking at the former Marine.

"I *am* interested," Jon declared.

"Good," said Addison. "Then, if you're interested, *really interested*, then be sure to be here tomorrow at ten."

"Ten at night?" asked Jon.

"No," said Addison. He grinned, unfolded his hands, and leaned back. "Ten in the morning. You got training to do."

"Training?"

"Lots of it," Addison barked at Jon as he began to make a turn.

"Okay, I'll...I'll be there," said Jon.

"Good," said Addison. "See you then, bright and early. Actually...not that far from now."

Jon marked this as the end of their conversation. He stood and nodded politely at Addison Krowe. Jon stepped back and the former Marine proceeded to the doors. Going on, Jon thought about the day ahead. He was also thinking about Billy, yet Jon didn't know how he was going to explain what happened. Jon thought about his mother and how he was going to tell her he was just hired to be a bouncer at New York's most exclusive nightclub.

Jon had to elaborate on the circumstances that led to his hiring.

There was so much piling up, and all Jon wanted to do now was think. On his way out of Addison's office, Jon spotted the same attractive bartender from before. Kya was her name. Jon remembered it suddenly. Kya's shirt was unbuttoned and she appeared scruffy, like she had just finished a long and brutal shift.

Jon raised his hand and gave Kya a gentle wave. He pretended like he knew her and he hoped the feeling was mutual. They had met before.

"Hey."

Kya stopped when she heard Jon's humble voice. Afterward, she tied her hair up and proceeded in Jon's direction. "Did you just come out of Addison's office?"

"Oh," said Jon, pretending like it was not a big deal that he did. "Yeah. Just had a meeting, actually."

"Really?"

"Yeah, he actually...offered me a job."

"To work *here*?" asked Kya. She pointed at the floor.

"Yeah," said Jon.

"As what?" Kya still sounded skeptical.

"A bouncer."

"A bouncer, really?"

"Yeah."

"Wow."

"Yeah, I...thought so too," replied Jon, doing his best not to sound surprised.

"Well, you did handle that situation pretty well today," said Kya. "It was actually quite good."

"You think so?"

"You tried to talk to 'em," Kya said. "You were nice. When that doesn't work, you—"

"Kicked one of them in the face," interrupted Jon.

This was only his attempt at humor, but Jon could see it wasn't his best move. As a waitress, Kya was likely harassed on a daily basis by men who wanted to book a one-way trip straight into her panties.

Maybe Jon didn't give himself the credit he deserved.

Perhaps this bouncing opportunity was sensible. Maybe it was even overdue.

"Yeah," said Kya, laughing.

Jon couldn't recall the last time he made someone laugh. He couldn't recall the last time he had laughed. But, when Jon heard Kya chortle and saw her smirk, he interpreted all of this as good. It was nice.

"So...I guess I'll see you around?" Kya asked Jon, still being casual.

"See *me* around?"

"Yeah, I mean..." replied Kya. "You do work here now, don't you?"

A smile began to form on Jon's face. His heart beat faster, and as his hand steadied, the pain inside Jon's head began to simmer. Everything became clearer. The next day, Jon accepted, it wouldn't be as bad as those before.

"Yeah," said Jon as euphoric feelings of satisfaction began to flourish throughout his insides. He began to feel giddy. "I do. I work here...at The Conquistador."

CHAPTER 10
A MOTHER'S FRAGILE HEART

WHEN JON WOKE THE FOLLOWING DAY, HE marched straight to his punching bag. This was purchased back in high school. It was actually a gift given to Jon by his father at Christmas. Once a fan of the sport, Jon trained often in his teenage years. He even won a few fights in an amateur boxing competition. However, he stopped training after he joined the Marines. And, now that he was back home, Jon commenced his days the way he had when he was ten years younger. He pounded with some jabs, solid hooks, and crosses.

The bag thumped and the chain above rattled. Wearing gloves, Jon heard some commotion in the kitchen after his tenth strike.

"Jon!" his mother shouted from behind the door.

And yet, Jon continued to beat the bag. His knuckles were wrapped up because of last night. Jon didn't tell his mother about the fight he had at the club, only that he and Billy had a very good time. And that he did have a job interview.

He didn't say where.

"Are you in *there*?"

"Yeah!"

"There's an omelet left from earlier this morning." Jon smiled at his mother. Always, she was a good mom. "When you're done exercising," she said, "it's down there waiting for you."

"Maybe," Jon replied. He didn't have much of an appetite. "Thanks a lot."

He slammed the bag again. Even though Jon didn't tell his mom where he was being interviewed, he did give her a brief description of the new job.

"I'm going to work security. I'm going to be a bouncer."

"A bouncer?" said Jon's mom, alarmed at the time. "Where?"

"The best club in the city."

Jon's mom did ask a lot of questions. And yet, she also trusted her son implicitly. Even in his fragile state, carrying much baggage and trauma, this trust did not change. It was because of this trust Jon didn't mind his mom's frequent questioning. After so many years, she continued to care, and that was good. So far, however, Jon didn't exactly know what his new job entailed.

"Where? Tell me everything. *Now*," demanded Jon's mother.

Jon looked at the bag. He had punched it so many times his hand made an imprint. A few more hits and Jon wouldn't be able to lift a damn thing.

"Don't worry," Jon said to her. "It's just a job. It'll be all right. I promise."

CHAPTER 11
DAY DAMN ONE

AFTER HIS QUICK TRAINING SESSION, JON ICED HIS hands and trekked down the steps. In the kitchen, Jon roamed to the fridge and pulled a slick carton of OJ. He guzzled the liquid knowing he didn't have a lot of time and it spilled past his lips and onto his shirt.

"Pour it into a glass, please!" Jon's mom's voice screeched.

Jon dropped the carton. He was so thirsty he could barely catch his breath.

"Sorry."

"What time are you heading out for your interview?" asked Betsy Haze.

"Soon." Jon filled a glass and looked ahead.

"Go now," said Jon's mother. "You don't want to cut it too close. You don't know what the traffic is going to be like."

"Going to take the subway, actually," Jon replied. He finished his OJ. "Shouldn't take too long."

Jon's mom held a fresh cup of coffee while he was

leaning against the counter. Jon could see his mother watching him as he moved across the kitchen.

"I hope not."

Jon placed the carton back in the fridge, shuffled down the hall, and headed toward the front door. "See ya later."

"Jon, wait!" Jon's mother yelled from the hall. Jon stopped dead and then he turned to see her rushing toward him.

"What?" Jon glanced at his watch and checked the time.

Now glimpsing over his shoulder, Jon could see his mother standing with a tall container that she gave to her son. For Jon, this served as a reminder that, often, he was too quick to go somewhere. Sometimes, he didn't have what he needed.

"You almost forgot about this." Jon squinted and a curious feeling began to emerge. He could see his mother. In her hand was Jon's protein shake. This gave him an incredible jumpstart so early in the day.

"Oh," Jon said. "Right. Good. Thanks."

When Jon was in high school, he would start his day in the same way. He'd complete a quick workout, take an even quicker shower, and down a shake before heading off to school.

Less than two years later, Jon was in the Marines. Six months after that, he was at war. While there, Jon tried not to think too much about home.

Remembering what life was like did help him through such brutal times. Mostly, it was just a distraction. Today, it was these simple gestures that reminded Jon of how lucky he was to be home and living with someone he cared about. Twenty-four and still living with his parent, on paper, it was everything a young person couldn't bear to think about. Before this, Jon's days were spent in a tent and marching through long stretches of sand and heat. Then, he accepted that anything could happen. When his mother handed him the shake, a small tear seeped out from the corner of Jon's eye.

Now he was home.

"Thanks."

"You sure you don't need a ride?" asked Jon's mom.

Still holding a 32 oz thermos, cold moisture appeared glazed around this tall plastic container. Jon grinned. Graciously, Jon took the container from his mother. Again, he said to himself, he had a good mother.

"No, thank you."

Jon kissed her cheek. Betsy Haze touched her son on the shoulder. She wrapped her arms around Jon so tight it was cutting off circulation. Jon understood a good parent gives more than love. They also give time. Jon felt his mother's warmth and recalled the joys experienced as a child.

Jon relied on these memories for the future. Sometimes, he had no idea how his mother had managed to remember all the things she did.

In the end, Jon supposed he just underestimated his mom.

He said goodbye and proceeded along. Work started soon. His mom was right.

Jon didn't want to be late.

CHAPTER 12
INTO THE DARK

JON TRAVELED ALL THE WAY FROM QUEENS, WHICH was quite a long trip, but didn't care. He sat with all the working-class folks while listening to his favorite beats and feeling the protein digesting in his gut.

Jon should be at The Conquistador soon.

Jon arrived early and stood at the club's front door. It looked different during the day.

Appearing immaculate, there were a few parked cars in the lot. Some of the doors were open. Nevertheless, Jon walked ahead. He breathed in all the alcohol and all the smoke.

Jon stepped into the dimness and saw the club completely empty. To him, it felt a lot like walking into a drab house. The club's energy, liveliness, and identity had all been stripped away. All that was left felt barren and eerie.

Dressed to impress—or comparatively impressed—Jon wore a jacket and leather shoes. Looking around The Conquistador, the booths were stripped to bare and the dance floor was now cleared.

Jon felt a chill tickle his neck.

While waiting, Jon went to the bar so he could sit and gather his thoughts before meeting with Addison. He adjusted his tie and was only wearing one because Jon thought it made him look more professional. He heard a voice speak to him from the stairs. It led all the way down to the second floor.

"Yo!"

Jon was soon greeted by a man he had seen one day before. He was the same man guarding the door. "Jamal?"

Jon remembered Jamal's name and the big doorman's response was a gratified blush. He walked up to the former Marine like he knew him. Jon felt as though they did.

"Hey," said Jon.

"Hey, brother," Jamal said. He began to stroll. "You're here now. Why?"

"Yeah," said Jon. "I'm actually here for work."

"*Word*?" Jamal's high voice indicated he was pleased with the news.

"Yeah, Addison, he's expecting *me*."

"I heard," said Jamal.

"You did?" asked Jon.

"Yeah," said Jamal. "Word moves pretty fast around here, and we all heard about your little demo last night. It was a good fight. At least, that's what the others are saying about it."

"Other people told you about it?" asked Jon, somewhat embarrassed.

"Just a few."

"Really?" Jon held the thought in his mind for as

long as he could. He was somewhat uncomfortable with this level of flattery.

Marines don't get thanked, they just get deployed.

People were talking about Jon and what he did, and this made him feel special. All Jon did, however, was hit someone before they hit him. He was careful and he was calm. He thought about when and how these tactics could be placed. And yet, the more he considered this, the more he could see why it would work so well with the crowd.

This was the right decision, and right decisions went a long way in this business.

"Yep. Danix told me all about it. Said you held your own really well."

"Danix?"

"The big-ass bouncer with the big-ass arms. In fact," added Jamal, "you should meet him officially. You should meet everyone officially."

"Meet?"

"Yeah," said Jamal. "Come. I'll introduce you to the guys."

Always friendly and seemingly kind, Jamal was gentle for a man who was six-nine. He escorted Jon to the back of the bar, where Jon saw Kya. She was by the bar cleaning glasses with a dishrag. Jon wanted to talk to her. He wanted to march right up to her and start courting her like he was so desperately wanted. Instead, Jon followed Jamal to a swirling staircase that circled a tight corner. There was a table and five men seated around it. They seemed like they were not doing much. Jon saw Danix, the bouncer he encountered yesterday.

"Danix Slade," Jamal introduced. "I know you met him."

"Nice to meet you, officially," said Jon, offering his hand.

When he addressed Danix, the chiseled man looked like a cluster of rocks jammed into a potato sack. Danix's grip was tight and his gaze firm. Jon listened to his every word and minded his posture. Danix deserved not just his attention, but also his respect.

"Same," said Danix. He was now so close Jon could feel it in his chest. "Heard you served in the Corps."

"Yeah," said Jon, forgetting his prosthetic but remembering his time in the service. He could never forget about this. "*You?*"

"SEALs," said Danix.

"Really?"

"Team Two," said Danix.

"Wow. That's...*impressive*," said Jon.

"Thanks."

"Two soldiers," said Jamal. "You two should get along."

Jon didn't say anything. However, people always assume soldiers have something in common just because they both underwent training and fought in a war. Yet, with so many who did serve, the similarities don't mean much. Jon admired the SEALs, not because of what they did, but because of who they were once they returned home. They were better, straighter, and did more with their lives. This was, of course, just Jon's opinion and not necessarily true. Still, Jon stood by his assumption.

"And over here is Sam," said Jamal. "Sam Vaughn."

The man with the peppered hair stood up from the table. This was the man Jon came across at the door. Jon offered his hand and Sam glared.

Jon thought this was odd. If Jon were passing Sam on the street, he wouldn't have thought of him in the same way he did Danix. While Danix was broad-chested and looked strong too, there was something about Sam that Jon couldn't quite grasp. There was something in his eyes, like he could see a black hole eating a thousand planets. Despite his unassuming appearance, Jon could gauge how Sam possessed a degree of experience that could shake most men to their core.

And when Sam touched Jon's hand, he felt whatever was inside of him burn like a match. He produced a jolt of pressure, and Jon nodded to acknowledge him.

"Nice to meet you."

"Same." Backstepping, Jon watched as Sam picked up his glass and took a drink.

"And this here is Li Huen."

Jamal raised his hand and gestured to an Asian man.

Unlike the others dressed in collared shirts, Li was wearing long sleeves that hung loosely around his wrists. When his name was called, Li stood and nodded at Jon.

This was the first show of respect he'd seen since he arrived.

"Hello." Li nodded and lent his hand. Jon accepted the gesture.

While it was done out of admiration, it also affirmed to Jon exactly where Li came from. He came from a place of profound respect and impeccable manners. Once he met Li, Jamal stepped closer and continued to point at everyone seated around the table.

"Here we have Divine," said Jamal. "She's another one of our waitresses."

A Black girl with cornrows and dark makeup turned to Jon. "You're the new guy, right?"

Head down, Jon considered the question. While he was new, and he was a guy, he still wasn't sure if he was the *new guy*.

"I guess."

"Cool."

"And that's pretty much everybody," said Jamal.

"Well, not everybody." A new voice chimed in from behind Jon.

Turning to see, the person who spoke seemed familiar. Standing in a three-piece suit and strolling onto the scene with slick hair and shiny shoes was Addison Krowe. He was the man responsible for bringing Jon to this club now. Addison Krowe roamed into this section where everyone was seated. He nodded at Jon and acknowledged the Marine like the two had known each other for a long time.

They didn't. They had only just met.

"You still haven't met Mr. Thomas, right?" Jamal asked Jon.

Jon's head shook. He didn't know Mr. Thomas personally, but did know he was the owner of The Conquistador.

"Figured I'd save that for another time," said Jamal. He sounded like he was joking.

And he was, sort of.

"Indeed," said Addison. "Thanks for coming."

"Thank you," said Jon.

"So, you've met almost everyone who works here," said Addison, "especially the bouncers."

"We were just getting acquainted," said Danix.

"Right," said Addison, looking across. "Before we get started with our meeting here, I would first like to officially welcome Jon Haze into The Conquistador family."

Addison's hand was now resting on Jon's shoulder. Now chummy, Addison and everyone else made the Marine feel welcomed and accepted. Being officially sworn into his new *brotherhood*, Jon thought Addison might wave the interview as well as the screening processes.

Wasn't Jon already hired?

The Conquistador was exclusive. It was also competitive.

And yet, Addison insisted on bringing Jon here without expressing even the slightest sign of hesitation. Jon deduced this to the fact that he was a Marine, a vet in need of assistance and compassion. He was also trained and had already proven himself. As well, Jon didn't think giving him a job at a nightclub would qualify as that.

Addison wasn't even a soldier.

Maybe he was pitying Jon because of his prosthetic?

Jon hoped that wasn't the case.

He was curious whether what he said was actually true?

Did he really see something in him?

Sitting there, Jon felt cold. Shivering, his hand trembled against his lap. He wouldn't describe his current state as nervous, only uncertain. Jon was now buried under a sea of thoughts. There were too many intruding ideas. Jon didn't care to determine the truth about any of them. Whenever he felt this way, the best course of action was to sit tight, to keep his ears open, and to not speak unless spoken to.

"So...Jon will be working night security with us," said Addison, "and so, he will need to be briefed on how we do things here, at this club. We have a strict no gun policy, and much of what we do follows a diligent step by step process. It's quite strenuous. But Jon here needs to make it through, Danix, so why don't you start prepping him for our *boot camp*, yeah?"

"Right," said Danix. "Not a problem."

"If he makes it more than halfway," said Addison, "then my thoughts about him are accurate."

Addison mulled Jon over for a second time. He stood with his hands on his hips.

Halfway was a word that stood out for Jon. Halfway meant there was an entire other part to Jon's journey that required completion. Addison didn't even think that Jon had what it took to make it farther.

Danix was up now and Jon's training was set to begin right here, right now.

"Okay."

"Follow Danix," said Addison. "He's going to take you through the basics."

"*The basics?*"

"Yeah," said Danix. "*This way.*"

Jon marched in kind of military strut. Danix was walking fast. Not looking back once, he didn't acknowledge Jon at all. Where he was taking Jon to was a new section of the club, away from everything else. Jon was under the impression he would have to shadow other bouncers as part of his training. Before he could do this, there was something else being expected of him. Jon ran through some of the ideas he had. He thought maybe he'd spend the day watching a training video or having to endure another session. He might fill out some paperwork or, at least this was what Addison alluded to.

However, to make it more than halfway seemed easier. Jon didn't exactly know.

Where was he going?

"Uh, so what is this? Is this a test?" Jon asked.

Danix chuckled as he motioned. The room was at the back and was somewhat hidden, yet it became clearer the more Jon followed Danix.

"Yes, you could say that."

Danix took a minute before stepping in. Jon could only interpret this pause as ominous. What Danix said after, however, confirmed Jon's suspicions.

"You might not understand everything you see behind these doors," said Danix, "but just know this: The Conquistador is a tough place. It pushes boundaries, and in some ways, we push back."

Jon squinted and his head bent with confusion.

Then Danix stepped aside and pushed open the door.

Taking a deep breath, more ideas flooded Jon's mind, but all of them had become clear. When Jon was allowed in, even with all the ideas in his mind, he was still unprepared.

It was nothing like Jon expected.

"Jesus," he said.

"Yeah," said Danix. "Get ready for a show."

CHAPTER 13
THE FIRST TEST

Now inside this new room, Jon smelled something so foul he had to hunch. He needed a minute to hold in his puke. The room smelled like the stench of a hundred dead bodies all crammed together and was rank with sweat and cheap perfume.

It was so putrid Jon covered his mouth soon as he was inside.

Why a room like this was at The Conquistador was something Jon hoped to discover once inside. While he was blinded, he couldn't bear the filth. When Danix stepped in to join Jon, he flicked on a light. Jon was struck by a new sensation. It was one that pained his pupils and forced him to turn away.

"Ah."

"Rise and shine, old boy," said Danix.

Gradually, Jon opened his eyes. And, with caution, kept his hand in front of his face. Jon stared and began to guess some of what was inside this space.

What he saw were people. Many, *many people.*

However, none of them were moving.

Jon squinted and honed his focus and gazed at all the silhouettes. From what he could see, Jon's assumptions were correct. However, to say that they were *real* people was not.

"What's going on?" Jon's voice broke. "What is this place?"

"*This,*" said Danix. "This is our own tactical training center and consider it your first step toward your greater understanding of the trade."

"The trade?"

Danix walked along the perimeter and stared at all the boxes located throughout the room. Although Jon couldn't see what was inside, he was still trying to make out what Danix was doing. While Jon's instincts were not on point, he was influenced by his inherent nose for danger. What Danix seemed to be doing was arming something. As he set up these new mannequins for the test, what Danix was saying to Jon carried great meaning.

It was truth, and that was why Jon was here now.

"Bouncing, you will find, is a matter of *tasking* and *assessment*," Danix explained. "It's a profession you can't just drop into until you learn all the basic steps, the basic rules."

"Basic rules?" asked Jon. "Right."

"Yeah," said Danix. He was now on the other side of the room. "And so, Addison set this place up for our new trainees to practice in. Before they're allowed to get on the floor, they first have to make it out of here, out of our Green Room."

"What?"

"It's what it's called," said Danix. *"The Green Room."*

"Why...why that?"

"You'll see," Danix said to Jon.

Above Danix's head was a giant banner with digital font. It looked like a shot clock with three numbers, and right now, all the digits were zero. Then, flicking the lights again, Danix blackened the space.

He then took a giant step backward and eyed Jon from behind the mannequins.

"Each group will be assigned a different scenario. You look at the banner overhead and then you have to try to solve the problem that's happening here. And, if you guess right, a green spotlight will shine, and you'll be free to move on to the next challenge."

"If I guess right?" said Jon. What he required now was more information. What Jon was told now, he did not understand.

"Correct," said Danix.

"And if I guess wrong?" Jon asked, a slight shake in his right hand.

Danix grinned. He was letting his expression do most of the talking. While piecing together what he could, in the back of his mind, Jon hadn't a clue what was happening.

"Just be on your guard, yeah?"

"I am," said Jon. "I will be."

"No, *be on your guard*," corrected Danix. "Guard is a state of mind, not as a means of waiting. As a bouncer, a good bouncer, you have to know the difference."

"Right," Jon replied, still somewhat confused.

"And your first scenario begins...*now*."

The room immediately darkened and a hard, loud,

ear-numbing beat thundered in the background. The booming sound was followed by a series of lights, which all made this small room into a micro-version of your everyday, run-of-the-mill nightclub.

"Concentrate," said Danix. "Be on your guard. Patrol and listen."

Jon surveyed the space. Jon heard Danix loud and clear. He saw the banner and the font changed:

TOO MANY DRINKS. GIRLS NIGHT OUT. ROWDY.

The font was now written in all capital letters. The words were angular. They appeared fat. Still, Jon saw every single one of them. A glowing circle brightened the mannequins and Jon's eyes shifted. Each one wore a frizzy, disheveled wig. All looked like they had been tossed together at the last minute.

"You have two minutes to resolve it. Go."

"What?" asked Jon. He could barely see Danix at all. Right now, he was just a figure sheathed in shadow. If not due to his large stature and his massive, encircling appearance, Danix too would have disappeared the same as everything else.

"Counting now."

"*Uh...*" Now frazzled, Jon tried to remember the reason why he was here. This was the difference that Danix recently outlined between being ready and *being on guard*.

It was all a state of mind, as Danix had specified.

Jon tried to transition to such a mindset. "*Go!*"

Jon raced to the crowd and followed the lights.

By doing this, Jon recalled the banner as well as the

scenario. It was all part of his training. Given so much time to resolve a single issue, these issues had changed after a certain timeframe. What happened afterward, *Jon wouldn't know*. He didn't have time to think or consider what the consequences might be.

He approached this crowd of *girls* and stopped dead in his tracks. Jon looked at each one of the statues and treated them like they were actual people.

He reviewed all the details and tried to absorb each one individually.

"What seems to be the problem here, ladies? How are you all doing tonight?"

Jon knew right away that this was a bad way to approach a rowdy crowd.

And the clock was ticking.

"Look, you ladies are getting really rowdy. You need to stop, *all right*? Otherwise, we're going to have to ask you to leave. Do you understand?"

Jon didn't know whether what he said was right or wrong. These mannequins couldn't react if what he was doing was correct. He thought about Danix and how the countdown was continuing. Danix shouted, the countdown ended, and Jon stopped.

"Time!"

With the first round down, Jon questioned whether or not he passed this first test. Was this what he was expected to do? Jon wanted to be sure he fulfilled all the expectations presented to him.

He wanted to do well. He wanted to succeed.

"Uh...I..." Jon's lips puckered and then separated. He wasn't parched, but he wanted a drink.

And soon as he began to construct a diligent response, the mannequins that were supposed to imitate an unscrupulous group of girls emitted a whirring siren. The sound reminded Jon of the sirens heard while in obstacle courses back in the Marines.

In fact, as soon as Jon heard it, he knew it wasn't good.

Well, when was a siren *ever* fucking good? "Shit."

The siren blared. Jon expected to be taken to the next part of the *course*. Yet, from inside one of the mannequins, a stream of scalding hot *green* water sprayed Jon's petrified face.

"Gah!"

Whatever it was, it fucking stung. This hurt less because of the temperature and more because it was composed of some kind of compound that burned like a motherfucker.

Spraying acid, if that's what this was?

How the hell was this a test?

Jon felt like he was in second grade. He was back to running relay races on the jungle gym and he didn't even know how to do it. He tried putting all the reasons together, but he still couldn't explain this test.

Danix snapped to attention and yelled at Jon. "Round Two!" he shouted. "Next problem! Go! Go! Go!"

"What?"

"Next station...now!"

Jon saw this first round as a complete and utter failure. And yet, he had no choice but to continue. Jon followed the lights and proceeded toward the next assembly, the next challenge. Now among a group of males, the effigies were sitting instead of standing.

The banner above provided the scenario.

FIGHT AT A BOOTH. OTHERS NEARBY.
GOAL: NEUTRALIZE.

Reading this, Jon stood in front of this *booth*. There, his head was cocked back and he was on the lookout for Danix.

"How do I neutralize a fucking mannequin?!" He didn't know where he was but heard Danix yelling from farther away.

"With words, motherfucker! With words!" Jon wanted to yell something back but he didn't.

The test continued to make little sense.

Jon couldn't determine how he was going to succeed in this next test. Whatever the reasons, whatever the price, Jon moved on to the next situation without saying a word. Jon held his own as he walked toward this crowd and did exactly as he did before.

"Gentlemen, we're getting some complaints about being too loud. Can we please keep it down?" Jon waited to see what would happen next.

He had no idea what may or may not follow. He declined to care or see how it ended for him. When Jon provided his response, he was hit by another stream. It sprayed Jon this time, and he shuffled back and almost fell over another table.

"Ah!" Jon screamed. Rubbing his eyes, he cleaned them as best he could.

From the corner of the room, right where Danix was positioned, he shouted again. He ordered Jon to keep moving. "Next! Go!"

Barely able to see and barely able to stand, Jon circled. Now in a daze, he headed to the left of the room, or what he thought was the left. Jon tripped over his feet and fell into another table. Now thinking the test would end here, Danix screamed.

"Go! New scenario! Next one! Move! Move!"

Falling over, Jon saw the banner. He saw it, but just barely.

FIGHT. FOUR PEOPLE. GOAL: REMOVE.

"Uh..."

"Go! Keep going! Keep going!" Danix yelled at Jon.

The Marine tipped and almost buckled. He did as he was ordered to. He went right to the next.

"Please. Keep it down. We don't want to—"

More spray!

"Next!" Danix shouted.

Jon was now forced into a tight corner and an even tighter scenario. It was these scenarios he could not understand. Not knowing what was going to happen or what he was doing, Jon couldn't comprehend so he just pushed on. Now in the middle of another fucking test, Jon did exactly as he had. He used words, he remained calm, and then he was struck again and again.

The intricacies and technology integrated into this tactical training center were incredible. All the tools and pieces were beyond Jon's comprehension.

But what was the point of this?

What was he supposed to do that he hadn't already?

Going from crowd to crowd and person to person, Jon was half-blind and in incredible pain. And yet, he proceeded while Danix screamed at him more.

"Go! Next! Keep moving! Keep moving!"

He endured much as a Marine. Jon fought, and he

conquered. He had been in trenches, amid gunfire, and had come face to face with death. And always, he was told, to keep moving.

Do. Not. Stop.

So Jon pushed still. He fought until the very end. Jon was someone who knew what it meant to never back down or surrender. And each time he heard Danix's screams, Jon fought harder. He rose up, and in doing this, Jon clashed with a new gathering of statues/ "people". He played through the scenarios again. He lost track of the many encounters and also lost track of where he was or *what he was doing*.

Nevertheless, when he stood up, he moved on to the next.

He crawled along the floor, but could not stand after.

And when he managed to gather the strength to get up, Jon was muttering incoherently. He babbled on like he'd been stripped of his ability to speak. He felt dizzy. He felt like throwing up. On his feet, Jon was in front of another mannequin, another cardboard cut-out of what was supposed to be a real person.

In the presence of this makeshift representation, something acting as a patron at the great Conquistador, Jon knelt and opened his hand. Halfway up, Jon was just starting to get his vision back. When it cleared and all the discomfort lifted, Jon found himself staring at Danix.

The big man looked at Jon with an intrigued smile.

Unable to speak, Jon's mind was still spinning.

Even in spite of what he experienced, Jon had experienced far worse. It was that worse that made him unable to stand up now.

"Well," said Danix, "I gotta say, Addison was right about you."

"What?" Out of breath, Jon's reply was accompanied by an exasperated sigh.

"You are *one* tough bastard."

With one eye opened, Danix had just put Jon through an absolute circus of confusion, misdirection, and pain.

"But I didn't get any of it right," said Jon. "I was a disaster. I got hit every time."

"That you did," said Danix. "Just like we *all* did."

"What?" Jon said, fatigued and perplexed. "What do you mean by that?"

"The game of bouncing is more often than not a *no-win* scenario," said Danix. "No matter what you do, how nice you are, shit's still gonna hit the fan. It's about strategy, problem solving, checking, and communicating, and so...you have to be ready for all that. Here is where you learn the most important rule in the game."

"*Which is?*" asked Jon. He coughed and grunted his response.

"Always...*always* stay calm," said Danix. "And always keep your head straight and never resort to violence unless absolutely necessary."

"But I didn't raise a single hand."

"No, no you did not," Danix replied. "And that's the *point*. That's why I said you did it."

Jon could still smell the smoke as well as the toxic scent of this green liquid that doused his cheeks and nose. Jon's skin was charred as if scalded with hot tea. Jon's eyes wobbled and looked elsewhere.

And yet, even so. Here he was, still up and still standing.

"And so, *you passed the first test.*"

"First?" asked Jon. "There's more?"

"Oh, brother," said Danix. He escorted Jon to the door and back into the club. "We're just getting started."

CHAPTER 14
FAMILY LEGACY

THE CONQUISTADOR OPENED ITS DOORS ON NEW Year's Day, at the dawning of a new decade, in the year 1980. From there, the club thrived as New York's hottest night scene. It offered a once-in-a-lifetime experience to all of its customers. At that time, Larry Thomas was the club's proprietor. He was also its chief executive officer. Therefore, he was the one in charge of creating its many decadent and lavish events. Larry was also someone who knew he had to have a clear vision for the company. It was about access for all people, with no guns allowed. It was to be built on a profound sense of respect and a clear set of unbreakable rules.

This vision was absolute and, at the time, utterly undeniable.

Bigger. Better. Different.

When the club first opened its doors, Larry wanted to do something new.

He wanted there to be more. There would be new experiences to offer, with the dance floor being wider and cleaner. The music would sound new and the drinks would be never-ending. They were ready to serve the top shelf of New York's finest selections of wines and other cool beverages. Larry wanted to make the prices high, but reasonable. What Larry also wanted was for the booths to be accessible and to include other top-notch décor. Always, he wanted more: more music, more seats, more tables, and more appearances by celebrities and other wealthy people. The way Larry saw it, when people come to nightclubs, they don't want to hold back.

They don't want to behave themselves in any capacity.

What they want more than anything is to let loose and to let go.

They want to get rid of all their problems and just be free.

Truly free or, as Larry called it, "golden." He wanted the club to be "pure gold".

But freedom is a subjective concept.

Opportunity and the methods granted as a result of freedom, however, are not.

To grant this to all of the people, Larry purchased a big space with a big parking lot and hired many employees. The new space was located just off the freeway and offered an in-house cab service, with added security and limousines designed specifically for pick-up and drop-off.

It was branded The Conquistador as if it were a hotel in Vegas.

Larry Thomas managed to increase attendance by fifty percent. Seeing such growth, Larry responded. He said he wanted to see more tourists and more people with money to come and join the party. He desired better service and better attendance.

"Everyone who comes into my club, I want them to feel famous and important."

"Everyone?" asked an employee at the time.

"Yes, everyone."

With such an attitude taken, there wasn't a single person who didn't desire such treatment. They were free from the confines of their daily lives, and this was an infectious strategy. It was the perfect way to reach people.

Ordinary People.

When all of them began joining The Conquistador, everything changed.

Everyone there felt like they were being deified. They felt like celebrities.

They were all but placed on the frontier of freedom, all manifesting into a prestige and indulging in certain moments of self-importance and expression. It elevated everyone to a level of themselves they did not know existed.

Larry pushed for a louder, more immersive club experience. Now with one of the largest spaces in the industry, attendance on Thursdays could be anywhere between one hundred to two hundred. On Fridays, it was a little more than the day before. Now Saturdays were the club's hottest day. The Conquistador saw anywhere between two hundred to two hundred and fifty.

It was an exploding empire and was growing more and more each day. Soon the reputation of The Conquistador skyrocketed, as did its revenue. After two weeks, it was accommodating A-list actors, musicians, and professional athletes. It opened its doors to Fortune 500 CEOs and other billionaire tycoons. And all had found their way to Larry Thomas's front door. Adoring Mr. Thomas's persona, most respected his entrepreneurial spirit as well as the *safe* environment. There was nothing like The Conquistador. It was "golden."

To everyone, Larry was more than the club's owner. No, he was its friend and its innovator. He was someone who would later be called a genius. As a pioneer ahead of his time, none of the other clubs were able to match The Conquistador's skill or reputation. As it grew, it secured its place as one of the hottest nightclubs in America. And because of this Larry accumulated more wealth, most of which became an absolute mystery to those who knew him. None were aware of what Larry did with his money, what he invested in, or how he managed to secure the permits to build this club here, in this city.

Yet, The Conquistador soon developed its own place among the guild of nightclubs and eventually, became something better. The Conquistador became more than just a club, it became a tradeable asset. It became currency—the *key* to something better.

———

Larry soon made many new friends. He also carved out a few enemies too. He was prepared for anything and anyone. His daughter Tanya introduced her dad to the man she was going to marry. She did just as the club was coming to its twenty-year anniversary.

Addison Krowe was Tanya's fiancé. He was also in

law school at the time of their introduction. Larry Thomas was a man who demanded instantaneous respect. However, Addison was actually more familiar with The Conquistador than the proprietor had anticipated. Not only did Addison possess knowledge of the law and the policy, he understood what needed to happen for the club to grow. "Have you thought about increasing your security?"

Until then, Larry Thomas had twenty bouncers on the floor at all times. He employed a cooler who had been working under him for almost a decade. And yet, it was Addison who pitched him a new and promising idea.

"If you're going to have the best nightclub in the city, then you're going to need the best security."

While Addison was bold to claim this, his intentions were not to offend Larry Thomas. Given the level of security Addison witnessed, he would be lying if he said he was impressed. Larry's original bouncers were nothing more than a bunch of thugs and washed-up tough guys from bad neighborhoods. As Addison said, *none of them were professional.* What Larry needed was men who were trained not only in the skills of fighting but were maybe ex-military, tough, smart but who understood how to be good guardians and not just good combatants. No, what Addison encouraged was a new breed of nightlife security that adhered to The Conquistador's creed and procedures.

All of this fell under the jurisdiction of the Nightclub Oversight Commission.

"Strong-willed, composed, unassuming, and very, *very* calm." Larry's attitude was always to find strength in numbers.

He wanted to swarm any threat until it was completely handled. Yet, as Addison had told him, this was only one way of thinking.

"Invest in one professional, train them the right way, and create a cohesive unit with only select vital members. You have an A squad and a B squad, all looking out for each other. They do this because, in the end, they care about each other. They're a brotherhood, a front, a unit."

"A unit?" Such an idea was new to Larry Thomas.

"They respect their professions," said Addison, "the artform that is bouncing."

Addison was the first one to label bouncing as an artform. He described it as being different than other professions. He compared it to the others that acquired pillars, methods, and mentalities that served to protect themselves and others.

Why should this job be any different?

"Sounds difficult," Larry commented as he stood in front of his future son-in-law.

"Difficult, but necessary," replied Addison. "We need real gatekeepers. We need...*Doormen*."

Soon after Addison made this proposal, Larry agreed to this new hiring process. He agreed to the set of rules that would govern his club. He never spoke about these rules to anyone, but Addison did make a few suggestions for the people he knew. The others Larry had himself selected. Soon The Conquistador had its Doormen, and their purposes were outlined and clear.

This was their new home.

————

The best of the best is a trite term given to anyone who deems themselves good at something. When Larry used the term, he actually meant it.

His men were the best.

They were because they all belonged to him. All under Larry's employ, everyone who was part of The Conquistador family was brought there for a specific purpose. It was to reach the highest level possible. They were all here to be better than the innumerable others working in this profession. Insisting always that they earn themselves the title, Addison Krowe promised Mr. Thomas that they would.

Addison was the overseer because he was not the physical type.

He was the smartest one at the club, but Addison prided himself on seeing everything all the time. He wanted to bring in people who he was convinced had something unique in their arsenal. If someone was physically capable, then the next recruit had to also be physically capable *and* endowed with another skill of some kind.

It needed to be something unique, something usable.

What Addison put together was an assembly of the best bouncers in the business.

Formidable yet calm, the Doormen were brutal yet tactful. They were decent and, at the same time, cunning. Addison Krowe insisted on giving them routine exercises as well as many health benefits. He fought for solid, reliable hours. And, as a result of the amount of money Larry Thomas was saving, this enabled the owner to deliver. Addison emphasized the concepts of loyalty and respect. Addison Krowe told

Larry he was now the best boss. Should his security respect him, then they would respect the club too.

And if they respected the club, then they would *always* respect him.

"Bouncers are not soldiers, and they are not cops. They are watchers and neutralizers. They are a force deployed only when necessary and they are ready at a moment's notice. Above all else, they're working top-scale professionals. They don't police, they escort, they communicate, and they interact. They do what they must to keep a venue safe, and that's all it is."

Larry knew this well before Addison said it. However, the fact Addison did say it made Larry feel much better.

"If this club is to be the best, then it needs to have the best security." These were the final words Addison provided before he was promoted as The Conquistador's official head of security.

Larry Thomas understood all of this now. And, like all good institutions with good reputations, it was soon the target of disruption and clandestine operations. While Larry was warned by Addison about what could potentially go wrong, celebrities weren't the only ones who came to The Conquistador.

Eventually, a new kind of clientele began to emerge and with a very different intention.

It started with the son of a mobster named Frankie Castellani.

He was someone who saw the club as something else...

As he said, *it had potential.*

CHAPTER 15
BACK IN THE GAME

"The Conquistador is a powder keg, and it's about to light up like the Fourth of fucking July." Frankie Castellani was relatively new to the world of criminality. Everyone in his family had a nickname for the son of New York's crime boss. What Frankie wanted most was to make a name for himself. His father, Giuliani, was the head of the family. He employed thieves, extortionists, and blackmailers. Everyone in the syndicate prided themselves on keeping things contained. They wanted fast and low, with few risks in between.

Frankie saw things differently.

He was an ambitious boy ever since he was small. Being the youngest in a family of five, Giuliani had made it clear to his children: "You don't do anything that will put our family at risk, do you understand?"

Frankie was low on the totem pole. There were many others far deadlier than he was, yet Frankie would never do anything to hurt his father or his family.

What Frankie wanted, he wanted *badly*.

And what he wanted was to have an operation of his own, one that stood apart from his family's, something small time on which he could build. Frankie wanted to make something even his dad would find impressive. It was not something dependent on his name. It was instead something that was about his intelligence. It played to his knowledge of what he learned being the son of a notorious gangster.

"A powder keg, huh?" asked Frankie's best friend, Rico. He was standing there too.

"Ready to pop," Frankie added. "And that means it's perfect."

"Perfect...for what?" Rico asked again.

Frankie stood in front of the balustrade outside the luxury apartment his dad had purchased for him. Although not officially affiliated with the Castellanis, Frankie's friend Rico did a few things for the family, but all of it was small-time. Being Frankie's confidant and bodyguard, Rico was someone whom Frankie hoped to bring into his operation despite not having permission to do so.

"Perfect for our own operation, our own path to greatness and glory."

Rico had ambition too. What he didn't have, however, was a death wish.

"But what about your dad?" asked Rico. "What does he have to say?"

Frankie smoked his cigarette and the gray cloud wafted in front of Rico's face. The friend's lips quivered as he spoke the man's name.

Frankie could sense the fear.

It was so palpable because Frankie was making the

decision to go behind his father's back. He was about to defy a very powerful man.

What was said needed to be said.

"He doesn't know. This is our thing, and we'll make sure that it stays that way."

"But your dad knows a lot of people. The Conquistador is a popular place. Lots of people go there."

"That I know," said Frankie.

"And I know you know," said Rico, "which is why I'm not sure you're really thinking this one through here."

"Look..." Frankie tossed his cigarette and stepped closer to his friend. Like the bro that he was, Frankie wrapped his hand around Rico's muscular neck and pulled him close.

"We can pull this off, buddy," he said. "We get into that club on a weekly basis. People down there, they know us already. We start pushing some product, build a base, and then we can trade. But we do it our way, on our own terms, and if we succeed, we'll have access to things beyond our wildest dreams."

"What about supply?" asked Rico.

This was a suitable question. Both were too young to have someone supply them with drugs to move in and out of the club.

"I have a *contact*."

"Who?"

"Someone on the inside. He's going to help us move under the radar. As soon as anyone gets a whiff of what we're doing, he's going to make sure no one asks any questions. Trust me, I got the whole thing under control."

"Man, I don't know...I..." Doubtful and a little

scared, Rico turned from Frankie. Although Frankie was not surprised to see his friend displaying such levels of conflict and uncertainty, what he wanted was very rebellious no doubt.

Frankie didn't have the authority to break such rules.

Also, it was something that, should it not go as planned, Frankie would be risking more than his family's name. He'd end any chance of having a future operation of his own.

It was a ballsy move, to say the least.

When Frankie stared at his friend, he channeled the ferocity and sternness observed in his father. By doing this, Frankie Castellani had reclaimed what he saw to be his well-deserved, much-owed birthright. "We can do this."

What Frankie wanted, essentially, was to set up an operation within the club itself. Instead of doing this through his father, Frankie would be using his own supplier. He would be choosing to move the product with the help of his friends, like Rico. He was going to set up something clandestine, a new means of distribution by reaching out to patrons and other high-class guests.

This was Frankie's plan.

"The Conquistador is a big place," said Rico. "It's a big place with a big history and, if we're in there, and we're setting up our own op, then we should all know who your contact on the inside is...right?"

"No one knows except for me." Emphatic, Frankie Castellani made it clear.

Whoever was on the inside, it was him and him alone who would be cooperating.

"You sure you won't want to give me a clue?" Rico asked Frankie.

Frankie shook his head. He was being abrupt and dismissive. Frankie, however, was confident in his decision. Chin up, Frankie pulled a fresh cigarette out of his pocket and lit it up. He smoked as he looked out at the city. His family and his name coursed through the vast metropolis like steam in a kettle.

It was a name that dominated the location. New York was the Castellani's home.

"This city is ripe," said Frankie, "and my family controls damn near all of it."

"I know," said Rico. "You're one lucky man there, Frankie boy."

"Lucky?" The comment was, in Frankie's opinion, condescending. He curled his tongue and licked his cigarette. "My father, my brothers, they all get more than I do," said Frankie. "There's never been a single part of my life where I haven't felt small. You ever feel like that way, Rico?"

"What?" said Rico. "Jealous of my siblings? Not really, bro."

"No," said Frankie. His eyes turned down and he was downcast as he replied. "*Small?*"

After a moment of silence, Frankie puffed and blew out smoke.

"I don't know. Sometimes," Rico replied eventually.

"What about...all the time?" asked Frankie.

There was no answer.

"Because all the time," said Frankie, "I feel like I'm too small and that I'm not good enough for anyone or anything."

Rico said nothing, but Frankie was aware that he

shared too much about his struggles. He'd already broken the chief rule of what it meant to be a *real boss*. The rules are clear.

Never talk outside the family.

"But all that's about to change. And the first step is to get moving, to get moving as quickly as possible."

"When?" asked Rico.

"This weekend," said Frankie, "I'm going to book us a booth at the club, talk to some of our dealers, and then we start rolling in our product as soon as possible. We're gonna pick our spots, *set up*, and get that money train churning. Once we have that, my contact is gonna hook us up with something even better, something *big* he said."

Frankie faced Rico.

Being his right-hand man, Rico was the one Frankie depended on the most. He was also the same person Frankie would be depending on in the future. He glared and summoned his inner mob boss role. Before, if Frankie disobeyed the cardinal rule of being a man in charge, he was now loyal to the main rule he and his father both abided by.

He was the boss, and bosses gave orders.

"You sure you want to do this?"

"No," Frankie said to Rico. "Not really, actually, but then I ain't into runnin' or bailin' either. If I'm gonna go legit, I gotta start treatin' myself as though I am already for the big time. And it won't just start here. It begins with an operation, a job where there's potential for growth, if you know what I mean?"

Rico nodded. He knew exactly what he meant.

"Okay," said Rico. "So...we start?"

Nodding, Frankie replied. "Yeah, we start...*big*."

CHAPTER 16
A WAY OF DOING THINGS

WHEN JON ENDED THE FIGHT, HE WENT TO THE bathroom to wash up. Blood dripped from his knuckles and into the sink. While his hand hurt, Jon's head hurt more. He thought it was all so clear. He wanted to avoid getting into fights. And yet, the one he had just partaken in was messy.

There was no backing down. There was no talking and no reasoning.

Although Jon did have backup, he only felt like he needed it because there was more than one person. Jon Haze had been employed at The Conquistador for two weeks. In that time, Jon had prevented several altercations. He had also managed to tangle in a few as well.

He was trained to avoid and to expect the unexpected.

For some reason, this particular engagement did not exactly align with these concepts.

Rubbing his hands with soap and water, Jon held his face over the sink and splashed his cheeks. The cold water felt absolutely rejuvenating. It awakened Jon soon as it touched his flesh.

He looked at himself in the mirror and he was all cut up and bruised. He was only now getting used to this. His face was always wrecked and banged up, and this reminded Jon that he was all done doing his job.

More than this, Jon was doing it well.

"Hey…" someone called to Jon from the door. Soon as Jon heard it, he looked.

Sam was standing there in his collared shirt, the one all Doormen were required to wear.

"You good?"

Jon tore a handful of paper towels from the dispenser above the sink. He wiped himself up nice and good and made sure he was cleaned up well. Jon then tossed the used towels into a bin and looked back at Sam. "I'll be fine."

Sam's lips were pressed together and he looked stoic, the same as Jon. The situation wasn't just Jon's. Sam was there too.

"What about the others?" asked Jon.

"The others in the fight?" Sam replied.

Jon nodded. "Yeah."

"Got rid of them. They're out."

"Good," said Jon. When he was done cleaning, he stepped back toward the door. Jon made his way back to the club, but before he could pass, Sam sidestepped into Jon's path.

Although Jon had handled the confrontation, he recalled an important detail yet to be discussed. While there, Jon found himself in a tussle with one of the guys at the table as the rest of the party scattered.

Jon did feel like a criminal. He had his hands full

with two guys. However, the others who raced away did manage to escape. When they did, they made sure they escaped to Sam.

"Why did you let them go by you?" Jon asked Sam.

"Who went by me?" Jon tossed another towel into the bin. He tried to hide how he really felt about the situation. He pretended like there was more to the story. He believed there were more details that might explain Sam's choices.

And, if Jon was honest, he was not impressed with what he was seeing so far. He was not impressed with Sam. Jon was getting his bell rung. He was being beat down and shaken, and although it was all a part of the game, there were other bouncers present.

There were more because you *needed* more.

Jon assumed Sam had his reasons for letting these guys go too far. Whether he did or didn't, Jon hadn't discussed any of this.

"There were three other guys who ran away," said Jon. "Did you see *them*?"

"Danix caught them all by the door, so yeah."

Jon nodded. What Sam said could have been true, or it might not have been either. Now Jon was unsure. He was actually glad someone managed to find the guys who tried to get away.

"And the guy who attacked me, what happened to him?"

"Name's Rico," said Sam.

Jon was intrigued by this response. His head was bent. Jon eyed Sam with one eye open.

"You *know* him?" Jon asked peculiarly.

Sam's chin moved in a slight nod. Yes, he did. "A little," said Sam.

There was an awkward pause. Jon was now by the door.

"Where is he now?"

"Gone," answered Sam. "Got his ass kicked out. *He's done.*"

"All right," said Jon. He was skeptical about the interaction. He almost hated it.

"Look, when you're done cleaning yourself up," continued Sam, "Addison wants to see you. You gotta fill out a police report."

"The police are here?"

"They are," said Sam.

Jon nodded and pockets of redness occupied his face. Then, getting feeling back in his hands, Jon held out his hand. He felt the same sting before he abruptly stopped.

He exhaled.

"You okay?" asked Sam.

What Jon wanted was time to get his head straight. Rage and nightmares echoed throughout his body. All Jon's movements ceased. He was now perfectly still.

"Yeah, I'm...I'm fine." Sam let Jon pass. As he went on, Jon didn't say a word. "Just fine."

———

In the kitchen inside the club, Jon stepped through the stark hallway. It was empty. Jon estimated what time it was when working a night job purely from how he felt at the time.

He was limber. He was lucid. It was now between eleven and two.

Jon's hands felt light. His feet did too. His legs were

stiff. It actually might be closer to four. The fight may have winded Jon, but he wasn't done for. Moving on, Jon was closer to the door when he heard the sound of Kya's voice.

Jon declined to walk. When hearing Kya's voice, a sensation coursed through Jon's entire body. It was both comforting and arousing. Jon had seen Kya each day and they were engaged in a chit-chat. It was nice going back and forth. While both were chummy, currently the two treated each other as though they were friends. Sometimes, there was a spark. There was a glimmer in Kya's eyes Jon felt like he could grab hold of.

Jon also felt like he knew her situation.

There was another guy in the picture, then again, Kya was a smokeshow.

Every guy wanted her. So, if many did want Kya, then Jon knew she was overwhelmed with options. There's always someone in the picture with girls like Kya. There's always someone available. The fact that Kya might have a boyfriend did not change how badly Jon wanted to be with her. One day, Jon believed he might be.

All he had to do was keep talking.

There was a breakroom situated off from the kitchen. It was an intimate setting, equipped with a table and small bar. With the shifts being so long, everyone needed a breather once and a while. Most would exit the floor and come here for five to fifteen.

Breaks in this kind of job worked differently. If it was a slow day, and it rarely was, one could incorporate breaks into their shift. This was something Jon did regularly. Also, if you were hurt or injured, then you weren't *taking* a break, you were resting because you *needed* to.

For now, Jon just wanted a little time, but he didn't want to spend it alone.

Jon hoped Kya was on the other side. As he pushed open the door, Jon listened to it squeak. He could hear laughter. Distinct and unique, it was liltingly feminine and Jon found this incredibly attractive. Kya was not alone. Li Huen was with her. He was having a drink and so was Jamal. They were wearing black shirts and Jamal laughed. Li smiled as he drank. When he was in, neither of the men noticed Jon, but Kya did.

She spotted Jon soon as he stepped inside.

"Jon." Kya's voice cracked as she called out to him. Soon as she did, the ears of both men pricked up and they turned to face him.

"You okay?" Kya asked. She stepped out from behind the bar. Moving at a moderate speed, she didn't seem in a rush to get to Jon, though she was speeding along. Therefore, Jon assumed it was because she was concerned about his injuries.

He tried not to blush as Kya inched closer.

"Heard what happened," said Jamal. "You good?"

"Fine," answered Jon. He nodded solemnly.

"Was pretty rough, huh?" said Kya. Now she was in front of Jon.

Jon iced his face. He held the blue pack tight and then proceeded to dab his chin. "Not that bad."

"How do you feel?" Jon looked at his hand. It pained him still, but the entire time, his mind was on Sam. He was there, but was holding himself back. Jon continued to ask the same question, and that question was *why*?

"I've felt worse," said Jon.

"Clearly," said Kya.

"How's your night?" Jon changed the subject. He didn't want to talk about the fight anymore. He was concerned, yes, but the fight was over, and he won.

"Not too bad," Kya said. "A few birthdays, and some assholes getting a little too handsy, you know how it is."

Jon nodded to show he did.

Bouncers got attacked, but bartenders got harassed. Here, in this setting, men prided themselves on taking things too far. They look out for those who are appealing and go until they can't anymore. Kya was a stone-cold fox and Jon imagined she was hired partially for this reason. She was asked to stay because no one knew how to handle a bar better than her. Being hit on, pointed to, and epically degraded was sadly a part of the job.

The rules were always clear in this place.

Never touch. Never cross the line.

Although Jon was asked to handle a few situations for Kya in the past. He had asked certain guys to take a step back and give Kya some space. On other occasions, Jon plainly asked them to leave. He dealt with the situation but didn't have time to assist Kya, if she did in fact acquire assistance. Jon read Kya's expression. She was plain and nonchalant, and her makeup was pristine. To Jon, this was a good sign.

"Not too bad. Not as bad as yours, I take it?"

"It isn't," said Jon. He looked down at his hand again. "Honestly. I'm...I'm good."

"Well, I'm glad it isn't." With a hint of charm, Jon shook his head. Yet, he had to remind himself that Kya was just being nice. And being nice didn't always mean a girl was into you.

It just meant she was kind and nice. Nothing more and nothing less.

Still, there was something in her words that made Jon think she wanted to know more. He would hardly call that flirting. Jon would, however, call it something. She was very sincere. Now, there was concern as well as show of grace for someone who was more than just a friend.

They were getting closer. Jon could feel it.

"Addison wants to see you," said Kya.

With their moment of sexual tension disrupted, all the feeling Jon once felt was now gone. He wanted it back. He wanted it all back.

———

Jon ventured through a hallway separate from the breakroom and walked to another stairwell apart from the others. If Jon were to proceed up these steps, he would be taken to the next floor of the club, not far from Addison's office. As Jon and the other Doormen were all aware, none were permitted to take such a route unless they had permission.

This permission was only granted to employees and friends. Fortunately, Jon was both.

Walking up the steps, Jon entered a hall with red velvet walls. He passed the framed photographs and proceeded to the door. He let out a long yawn as he headed into this strange passage. Though completely exhausted, the last chore Jon wanted to complete was to talk about the fight. Then again, protocol was protocol, and rules were rules.

That's just the way it was.

Jon knocked at Addison's door only once. He saw the box to enter the code. He thought he remembered it, but chose to knock. Soon as Jon's knuckles connected with the crisp wood, he could hear Addison on the other side.

"Come in!"

Jon opened the door and expected to see Addison sitting behind his desk, alone. He was seated, but alone? No. Standing next to him, in a three-piece red suit, was the man—Mr. Larry Thomas himself! Wearing a gold watch and fat rings, his gray hair was thick and extended down to his neck.

Sternly, Larry looked at Jon as he entered.

"Jon," said Addison. "Welcome."

"Hi." Now anxious, the quakes in Jon's hands returned. His vision blurred. Then with a few quick blinks, Jon was back.

"Thanks for coming in." Although Addison was the one speaking, Jon refused to look.

He did this not because he was afraid or because Jon had any regrets about the fight. No, who Jon was seeing now was the same man who owned it all. He was also someone who rarely showed his face unless he absolutely needed to. And, if Larry absolutely needed to now, then it had to be because someone did something they weren't supposed to. And the only person who could have done that *was Jon.*

"You know *Larry Thomas.*"

"Yes," said Jon. Now nervous, his hand trembled, so he wrapped his opposite one around it. *Why was the boss here?* "Nice to see you again."

"You too, Jon."

Jon was surprised Larry knew him by his first name.

However, Jon had only seen Mr. Thomas on a few occasions. Until now, Jon didn't think they were on a first-name basis.

He was wrong.

"So..." Jon said, turning to Addison. "I was told you needed me to fill in some paperwork, a report. It's protocol, I know, in case of a..." Jon coughed into his hand. "Violent situation."

"Right," replied Addison Krowe.

Jon watched Addison's gaze shift to Larry Thomas.

Suddenly, the situation was tense and uncomfortable. Questioning himself, Jon was starting to feel like he had done something wrong.

Maybe he didn't do his job as well as he should have.

Maybe he didn't do exactly what his training dictated he do.

Maybe Jon did step out of line. Maybe Larry was discussing with Addison about how the Marine should be reprimanded or handled. At this moment, Jon's head was spinning. Now in a panic, he couldn't understand how or why.

"But before we do any of that, we need to talk first."

"To me?" Jon pressed his finger to his chest.

Such a statement was ominous. Whenever someone says these words, it can only be interpreted in one way.

"Yes," said Larry.

A jitter trailed through Jon's shoulders. If Larry was speaking, then...

"Please...*have a seat*," Larry continued. His voice was weak. To Jon, Larry Thomas seemed brittle and ill.

"Okay." Jon did as he was told.

He couldn't refuse or deny what was being asked of him.

Larry Thomas was still his boss. And until now, Jon had dealt with Addison and no one else. So, if Mr. Thomas was here, then it *was* serious. There was no point in pretending it wasn't.

"That fight you were in today," said Addison, "do you remember it?"

"Of course," said Jon. "I remember *all* of it."

"Good," said Larry.

Jon meant what he said. He recalled every detail about the altercation.

Jon did this because he had to do it. Bouncers needed to summon all their moves, tactics, and techniques in an instant. They are questioned and they are reviewed. It was not so different from police tactics both in terms of strategy and approach. In this case, however, Jon was speaking to people he knew. He was with people who knew him too. He chose to leave this part of the story out. It was the part whereby he lost his memory and was in the middle of another damn flashback.

"Then you will know the man who you were fighting?" Addison asked again.

Jon nodded.

"Did you manage to get his name?" asked Larry.

Jon shook his head. The answer he provided was a clear *no*.

Why Addison had yet to speak was beginning to worry Jon. He was the head of security, but Larry owned the club. Again, the same odd scenario was surfacing in Jon's increasingly worrisome mind.

Why was Larry Thomas here?

"His name is Frankie Castellani. Ever heard of him?"

"I haven't."

"His father is Giuliani Castellani," Addison said to Jon. "He's the head of the Castellani crime family."

"Castellani crime family?" Jon was less worried about this and more concerned about what he should have done. Jon didn't doubt himself during the altercation. Jon's training was sufficient. He knew everything that happened. Jon was pushed. He was knocked down. It was rowdy, and it was getting rowdier. Jon did what he was told. Yet, simultaneously, he managed to piss off the heir to a rising criminal empire.

Not smart.

Still, this job wasn't personal. It didn't choose who it reprimanded or who it hurt. Its decisions were made only when rules were broken. After this, the consequences would follow. This was the rule of the club business as much as it was the rule for life.

"The same."

"Well, he was out of line," said Jon. "He was pushing, shoving, and breaking the rules, as you know. I needed to do something, so I followed my training. And that's all I did."

"No one is questioning your strategy, Jon," Addison said.

"Then why am I here?"

"Protection," said Larry.

"*What?*"

"Son of a local mobster," Larry stated, "and well, you just don't know this city as well as we do."

"But I didn't do anything wrong," declared Jon.

He wanted to make this point clear.

Jon had unapologetically declared he regretted nothing. He spoke vehemently and did so in the company of the man who was more than his boss. He was, right now, his entire future.

"No, you didn't," said Addison. "You were *doing* your job."

"Yes," said Larry, "but we're just giving you a word of warning, in case—"

"In case," Jon said, feeling a bit bolder now. He finished the rest of Larry's sentence and then he closed his hand over his wrist to stop the shaking. "Of what?"

And then there was silence.

No one wanted to talk, no one except for Jon. He was beginning to feel similar to what happened to him back in Iraq. He did his job targeting enemy insurgents. This was his purpose. Even if he fulfilled it with the utmost perfection, there were always consequences and lessons to be learned.

Jon reminded himself that bouncing is a game of assessment, with little doubt and many rules. It's not about combat, destruction, or attack. It's not about hurting people but communication, calmness, and sincerity. Jon was taught to channel these principles before anything else. Jon stood by and thought about what happened.

And doing this, Jon began to relentlessly question himself.

Did he do it right? Was he maybe too *rough*?

Did he follow *orders*, their orders, or did he follow only his own?

"Nothing," Larry said. Jon's rapid blinking continued. He was suddenly back in the Green Room where he was trained. "We just look out for our own," explained Larry. "And we thought you should know, and to...well, be careful, that's all."

Larry stood and retrieved his hat off Addison's desk. He owned a sleek fedora. It was red and matched the trimmings of his suit. Before Larry could leave the office, he wobbled and he blinked. He was old but not too spry. He looked weak, but this meant little to Jon.

He was still the boss.

The Marine exhaled.

"Well...that was something, wasn't it?" Addison made the comment. Jon's heart thumped, and he held his wrist tighter.

Whenever Jon felt stressed or doubtful and like he wasn't in the right headspace, his therapist suggested a few strategies. One of them was known as a wrist stretch. It was helping Jon now, so he delivered a comment of his own.

"Yes, it was. What the hell was that about, Addison?"

Addison was dressed in a black suit, his collar loose around his neck. He leaned back, casual yet also exhausted. Addison sighed and then he replied. "Do you really want to know?"

Jon shrugged. His impulse was to sarcastically respond by saying: *No, I only asked because I didn't want a reason.*

Of course, Jon didn't *say* this. All he did was nod. Addison leaned forward. "I do."

"Well," said Addison, "a low-level mobster who got taken down by one of our Doormen is a new trend happening at The Conquistador."

Jon squinted. Confused by the statement, everything about this conversation was bewildering.

"You're telling me no other sons of criminals have visited his club before? They weren't bounced? I find that very hard to believe."

"Well," said Addison, "some have, but if you want me to be honest with you—"

"I do," Jon piped in right away.

Now, he was fed up. He felt cornered, and the doubt he was experiencing had heightened. Jon wanted more than he was getting.

"Sort of an unwritten rule here at The Conquistador. Powerful people get different treatment."

Jon's forehead began to wrinkle and his hand began to shake. He did not like what he was hearing, not at all.

"We favor the bad guys?" Jon asked. "Is that what you're saying?"

"Not exactly," said Addison. "We just have to be careful. I mean, people who break the rules, sure they're asked to leave and everything, but there's sort of an unwritten rule that if some of the clients are linked to organized crime, we handle them more carefully. Some might even say we handle them *very* carefully. We do this because, well...we might be a solid club with solid security, we are still, at the end of the day, an *important* club. There are rules here, some people follow them, but other people have a harder time understanding them."

"By some other people, you mean...*criminals*?" Despondent and ashamed, Jon looked down at his feet.

He could sense similar feelings from Addison too. In fact, Jon knew Addison better than all his other coworkers. When Jon wasn't looking him in the eye, the act suggested he struggled to accept what Larry Thomas was giving now.

"Larry has kept our club on top for many years," said Addison, "because of how he chooses to engage not only with his customers, but with the people of this city too. You didn't cross any line, so don't think that you did. No, Jon, you did your job and you did it well. It's just...at the end of the day, you're still a rookie. And a rookie, by definition, has a lot of learning to do. So, don't consider this to be a confrontation or that you're being reprimanded in any way. Just take it more as a...*heads up*, so to speak."

"A heads up?" asked Jon.

"Yes," said Addison. "And don't worry, whatever happens, everyone here protects the next guy. We look out for each other, and you can be damn sure...we're going to be looking out for you."

"Thanks."

"So...are we good?" Addison asked Jon. The Marine's hands slid down to his leg.

He was conflicted and somewhat worried about the conversation he just had. Larry Thomas, up until this point, was still thought of as an honorable, good man. For Jon, he was a man with secrets, a man with a code. As Addison described, the club had its *own way of doing things*.

Here for almost six weeks at The Conquistador, Addison wasn't wrong when he referred to Jon as a rookie. Still, with much to learn, the familiarity that was beginning to strike him was his time in the Marines. He was a man following orders.

The more orders he followed, the more he learned.

Corporals, colonels, generals, their outlook was synonymous with Larry's.

Their way was the only way.

There were to be no questions asked, and everyone was to follow protocol and obey.

Jon knew well to do this. And so, without asking questions, he stepped through the door. He walked on without saying a word, and the entire time, he was thinking about that face in the crowd.

Frankie Castellani...*see you soon*.

CHAPTER 17
SOMETHING IN THE WAY

SINCE BEGINNING HIS NEW JOB AS A BOUNCER, JON Haze's life had drastically changed. What was once a broken, uncertain day-to-day routine had become regimented and strict, upheld and adhered to no matter what. It must never fail, and neither could Jon.

At least, this was Jon's perception of his new life.

Working late nights, Jon's days at The Conquistador went from Tuesday to Saturday. The club was officially closed on Sundays, with no special events or appearances scheduled. Therefore, there were no people who needed to be tended to and no meetings or plans for any of the Doormen.

Yet, even when the Doormen weren't working, they were still working.

Still a morning riser, Jon slept for only a few hours.

The Marines ruined his sleeping patterns and Jon's bed felt too soft. This, combined with the quiet, Jon did get some good shuteye most nights. He liked how safe he felt.

Home helped. It helped a lot.

After this, Jon would have a protein shake and run to the gym. He was just starting to get into MMA and would frequent Danix's gym for training. Danix was a former SEAL who actually competed in the UFC. He managed to use some of his private contract money to open a garage. He trained aspiring fighters, some of whom were former Marines like Jon. Jon would hit the bag and roll on the mats. When he wasn't working, he was there training to get stronger, faster, and harder.

Endurance was what Jon desired most of all.

And when Jon wasn't doing all of this, he was helping his mother. He was either getting groceries or assisting her when she cleaned the house. Jon tried to be there whenever she needed him to be. This was not to say Jon's mom *did* need him. It was nice, as she said, just to have him around. What Jon's mom really meant to say was she was happy. She was happy to have Jon here, back home. Sometimes Jon would go out and do other things. He would catch a movie before work or use some of his money to buy himself something nice. He'd visit a shooting range and fire guns with either Jamal or Li, who both enjoyed the hobby too.

Jon was learning how to make the most out of a single day.

To even be allowed to do this, Jon considered himself lucky.

He was home, alive, and employed. He had what some vets don't after they return home. He had somewhere to go. He had purpose. Before work started, Jon went to the bar early so he could talk with Kya.

She would work nights, but during the day, Kya was in school.

She was at NYU studying education. She said she

wanted to be an elementary school teacher at a private school like Exeter or some other institution that paid more money. Jon had the answers to many things. However, the one part of his life that remained unsolved was the question:

What do you want to do for the rest of your life?

To be frank, Jon didn't know what he wanted.

He didn't know what he wanted to do beyond the next twenty-four hours. Jon didn't know who he was or what lay ahead of him. Jon also knew that his bouncer job wasn't permanent, and it didn't make promises for a steady future.

It was just another dead end. It was just another path for Jon to walk at the time.

He emphatically defended his decision, though. No, Jon didn't need to know where he was going or why. What he needed to do was stay alive and keep his head above water. As far as Jon knew, that's exactly what he was doing now.

———

Since Jon started working, he spoke to his doctor about getting a new prosthetic. Most of the time, no one noticed how Jon was someone with an amputation. He didn't go out of his way to make it known to anyone either. He suspected Kya knew.

Sometimes, he was worried about what she might think. Jon believed she wouldn't care.

Whenever he was exercising, he was sure to do some extra exercises for his only leg.

He could squat and he could press. What he struggled with most was mobility. This was what his new prosthetic was designed to do. At the time, Jon was joined by his mother. They went to see a doctor named Tuttle. Afterward, Dr. Tuttle provided Jon with a more durable and lighter prosthetic that enabled him to move faster and easier. He could stand without feeling encumbered. The new piece was something made for athletes. And, since Jon was on his feet all the time, there was a certain degree of discomfort he was faced with.

Nevertheless, Jon could stand and he could move. But, as Dr. Tuttle explained, he would be able to maneuver in a much quicker, much easier way.

"Titanium alloy, with a bendable joint, flexible, and not too heavy. Try it. See what you think."

Jon unfastened his old prosthetic and inserted the updated model. He secured it tightly, clipped into place, and felt the cool material against his skin.

"And?" Jon's mom stood by his shoulder and looked into her son's exhausted eyes.

"Not bad," said Jon.

"Good?"

Jon nodded. He stood up so he could take a short walk around the room to test the piece out. So far, he was satisfied. *Very.* While the prosthetic was successfully installed, Jon Haze may have lost his leg, but he lost a friend too. Only in the spaces in between did Jon remember what he truly did not have. It was because of this that Jon could not stop moving. He pushed on and he kept fighting. A missing leg wasn't the same as the other missing things. Jon was concerned. He had replaced the one thing he could get back.

It was the same as he had replaced most of his life.

———

After leaving the doctor's office, Jon stopped by his favorite coffee shop in Queens to get a cup. He ordered a medium black and proceeded to drink it as he hailed a cab despite having access to a car. It was the Civic Jon's mother had lent him. Some nights, Jon was too tired to drive. On the subway, some nights were easier than others were. Jon relied on public transportation. He began to appreciate and further understand the city that he lived in for most of his life.

Into the foyer, Jon looked on and saw Danix and Jamal, both by the bar.

"S'up." Jamal was drinking a tall glass of what looked like cranberry juice. Jon acknowledged Jamal with a quick nod. Jon saw Danix dressed in a muscle shirt and his Doormen pants.

Jon had come across some big guys in his life. Few were as big as Danix.

His arms looked inflated. His chest was wide but his waist was narrow, which was weird. Back at the gym, Jon had taken a few punches from Danix. Even with padded gloves, Jon felt like he was being hit with a baseball bat. Jon was not afraid of his coworkers, but he was aware of the sheer damage they were capable of if pushed too far.

Everyone was unique in their own way, but all were certainly deadly.

When Jon looked at Danix, he nodded to acknowledge. "Hey."

"Hey." Danix nodded to show grace. As far as Jon knew, it was all normal. Before every shift, certain tasks needed to be completed.

Check and review the night's itinerary.

Every bouncer was to be given a section of the club to take care of. Once the night was underway, they all took their positions. Some were on the dance floor while others were supposed to watch the door with Jamal. Some were in charge of the bar as well as the second level. All were to watch and all were to observe. The goal of a Doorman is not to simply stand around but also to reflect. Doormen needed to study and assess. It was exactly as Jon was taught to do during his training.

Tonight, he was assigned to the door.

All of this was written on a tablet provided by Addison during daily briefings. All used their tablet to punch in, report, and sign out once the evening ended. It contained all the Doormen's names, while Jon, being the newest recruit, was at the very bottom of the list. When Jon looked at his again, he realized he was actually outside for the first time. Always, he was on the floor in some capacity. Now that he was going outdoors, he had to wonder why.

Jon grunted.

Holding a plastic cup filled with water, Jon felt stagnant, almost useless.

The door saw the least amount of action. It was also a painfully boring place to be. Jon turned to question Danix, Li, and Jamal but stopped when he saw Sam. He was just starting to make his way onto the empty floor.

"Hey, Jon?" Sam said to Jon.

While Jon had yet to question Sam about the recent incident, the Marine believed this was all worth mentioning.

"Did you see today's schedule?" Jon asked.

Jon drank his water while Sam drank coffee from a Styrofoam cup. Sam's hair was gelled tonight. He nodded at Jon. "I did."

"Did you see where I was posted?" Jon asked again.

"No," Sam said, shaking his head. He came off as stern as he came forward to check. "Where are you?"

Sam moved past Jon and he pinched the corner of the page. He turned it up and looked to where Jon's name was written.

"I'm at the door."

"Oh?"

"I'm *never* at the door," said Jon. "In fact, isn't that where you usually are?"

"Sometimes," answered Sam. He was looking elsewhere and avoiding eye contact with Jon.

Sam stepped to his right and was about to carry on through the kitchen when he was suddenly stopped by the Marine.

"Hey, what happened the other night?" Jon asked.

Right now, Jon was refusing to pull any punches. He wanted to know about the Castellani situation, why Sam insisted on holding back and why he didn't help Jon at the time?

Why did he leave Jon to fight on his own and why did he act like such a fucking coward?

"What?" replied Sam.

"You know what I mean," snapped Jon. "There was a fight, and you could see I needed backup, and you were my spotter that night, weren't you? So I gotta ask, what the hell happened?"

Jon glared. He could see through Sam's bullshit. He ached to hear his response.

"I don't know what you mean," said Sam.

Jon shook his head and sighed. He was disappointed with Sam's explanation. Jon knew Sam was a tough one. There was no doubt he could ring Jon's bell. Being the more experienced bouncer, Sam was a killer one in fact. He had two black belts and some solid fighting experience. Although a Marine, Jon hadn't been in as many fights. Nonetheless, Jon felt he was tough enough to go toe-to-toe with someone like Sam. However, to confront and to not back down also made room for potential escalation and trouble.

"Come on, man," Jon said to Sam. "You know what I'm talking about here, yeah? I was taking on five guys, one of them was a mobster's son. You were there, and things got out of hand, and you weren't there to stop it or to help me. I needed you."

"No, man, I was there," said Sam. "I was just busy with a few other guys who wanted to step in. That's all."

"I didn't see anyone else trying to step in."

"Well, they were there," insisted Sam. "Trust me. And I needed to keep them away, and honestly, I thought you could handle all of it yourself."

"And I could," added Jon, now defending his honor and pride. "That's not the point, though. I did handle it, but I didn't know *who* I was handling, see?"

"And you think I did?" asked Sam.

He wasn't nodding, but then he wasn't shaking his head either. Jon recalled the incident as best he could. He remembered clearly where Sam was and what he was doing.

"You two looked pretty chummy before things got out of hand."

"Nah," Sam defended. There was a long pause

before he took a step back. He was about to move on as if finished with the whole conversation.

Jon might have been too, but then he wasn't. In fact, he wasn't even close.

"That's not what happened, man. Not at all." Sam was now the one choosing to walk away. Jon watched him as he went. He knew when a person was avoiding him, and that's exactly what Sam was doing. Most people chose to walk away because they were being confronted or worse, they were called a liar or a snake.

For Jon, Sam was now a bouncer who set his coworkers up to fail.

This is exactly how Jon saw him. Jon was in a fight and Sam watched.

He was in a death battle with a boy named Frankie Castellani. At the time, Jon remembered seeing Sam perfectly. His hand was on Frankie's chest. He stood in front of him like he was telling him something. Whenever a person's hand was in such a position, it meant not to come any farther or not to get involved.

While Sam did this, he also watched as Jon took a hard beating.

No matter now, Jon couldn't keep making it an issue, especially when they were beginning their shift soon. Everyone needed to be on point. Jon wasn't going to bring any drama to the Doormen, but then he should have.

————

When Jon finished drinking his water, he crushed the cup and tossed it into the bin by the bar. He was through the door, on his way out, and then he spotted

Kya. Working with another bar-keep, she was taking bottles from boxes and shelving them one after the other. Jon wanted to ask her if she needed any help. He reflected on the solid piece of advice he was told by so many.

Always be useful, especially in the company of women.

Ladies adore someone who they can rely on, someone who is not helpless or without purpose. He prided himself on living up to this reputation. Jon wanted to ask Kya if she did need help. Soon after he was about to, someone else came to do it. Sam strolled onto the scene. He stood with his arms apart and smirked at Kya. Suddenly, Jon felt a pain in his chest. He wanted to hit Sam hard in the face and shame him for not doing what was right.

But, Jon could do neither, or so he said to himself. *Stay calm.*

Jon looked Kya up and down. Dressed in a pair of tight black pants, Kya's shirt was tied around her stomach. When Sam came in to stand next to her, he leered. He grabbed one of the boxes while Jon had to stay by the door. Jon was now attempting to assess the situation like he did as if he was on the floor. He wasn't looking for a fight, but sparks—chemistry. Jon looked deep into Kya's eyes and tried to see if there was any attraction, if Kya was responding to Sam in an intimate way.

Both handsome Sam's arms were bigger than Jon's. His eyes were a more alluring shade of blue. He was also older and presumably more experienced. Sam possessed a certain confidence that could only belong to a man who had talked to many girls like Kya. He talked to them and he knew them. Sam was like the boys Jon knew back in high school. They were the football players who'd swoop in and date all the sophomore and freshman girls. They would lay waste to all the other boys in lower grades simply because they had more autonomy and respect.

Jon didn't wish to stand for much longer.

He pushed through the door and walked on like he didn't see a damn thing.

Problem is...*he did.*

CHAPTER 18
BACK AT IT

THE DOORS OPENED AND THE CUSTOMERS STOOD IN a long line outside on what was a blissful summer evening. The air was cool, and the fading sunlight covered the whole sky. At this point, The Conquistador was still undergoing preparations before fully opening. It was close to dinner, so sometimes the staff were given food if it was going to be a busy night.

Tonight, it might be.

Tonight, the club was hosting a famous internet celebrity called Mack Tilerian. He was an influencer with a significant following and the club was hosting him as well as DJ North Star, a known pop star. Set to a blazing night of fun and enjoyment, all of this was booked and arranged by Addison. Despite being older, Addison prided himself on remaining up-to-date on who was hot among teens and subscribers. He was on social media the same as any other person and so he managed to book both for tonight. Addison had also been promoting the event for close to two months.

Jon finished his meal and he was sitting with Danix

and with Addison. Sam was with Li and a few other waiters and barkeeps. Once done, Jon made his way to the doors and bought Jamal a drink once he was there.

"Hey, big man." Although Jon was close with everyone he worked with, he enjoyed spending most of his time with Jamal.

Friendly and kind, Jamal was someone who made Jon relaxed and cool. He was good, particularly under the pressures that came with this environment.

"Hey, brother," said Jamal. He was wearing a shirt loosely fitted to his long arms. Holding a cigarette between his fingers, Jamal smoked as the full moon hung just above the breathtaking skyline.

"What's going on?" Jon asked.

"Not much, y'know," said Jamal. "Just getting set up."

"Right," answered Jon. "Here, brought you this." Jon handed Jamal a cup.

Jamal grinned as he took it from Jon, who was his friend. "Thanks, man. Appreciate it."

"No problem."

Jon trusted a lot of the people he worked with. He trusted Addison, he trusted Danix, and he trusted Li. He trusted Jamal, sure, but he also liked him. In fact, Jon liked Jamal a lot, and because he did, it always seemed like he was reliable. Jon liked talking to Jamal whenever he could. After all, he did *serve* too.

"Hey, is it all right if I ask you something...*private*?"

Jamal finished his drink. "Sure."

"Did you hear what happened?" asked Jon. He looked back to make sure no one else was around.

"What?" asked Jamal. "You mean about you in a tussle with Castellani's boy?"

Jon nodded and couldn't help but smile. "Yeah."

Jamal gulped more of his drink. "Yeah, I heard."

"And what do you think?"

Jamal shrugged. He stared at Jon and showed the same smile as before. "I think you were doing your job, and doing it well. That's what I think."

"Thanks."

"Why?" asked Jamal. "What do *you* think about what happened?"

"I think..." Jon knew exactly what he thought, so he decided to say the whole truth and nothing more.

"I think that Sam knows some shit we don't."

"Sam?" Jamal snapped back. He was actually surprised Jon mentioned another Doorman.

"Yeah."

"You think Sam is involved?" Jamal asked. "What makes you say that?"

"When the fight went down," explained Jon, "I saw him standing there, but he wasn't helping or doing anything. Actually, it looked like he was communicating, *communicating* with Frankie Castellani."

"You mean...he was what, like talking to him?"

"Yeah," said Jon, "looking at him and nodding. Exactly."

"You sure you saw that?" It was no secret Jamal would be skeptical.

In a fight, everything gets fuzzy and unclear. There was this, and not to mention the problems Jon had staying stable and not flashing back to the war when things got rough. So far, Jon was okay. He hadn't experienced an episode since he had that tussle with those fellas a while back. Since then, Jon has been good, very good. However, Jon was taking on two guys at once and was waiting for more bouncers. In the midst of doing this, that's when Frankie saw Sam, that's when Jon saw Sam too, and that's when he saw the two of them start *talking*.

Jon didn't tell anyone about this, not yet. At The Conquistador, Sam was unaware of Jon's struggles. If Sam was aware, then everyone might see that it could potentially affect Jon's work. This was the last thing Jon wanted. Being here was the best thing in Jon's life. He wouldn't do anything to jeopardize it.

"I'm sure," said Jon.

"Well, just a mishap, maybe," said Jamal. "You know how things get sometimes. It's rough. Too much at one time. Sometimes, you just gotta do what you can, that's all."

"Yeah."

Jon was dubious. He actually expected this response. Still, it didn't change how he felt.

"Why?" asked Jamal. "What do you think?"

"What do I think?" Jon was surprised to see he was the one being asked to consider. Having thought this on only a few occasions, Jon undoubtedly had his own thoughts.

"I think they know each other."

"Who?"

"Frankie Castellani and Sam. I think they know each other. More than this, I think they're *friends*."

"With Castellani?" asked Jamal. He was shocked by Jon's suspicions.

"Yeah."

"Are you being serious right now?" Jamal asked Jon.

"I am," Jon declared.

"And what makes you say all of this? Why do you think it's true?"

"A hunch," said Jon. "I know how he acted when the fight broke out, and I know how he *reacted* once it was all over and done."

"So, what? You think he hung you out to dry on purpose? Is that what you're saying?"

Jon nodded at Jamal and bit his lip.

"That's *exactly* what I'm saying."

"Oh, come on, now," Jamal replied. "Sam might be a tough bastard, but he ain't cold or corrupt. You two work together for chrissake. The Doormen and all that shit. He wouldn't bail on you."

"Unless there was a reason to bail," said Jon.

"A reason?" asked Jamal.

"Yeah," said Jon. "Maybe, a *big* reason."

There was a pause as the conversation took an ominous turn. The reason Jon was proposing suggested conspiracy, maybe even treason. More than this, it was corruption. It was death.

"Well, since we're talkin' about it, what do you think the *reason* is?"

"I think he was *in* on it."

"What?" asked Jamal. He was so shocked and chagrined to see Jon would even suggest such an idea. "You're not serious, are you?"

"I got a feeling, that's all."

"Yeah, well, we all get feelings," Jamal said to Jon. "Part of this game is to not let your feelings come to the forefront of what we do around here. Assess first, *remember*? And stay calm. I hope you remember that too."

"Yeah, I remember it. I remember all of it."

———

Jon scanned the line after speaking with Jamal and remained by the front door.

People were just starting to assemble in big crowds along the sidewalk. It didn't take long for The Conquistador to build its list of willing attendees, guests, and all it would take was a few hours before everything became jammed.

Jon hated lots of things in his life.

What he hated most was when people told him he was being paranoid. Jon hated when someone said that what he was seeing wasn't real or true. This would always be a hard reality for the Marine to accept. It was even harder to accept that something he felt in his gut could be cast aside.

It could be denied so easily.

When Jon served in the Marines, a hunch was everything. If someone had a bad feeling about anything, right away it was taken seriously. It was adhered to. By doing this, everyone stayed prepared for the worst. Suggesting that someone inside might be a traitor, Jon had a difficult time accepting this as real. No doubt The Conquistador employed some elite and deadly men. Most of whom would do anything to help another employee. In the end, Jon saw what he saw. He knew what was real and he knew what might happen if he didn't respond.

Jon stepped back and was about to move into the door but saw a car pull up.

An Escalade with sparkling rims approached the curb. What Jon could see was a stunning vehicle. Soon after it parked, its doors opened, and from inside, four men in suits exited onto the sidewalk.

Jon gazed to examine who they were. He learned quickly they weren't really men.

No, they were boys. Most were around Jon's age. Although Jon recognized them soon as they made their appearances, he classified them as a band of brats. All were led by the same person he saw just three days ago. Frankie Castellani and his band of merry men had returned to The Conquistador. The fools in his company all clung to their leader. They acted like just being with him was impressive.

Jon did not break eye contact.

Glaring at Frankie, the son of the mobster walked ahead. There, a group of girls in skimpy dresses and short skirts screamed his name. Frankie gave them all a wave. He was a movie star in his own right, but Jon had to ask: *what was a celebrity if not someone with adoring fans?*

As Frankie approached the rope guarding the door, Jamal lifted it.

"Always on the list," Jamal said to Frankie.

Jon squinted. He didn't look away for a second. His intention was to elicit an ominous feeling, one he wanted to be read loudly and clearly.

Always in bouncing, everyone is waiting for that one big fight to go down.

For Jon, it almost always occurred at the beginning of his shift. He was ordered to stay away from Frankie. Jon was also told to watch his back. He spent almost two hours by the door. Throughout his time there, Jon saw a girl celebrating her twenty-fifth and some frat boys from a few different colleges. He saw a few dimwitted young girls who tried to get in with a fake ID. Jon and Jamal sent them all packing. He saw a few older women who had just come to celebrate the promotion of a coworker. After this, there were a bunch of randoms who were just there to have a good time.

Jon didn't mind any of them.

He was once under the impression that the job would be boring, but it was actually quite pleasant being outside. Also, while Jon's leg wasn't acting up, his new prosthetic was light and it was easy. All of this was good. In fact, it was *perfect*.

———

Once Jon spent enough time by the door, he was called back into the club. Addison contacted Jon using his walkie. Back in the club, Jon stayed with Li and Danix. They were behind the railing overlooking the dance floor.

The floor was loaded.

"Hey!" Jon raised his voice so he could be heard over the music. He lined himself up with the other bouncers and stood guard.

"How's it going?" Danix's voice was raised too.

Jon eyed Frankie. He was walking around the dance floor and heading to the VIP section along with his boys. There, Frankie waved down another waitress.

"Fine!" Jon didn't look at Danix while responding. In the presence of the rotten prick, Frankie Castellani, garnered every ounce of Jon's focus. Funny how much a person's attitude changes after joining the military. Training alongside Marines, Jon was built to be solid and tough. He was taught to know the importance of remaining loyal to one's unit as well as to one's mission.

Everywhere Jon looked, he saw people who only thought they were tough.

Although Frankie's boys possessed certain traits, Jon pictured what they would be like on the battlefield. He imagined them among grenades and fucking bullets. No matter how tough one appears to be, real toughness comes from failure and from looking down the barrel of a gun, of coming too close to death.

"Don't worry!" Danix assured as he leaned into Jon's left ear. "We got our eye on him!"

"Thanks!" Jon replied. Li stood near Jon's shoulder. Resting his hand there, he completed the friendly gesture and Jon acknowledged him with a nod.

Now aligned with some of the deadliest of all Doormen, Jon looked up at the second level. He saw Addison. He was dressed in a navy, three-piece, checkered suit and was speaking to two women. All were of them part of The Conquistador's club-promoting team. Jon held his walkie two inches from his face and tried to read Addison's lips. He couldn't read or understand a goddamn thing.

Jon shuddered.

What he wanted to know, he absolutely needed to know.

CHAPTER 19
FIST BUMPS AND HANDSHAKES

Mack Tilerian and DJ North Star were both waiting upstairs in the lounge. The room was equipped with its own bar and its own waiting staff. There was a gourmet spread for both guests and Kya was selected as Mack's host.

Kya was all Jon thought of now.

Kind and pretty, while Tilerian was known to keep the company of many women, Kya was never known to mix business with pleasure. Still, Jon thought about how she was being hit on constantly.

She was now probably being swarmed by inebriated and filthy men.

Jon kept his eyes on the dance floor. He read as many faces as he could. So far, everything appeared to be tamed. Yet there was only one place Jon's mind could go. Jon looked back at Frankie as he frolicked about in the VIP. Jon watched as he and his friends toasted to each other and shouted, "Salute!" As of now, it wasn't too rowdy. So far, it seemed to be okay. Something about this gave Jon a bad feeling. It was how he felt when he had to sweep a field for mines. It was clear, open, and all on the surface. At any moment, this place could light up in a blaze of fire. It could explode into a dozen pieces. Frankie was in the booth. A bright light shined over him and all his guests. Within this light, Jon could see him glancing repeatedly at the floor.

He was not glancing because he liked the music. He was not glancing because he noticed girls on the floor. As far as Jon could see, there were too many booths already. Frankie was scoping the guests. He knew when someone was studying a scene. For whatever reason, that was exactly what Frankie was doing now.

Why? Jon hadn't a clue.

Jon motioned across the floor and nodded at Danix and Li. The look said Jon was getting work done. Jon pushed forward and kept his chest and his chin up. Minding the people now around him, he looked at a table filled with girls. One of them was wearing a crown and a sash.

Among her friends, she shouted at Jon. He stopped and turned.

"Hey, you! Hot-ass bouncer!"

"Karla!" The girl, Karla, was promptly scolded by her friend. Still, Jon had enough experience to know what was actually happening. Karla was a basic birthday girl. The booze was just starting to hit her and she was primed to get wild and loose.

"Take a picture with me, please!"

"What?" Jon was distracted. All he wanted to do was get to the second floor.

He had to keep an eye on Castellani.

"Please, take a picture with us!" Karla shouted again.

"Uh..." This was not the first time Jon was asked to take a picture with his guests.

No, being a bouncer, you were basically a fuck boy. Although Jon never crossed any professional boundaries, he didn't do anything he thought was inappropriate or invasive.

He never used his authority to get any girl's attention.

When he enlisted, people had tremendous respect for Marines. People adored those who served their country and served it well. As a result, Jon received a lot of praise and adoration for this. Sometimes it pulled Jon in too much. Women offered him things, casual things. While he acted on only a few occasions, Jon remembered these days quite well. None of them compared to his time in nightlife security. Some customers wanted what they knew they could not have. They wanted privileges they were not allowed to take.

Then, girls do have certain methods of persuasion. The Doormen were ordered to never engage with anyone while on the job.

They were required to be on their game at all times and never step out of line.

To be off course for even a second could potentially cause a chain reaction of consequences. It might also put the people Jon trusted at risk. Even something as innocent as a photograph had taken Jon aside for time that was too long. And yet, Jon was no jerk-off. He didn't want to ruin the enthusiasm or the excitement now flourishing throughout the club.

The cute blonde fell into Jon's arms. She gave him a peace sign as she nestled against his chest.

"Thanks!"

"We love you!"

"You're hot AF!"

Among the chuckles and comments, smiles and selfies, Jon nodded to show his appreciation. Then he moved on.

———

On the second floor, Jon passed by a few groups who were dancing and talking, talking and dancing. The lights flashed from high above the stage. Halfway up, Jon looked at the booth. He saw two of Frankie's cronies splitting up from the table. All were coming straight for Jon.

The Marine, however, stood his ground. These fellas marched as if on a mission. They were stoic, as if pretending to be soldiers, but all were so very bad at this.

In the end, they all lacked the one quality that every soldier had. What solidified them were things like loyalty and prowess. And still, Jon watched them as they moved. Whatever they were up to, they were moving fast.

Jon hid behind a pillar. He kept an eye on each one of them as they walked. These boys went to two separate areas.

The one in the red suit walked to the bathroom. Another one followed. None of this made Jon interested. People join other people in the bathrooms often at clubs. Mostly, it's to do one thing only, to deal.

Jon examined the appearance of the other man he was following. He was raggedy and wiry. He didn't wear a suit so well designed or as fashionable. When

Jon went in, he watched the other guy who worked with Frankie make his way through the club. Unlike his counterpart, he went straight to the dance floor and was joined by two others.

Tradecraft, as it's known in the military, was what these men were practicing.

They wanted none to notice them. Almost none did. Jon watched their hands.

This is the part of the body Doormen have to watch out for the most. Jon could see them switching back and forth. *Was it a hand-off, maybe?*

If it was, it was happening right under everyone's noses.

Jon blinked.

The lights stopped flashing at their usual intervals and switched to intermittent blinks. Jon stood back. If he were to tell any of the other bouncers he was witnessing a "trade," then the Doormen would immediately ask Jon about his location.

But before he would have the chance to reply, Jon questioned whether or not he was sure.

Therefore, at this very moment, as Jon stood and watched...this is exactly what he was telling himself. He was damn sure of this.

Jon kept his eyes on more hands. All were exchanging in the middle of the floor! It was so obvious Jon couldn't take it. All anyone had to do was take a second and look. Yet, none of them *were* looking. Everyone who was there was either dancing, gyrating, drinking, or yelling. No one could see what was unfolding, but Jon could. He did!

Standing by the railing, Jon was precariously

perched. Soon as one hand shifted, another one followed. While everything was present, Jon insisted.

Something was going down. Jon was smack down in the middle of it!

The entire time, Jon remained calm because calmness is key.

He only had so much time before the two men here with Frankie Castellani dispersed into another section of the club. Everywhere Jon looked, swarms of bodies were packed in thick, clustered groupings. Each one was spread throughout the space, and it was so crammed Jon could barely move. Jon scoped Frankie's goons in the middle of the floor. He knew now was the time to move. If he didn't, Jon would lose this lead. As he made the first move, Jon stepped down the staircase that led to the floor. He pushed other people aside and moved in.

"Hey!"

"Yo, bro!" More comments sounded from inside the crowd. Whoever these people were, they were unaware that Jon was security. Doing what he could, Jon curved in and out. He did not break speed because he couldn't. As the two guys parted, the music blared. The lights obscured Jon's vision. In the end, Jon saw only what he could see.

He marched.

Now approaching the first guy, Jon was amped. Adrenaline was pumping through his body and he was about to make a serious bust and was also ready for the fallout, if there was any.

"Hey!" Jon yelled loud as he could. His lungs hurt and his hands trembled.

He screamed to alert the two guys he was in pursuit

of. Some stopped to look. The fear surfaced. Soon as Jon was close, the other guests could see from his coiled lips and clenched fists that his anger was clear.

He could feel the intensity of this confrontation. The boys then began to split.

"Wait! Stop!" Jon urged them to stay still. When they refused, he reached out and grabbed one of the guy's shoulders. "Stop!"

"Yo, bro!" the guy yelled. "What the hell do you think you're doing, man?"

"I said stop!" Jon was in a fit of rage.

He hated when people didn't respect. They knew exactly who Jon was. They were just pretending like they didn't. While Jon was infuriated by this lack of care, he pointed at the man's face. Another one took a step back and threw his hands up. Acting innocent, it was like these guys didn't know a damn thing.

Jon channeled the lessons learned during training. He knew how to use his voice. He spoke slowly when there was a situation. Jon didn't need to use his body, not yet. He needed to make that clear right now. These two had to be confronted.

"What the fuck, man!"

"Enough!" Jon's shouts turned vicious and cutting. Right now, he was in the dead center. With little room to move or defend himself, it was time to let these boys know just what the hell was going on.

"I saw it!" screamed Jon. "I know you guys are movin' shit! I saw!" Jon did his best not to sound like a cop. What he was doing didn't fall under the Doormen's jurisdiction. Rules at The Conquistador dictate if there are drugs, then you throw the people out and call the police. Jon was attempting to take care of these two guys entirely on his own. As far as getting the police involved, he was inadvertently taking on that rule himself.

"Packin' what, man?" Now the second man was talking. The two were squaring off with Jon. Chests out, their lips curled into their smug mouths. Though their fury was present, their displeasure concerning the intervention was also there.

"Contraband!" yelled Jon. Using the official term, Jon didn't say *drugs*. To him, the word sounded dirty and amateur. So, Jon refused to refer to as such. He decided to refer to it as what it was.

"Drugs, man?!" The first man was the one talking now. Jon examined this man with a grim, focused look. He was becoming more like a cop than he cared to admit. "That's what you think?!"

"That's what I know," Jon said back. "Open your hand!"

Jon pulled away and the man who he confronted backed off.

"Nah, man!"

"Open it!" Jon's hand twitched against his thigh. Right now, Jon was fighting more adrenaline, more memories, and more flashbacks.

He refused to be as nice as he was. This wasn't a situation that required cordiality or patience. Drugs are not fights. Drugs contaminate, they pollute, and they corrupt.

With The Conquistador's reputation and its security on the line, this kind of action was unacceptable. Jon was doing what he could to drive this notion home.

It was either surrender or resist. Jon would rather fall to his knees than give up on what he was doing.

"I...I..." The first man was caught up in a stammer while the other looked at the balcony and at Frankie. Jon checked to see if he was seeing what they were. Jon refused to take his focus off the confrontation.

In the midst of him trying to explain, the first guy took another step back. Jon was ordered by Addison and the other Doormen to never start anything inside the club, especially not on the dance floor. But again, Jon had consistently reminded himself of this situation's seriousness.

"Hey!" In the middle of the escape, Jon refused to stand back. He refused because, to endure this, Jon would need to unleash all his power, at least whatever was left of it.

Jon grabbed the man by the shoulder and pulled.

Immediately after making contact, the response was demonstrably predictable. The man swung and tried to land a defensive punch. This was something Jon was ready for. Arm up, Jon completed a clean cross-block and deflected the punch. His right leg then shot out and Jon glided it around the back of his attacker's for a nice takedown.

Encouraged not to strike or to use any striking techniques, Jon's goal was always about neutralization. It's to take them out of the space with ease. Locks, pins, and throws are the main strategies. In this case, Jon's prosthetic made everything more effective.

Straight down, Jon grunted. He looked to the left and searched for the next hitter.

The second man was now inching closer. The flashing lights blinded Jon. Unable to see as perfectly as he needed to, Jon pushed his feet hard into the ground. He kept himself solid.

He kept himself protected.

Jon raised his hands while the second man dove in for a prototypical punch.

Jon straightened his back leg and splayed his fingers. The technique used was taught by Addison. Although Addison wasn't someone who normally trained, this was mostly Danix and Li's responsibility. Still, sometimes Addison would stop by and show him some things too.

Kotegaeshi.

Aikido was Addison's primary martial art. Kotegaeshi was Aikido's dynamic wrist lock. It could either break the opponent's joint or lock them up nice and tight. And when Jon stepped aside, he blocked and tightened his grip on the man's wrist until he felt bone. Jon then contorted the fool's joint, pressed down hard with both his hands, and shifted to gain momentum.

Jon pushed and threw his attacker back and then away. Jon was always urged to do the move quickly. However, in this case, Jon had to drop to his knees in order to do it in the best way possible. He was able to send his attacker straight down. He was the first was up but he was not alone.

"The fuck!" Jon screamed. His body was tense. The man roared at his friend just as the group began to disperse. Frankie entered the scene shortly after.

"What the hell is going on?"

CHAPTER 20
POINTED FINGERS AND NEW PLANS

WITH FRANKIE NOW ON THE FLOOR, HE STOOD among the boys Jon just took for a ride. He glared at the Doorman and stomped after the former Marine.

"What do you think you're doing, man? Who the hell do you think you are? Do you know how many people I know who work here! You can't just come down and start shit for no reason!"

"Your friends are dealing!" Jon shouted. "I'm going to have to ask you to leave right now!"

"Dealin'!" Frankie snapped back at Jon. "Who the fuck's dealin'? Show me!"

Frankie raised his hand and pointed. Soon after Jon said what he did, more Doormen amassed around the floor. Jon quickly spotted Danix. Then, he came across Li, and Sam. The four squared off. Frankie noticed this additional security and then bolted after them.

"One of your guys is harassing my friends, man!" Frankie screamed.

"What?" Sam said back.

Standing with Jon were Danix and Li. Sam eyed

Frankie. He and his two asshole friends looked scornfully at the Doormen. Now shaken, Frankie's collar was bent and uneven. Jon stood with Sam. He screamed again.

"This asshole keeps pushin' ass, man!" shouted one of Frankie's assholes.

"I saw contraband!" Jon yelled back. "We need to get them outta here!"

"Hold up!" yelled Danix. "Drugs?"

Jon glowered back at Frankie. "Saw them both." Jon pointed at the two he saw making an exchange.

"Fuck no!" yelled the guy who Jon flipped over on the floor.

"I asked them to show me their hands! They wouldn't!"

"All right!" shouted Sam. "Let's just get off the floor! Come on! Before this shit escalates!"

"Okay," said Frankie.

When he was with Sam, Jon looked on, confused.

Now with his head bent and his neck craned, the suggestion to get off the floor was not the proposed plan. It was also one Jon didn't want to hear right now. On paper, it all seemed like a good idea. Get out of the way and solve this problem away from guests. Easy. By doing this, Sam had inadvertently given Frankie and his boys exactly what they wanted.

They now had time to reconvene because the walk to the dance floor was fifteen meters.

This, combined with all the bodies in their vicinity, they could easily switch places. They could easily do something new, like empty their pockets or go somewhere they shouldn't.

Frankie agreed to this strategy and Jon watched as

he walked away. Jon also noticed some changes to Frankie's appearance. Now with a boyish smirk, Frankie giddily glanced back to give Jon a smug look. It was an in-your-face show of conceitedness that further proved that what was about to happen *was exactly what he wanted.*

Jon stood with Danix and he could see Frankie and his boys walking away.

In a fit of fury and unhinged rage, Jon lunged and tackled Frankie to the ground.

"I said show me your damn pockets!" Jon pushed Frankie's face and contorted his hands. By doing this, Jon was targeting all of Frankie's joints.

Bending and twisting, Jon continued to push down and around.

The altercation went on while everyone else stood by and watched.

"Get 'em! Get 'em off!" As Frankie tried to get his hands in, Danix tried to do the same.

He was trying to protect Jon, as was Li. However, with Sam standing alongside Frankie, he was doing his best to make sure the temperamental son of a mobster didn't get hurt.

Sam was protecting Frankie and not his fellow Doorman, Jon.

"Get off me!" Frankie yelled at Sam. He was too close to Frankie's pocket. Within an arm's reach, Jon was so close to getting his hand what was inside his face broke into a slight smile.

Jon stopped after he was hit.

"Gah!" Jon was kicked by a new attacker. Jon fell and, landing on his back, looked up and saw this beast of a man standing over him. This new guy was almost as big as Jamal was, although not quite. He had a wide back and big biceps. He wore a baggy Ed Hardy shirt and looked like a typical juiced-up Guido idiot Jon saw all the time. He was someone so here with Frankie. Although, Jon didn't see him come in.

Big and thick, this roided out asshole tried grabbing Jon's neck.

Down on the ground, Jon was winded. He gasped and gawked at his new opponent and breathed.

"Don't touch my boy!" yelled the juicehead.

"Fuck you!" Jon shouted back. The Marine was primed for another attack. He wanted to hit the roided freak right in his knee. Then he realized he didn't have to.

Danix had exploded onto the scene. Moving in, Danix cut between this roided dude. While this man stood at the same height, Danix was only a few pounds lighter. No doubt, though, the two were in the same weight class.

"Back off!" Now in the guy's face, Danix's intent wasn't to escalate. Yet Danix was pissed after seeing Jon kicked down to the floor. There was also Frankie and his goon. There were three of his buddies, and then there was Jon, Danix, Li, and Sam. All were smack in the middle of the booming conflict unfolding in the densest section of the club.

"Fuck you!" yelled the Guido. He swung for Danix. Instantly, Danix pulled his arm up and blocked to absorb the blow. Danix jabbed the Guido three times, and all of Danix's strikes were hard and fierce. Danix could knock out most people with one hit. And although this Guido was big, he lacked stamina. And so, once Danix smoked him with five more smacks, he finished with a solid push kick to the face.

"Hey!" The second guy stomped and vehemently moved after Danix. It was then Jon saw Li.

He was going in too.

Hands straight, Li made his fingers flat as knives. He was looking at the man who had called out earlier. Li chopped him in his neck and leveled the guy directly in the throat. Then, he added an elbow and a boot to the fool's knee.

Li snatched the fool by the neck with both hands, pulled, and flipped him down.

Two of Frankie's boys were fallen now. Jon was with Frankie. Both glared at each other with pure hatred. With both of them up, the situation was real.

Sam was hanging back.

So far, all the Doormen were on the floor. They wanted a piece of the fight, but not Sam.

No, he was standing back. He was neutral. No aggression.

Almost as though he didn't care, when Frankie stomped in, he went for Jon. After he saw what he did, Jon moved away. He raised his hands and was ready for another throwdown. Jon hit Frankie square in the nose. It was a clean, straight shot to the face. Jon felt Frankie's nose crack beneath his knuckles. Jon hooked and aimed for Frankie's left cheek. Instead of hitting there, Jon clobbered him right in his ear.

"Gah!"

The hit was intentional and very effective. If there was ever a painful place to be hit, it was in the fucking ear. Jon backed off and switched his stance.

Once in Southpaw, Jon widened his stance. Now on the defensive, Jon's arms were up and bent. He flexed his arms and was prepared for Frankie to retaliate. Jon could see the rage brimming in his gaze. His suit was disheveled, as was his hair. Frankie was swinging, not punching. When seeing every approaching blow, Jon cross-blocked and let the first punch connect with his forearm.

After Jon connected with a hook, he pounded Frankie's smug face. Frankie stumbled. Falling down, Frankie pancaked the dance floor and looked up. His lip was bleeding as Jon stood over him. Now done fighting, Sam stepped in.

He looked at Frankie and at Jon. "Shit," Sam said.

After hitting Frankie, the defeated pretty boy was peeved. Frankie stood , and using all his anger, tackled Jon to the ground. "Fucker!"

The two rolled on the floor like two high schoolers engaged in a silly romp.

They plowed through the crowd while Danix and Li raced. However, Jon didn't require assistance. No, what he required now was only his fists and his legs. While on the ground, Jon felt ashamed that he had let a brawler like this successfully take him down. As the better fighter, Jon was no doubt prepared. But now that the two were on the floor, things had changed.

They changed quickly.

———

Frankie went for Jon's wrists and tried to pin him down.

But Jon was smart. He knew exactly what to do. He looped his leg against Frankie's shin and pulled him to the ground. Then, Jon rammed his elbow into the side of Frankie's face. Jon hit hard. He was merciless as he knocked Frankie down again.

"Gah!" Jon snaked behind Frankie and wrapped his legs securely around his opponent's thighs. Jon slipped his arms around Frankie's neck and squeezed to initiate an effective rear-naked choke. This was the ideal move needed to finish him off.

"Ah!" Frankie screamed like a weeping little boy.

It was at this point that the dance floor was turned into pandemonium.

Patrons shouted as they ran and people moved in. They tried to get into the fight, but Danix and Li did their best to hold everyone back. Lastly, the sound of Sam screaming at Jon to let Frankie go was heard perfectly. Jon was also now holding Frankie Castellani so tight he felt pressure in his arms and in his backside.

Jon refused to break the hold.

"Jon!" someone yelled.

Now relentlessly squeezing Frankie's throat, Jon pushed with everything he had left inside. Gritting his teeth, Jon stopped seeing the lights from the dance floor. No, he was back in the desert, standing with his fellow Marines. Up against so many insurgents and among so many other enemies, Jon didn't think of anything other than the targets.

No, in the end, Jon needed to get them before they got him.

He used the same dark energy he did back in war. Jon knew if he stopped then, he was dead. Although this particular situation was not the same as being in a war, right now, Jon felt exactly as if it was. He didn't stop. He pushed. And, still pushing hard, he heard

Frankie's choke while also hearing the sound of Danix's terrible scream. "Jon, stop!"

———

Stopping, Jon's gaze blurred and he felt like he was waking from a deep sleep. The first person he saw after was Danix. He was brooding and looking at Jon with furrowed eyebrows. Showing concern, Danix was not the only one who was shocked to see Jon reach such a pinnacle level of violence.

Jon had slipped. He lost control!

He had used too much force, and not knowing when to stop is not what happens at The Conquistador. With a protocol set to follow, Jon had not released Frankie. He could have injured him or worse.

When Jon released the hold, he pushed off and rolled up onto one knee.

He took a deep breath and looked dead ahead. Frankie coughed and Jon did too. By now, all the Doormen had gathered and were looking at the winded boy. Frankie had been taken for quite a spin and Jon was primed for what was to be another hard-hitting rumble. Sam was in the middle, with both hands out, and acting like a referee. He did this despite the fact that he was already on a team.

"Everyone just relax. Just—" As Sam did his best to mediate, Frankie's grip on reality returned and he raced after Jon.

"You mother—!"

"Whoa! Hey!" Sam shouted.

Both parties were locked in a stand-off, but Jon

wasn't charging or attempting to break free. He stared at Frankie and the son of the mobster glowered.

Jon had him. Jon beat him.

"Back up! Move!" Another voice emerged from inside the crowd. Jon stopped and Danix stepped aside while Addison Krowe came forth. Holding a flashlight, Addison shined the light into the face of anyone standing too close. Forcing them, in a very clever way, to back up, Addison questioned everyone like a detective.

"What's going on? What happened?"

"A scrap," Danix said to Addison. "But it's all over and done now."

"Shit it is," said Frankie. He moved from his boys and stepped to Addison.

"Your fucking bouncer attacked me!" Frankie yelled. "This asshole attacked my friends for no reason! Fuck him!"

Addison glimpsed at Jon.

The Marine did nothing to absolve himself. As far as Jon understood, everything he did was justified, the same as always. Every action taken was the right one. Jon was prepared to explain himself when the time came. However, being smack in the middle of the floor, now was not the time to do that.

Addison knew this too, hence why he slipped his flashlight into his jacket and turned to Danix.

"Get off the floor, now," he said.

Danix nodded and backstepped. The space cleared.

"You two," Addison said, pointing at Frankie and his friend. It was the first guy whom Jon popped earlier. "You two come with me."

"What?" snapped Frankie. "Are you fucking serious right now?"

"Hey," said Addison, and he took a big step forward. Addison asserted his position as the cooler. He pointed his finger at Frankie and continued to exact his authority. "Either you're going to come with me now and we can get this thing straight, or I call the cops and let them sort it. Now, what do you want to do?"

Frankie didn't answer, but Sam was here. He moved and nudged the Frankie forward.

"He's coming. Let's go." Frankie smugly threw his hands up in the air and walked with Sam.

Jon didn't move. He waited with Danix, Li, and Addison. Exhaling like he just sprinted a mile, Jon was too exasperated to say anything. His heart was beating hard and fast, and as the seconds passed, he was able to cultivate more calm. The music boomed, but no one had brought out the celebrity guests. The people on the dance floor had returned to getting their freak on, but again, none of the Doormen went anywhere. Still, Jon waited for Addison to say something.

Jon felt he already knew how Danix and Li felt. They were in the fight, same as he was.

As Jon rarely admitted, he cared more about what Addison thought of him than anyone else. Jon had a profound respect for the man who gave him his opportunity. He enjoyed working at The Conquistador, even under difficult circumstances. He didn't regret his choices. Jon also didn't know what Addison thought or what he was going to say.

Jon was justified in his strategy, absolutely. He did what he was told not to. He disobeyed Addison because Frankie was connected. Jon wasn't. Frankie was somebody, and Jon was nobody. Frankie was dangerous, but then again...Jon was dangerous too.

When Jon stepped closer, Addison's hands went from being in front of his face to now down by his hips. He looked at Jon from top to bottom. He inspected him like a tailor about to complete a fitting.

"You okay?" Addison asked.

Jon shook his head. He wasn't hurt, but that damn well didn't mean he was bloody okay.

"My office," said Addison. "Come now."

CHAPTER 21
SEARCHED AND SEIZED

THE IDEA OF ADDISON INVITING JON INTO HIS office was terrifying.

It was mayhem.

This was a big night for The Conquistador. There were big guests, lots of people, and most importantly, a lot of money was being paid in order to deliver quality entertainment. And the way it started was with a brawl and with injuries. Yet, now that Jon was off the floor, the second string of bouncers came in to keep watch. They were Doormen too, just different. They had less responsibility and weren't given nearly as many privileges. They are known as tier two bouncers. This was a classification given by Addison himself.

During big evenings, extra security needed to be added. This included a tier two team unit that could assist the Doormen. Sam and Danix stayed outside Addison's office. There was Frankie and then there were some of the others present in Addison's space. Still, everyone who needed to be present was there now.

Not a word was spoken, but Sam continued to stand next to Frankie for some reason.

Jon glared. The entire time, all the Marine did was stare back at the son of a mobster. Frankie was so connected and wealthy, while Jon lived at home in Queens with his mother. He had barely enough money to afford the basic things. What Jon earned at the club went mostly to savings and fun things like gym and training. Nevertheless, Jon was neither intimidated nor impressed. And, as far as he was concerned, he won the fight.

He owned Frankie's sorry ass.

"Gentlemen, please have a seat," said Addison. He gestured to the chairs, but Jon didn't sit, not right away.

"After you," Jon said to Frankie.

Frankie Castellani wore a silk suit, which was a shade of navy. It was actually quite nice, but it looked somewhat disheveled. The shirt was untucked and crinkled around the chest and waist.

"Fuck you, man."

"Enough!" yelled Addison. "Just sit."

Once all the bouncers were in Addison's office, the cooler was sitting behind his desk. Through the window in Addison's office, Jon could see the entire dance floor and most of the stage. From here, what he had was a solid view of the club. As he proceeded, Jon peeked out the window. From here, everything below seemed normal.

It was active and exactly as it should be. *Almost.*

There was no more security on the stage. This was the section where the fight went down, and it was now being cleaned by The Conquistador's maintenance staff. Now, from what Jon could recall, there was a little blood on the scene. Actually, he was spared of most of it.

"Sit," Addison said to Jon.

Jon followed the instruction. Addison was not the only one in the office. Two uniformed officers were present too.

They glared at Jon as he stepped inside. Jon's dog tags slipped out from under his shirt. He refused to put them back in. He wanted the cops to know of his veteran status. He fought and almost died for his country while Frankie and his boys lived in a posh Manhattan neighborhood.

What did they fight for? They only watched as others did the fighting for them, namely the people, all of whom were likely too weak to resist.

"This is Officer Merchant and Officer Clanistan from the NYPD. I called them after the assault."

"Assault?" Jon said to Addison. "I think you mean the act of self-defense." Jon wasn't correcting Addison. He was just saying what he felt he needed to. He had to be absolutely clear now the cops were here. Both officers stood in front of Jon, arms folded and not saying a word.

"Until we get all the facts in order, it's assault," said one of the cops.

The one that spoke, Jon thought, could be Officer Merchant. He was standing to Jon's right. He was the one who Addison had introduced first from the pair.

Oddly, this person looked familiar to Jon. He saw him at some point, but he couldn't remember when exactly. Jon vaguely recalled his face, yet the déjà vu was distracting him as he stood in the office.

"And that's what we're here to do," said Addison.

"What we're here to do," said Frankie. He referred to himself and the people in his company. "We're going to get my lawyer down here before I answer any more of your dumbass questions."

"You're welcome to do that," invited Addison, "though we're not here to question you as much as we're here to look at this."

Addison removed a remote from his pocket. He turned to face the corner of his office and raised the hand holding the controller. He pointed it to a bank of screens positioned in the shape of a grid near his desk. Here was the club's surveillance cameras—the chief tool in not only nightclubs, but everywhere now.

Even when surveying personal property or people who might be up to no good, these tools were absolutely essential. Addison turned toward the screen in the dead center. He was right in front of it, as were the officers Merchant and Clanistan.

All watched while Frankie stood with his two friends. Jon stood away. He knew what he was seeing. He didn't need a camera to confirm it.

Eyeing Addison from where he was standing, Jon watched his boss fast-forward the video. He waited as the footage zipped along and the camera magnified. From Jon's point of view, he could see exactly what he had seen almost two hours ago.

It showed Frankie and his friends. They were in the middle of the frame, next to each other. Closing in on their hands, an item slipped out from one and into the other.

"Pause," ordered Addison. He magnified the image in a series of quick snaps. The picture focused, and the shot of the two hands consumed the entire screen.

"Well," Addison continued, "looks like we might have a hand-off happening here."

"*It would appear that way*," acknowledged Officer Merchant.

The officer turned to Frankie. Jon's arms folded as he watched. "You two movin' product?"

"No," said Frankie's friend. He was with Frankie at the time of the fight. "I was giving him some Advil, that's all. Guy gets headaches. Giving him Advil."

"Really?" asked Merchant, doubtful. This excuse sounded like a punchline to a bad joke.

Jon scoffed. Shaking his head, he looked at Addison. Jon's boss's expression was the same as his own. Both were unimpressed by another lame excuse delivered by Frankie's idiot friends. None of them really had any idea. Due to this, the mobster's son continued to grin.

"Yeah, really," Frankie's friend snapped at Officer Merchant.

"Don't worry," said Frankie. He tapped his friend on the chest. "We don't gotta do nothin' until the lawyer gets here. They don't have grounds to search us."

"You sure about that?" asked Merchant.

Frankie's lips puckered. The gum in his mouth rolled around as he leered at the detective.

"Definitely sure."

"Well, you can wait for your lawyer to get here if you want to, but while he's doing that, we have to clear our security for any wrongdoing," said Addison. "My guy thought he saw something shady, and so, you had grounds for ejection. He was well within his job parameters, no question about that."

Addison gazed at Jon. Besides holding a raised fist

to let Jon know he was with him, there was solemnity in Addison's eyes. His fist said more than his words did.

"Okay," said Officer Merchant.

"Okay?" snapped Frankie. "Last time I checked, you need to be a cop in order to search somebody or eject someone. This asshole over here..." And Frankie pointed at Jon. He flapped his mouth and spat out his last few words. "Sure as shit ain't a fucking cop."

"And we're well aware of that fact," said Addison, "but I know he tried calling. And, when your friend ran, he went after him."

"I ran, yeah," said Frankie's friend. He was the same guy Addison mentioned earlier. "I ran because I was being chased."

"You were being chased because you had something to hide."

The one who said this was Danix. Jon looked in his direction.

Danix was the strong and silent type. Although friendly, he rarely spoke or offered his opinions. Choosing to do this now only let Jon know he was right in his decision. He garnered the reluctant input of another Doorman and it came from the chief himself.

"Look, enough of this," said Frankie, "unless you actually found contraband, we could have just been passin' shit that ain't suspicious. And whether you found shit on us or not, you know you ain't got nothing."

"Well, still...we have grounds to search you," said Addison.

"You wanna search me," said Frankie. "You go right ahead and search me."

With his arms spread out, Frankie now offered himself up to the cops like he was in a music video. He waited for either cop to come forward and do what they were invited to do. Frankie strutted like the wannabe gangster he was and Jon scoffed. The Marine was anything but impressed. Then again, the entire exchange didn't seem typical or, for that matter, *real*.

Jon sensed something else. He waited.

As Merchant chose to come forward, he frisked Frankie while he snickered. Jon and his fellow Doormen endure the sight. But, based on the look he received from Addison, there was nothing to worry about. Still, just because he was in the clear, it did not mean everything else was too.

And more suspicions did emerge.

"Find anything?" snapped Frankie.

"The product *wasn't* on him," said Jon. By stating such an obvious fact, he felt the impulse to stand. Jon addressed Frankie Castellani while on his feet. "It was on his friend."

"Search him!" yelled Frankie. "Won't find anything there either."

"I know what the hell happened."

"So do I," said Danix. He spoke up in defense of not only Jon but all the Doormen involved.

"We all do," said Addison, now in it with the rest.

Once the cop was done searching, the officer looked at Addison. "He's clean."

"Told ya," Frankie piped in.

"Okay, well, we have grounds to search all of them, isn't that right, officer?"

"Well..." Officer Merchant trailed off. He looked dolefully at Addison and Jon. The Marine observed his conflicted look. The response conjured was *not* the one any of them wanted to hear.

"We could, but we don't feel that it's necessary."

"What?" snapped Jon.

"You *serious?*" piped in Danix.

So far, Jon hadn't heard anything from Li. Judging by his crossed arms, Li was just as displeased as everyone else in the room.

"Officer, you must be joking," said Addison. "We have grounds to ban them from this establishment, no question."

"Actually," added a man by the door. Jon could hear his smug voice. Everyone who heard it then turned to face him. "My client is right. *You got nothing.*"

CHAPTER 22
CHEAP BACK AND FORTHS

A NEW MAN ARRIVED WEARING A THREE-PIECE gray suit and carrying a briefcase by his side. His hair was slick and his body rank with putrid cologne. Jon mulled this guy over like he was a piece of meat gone bad. The comparison, Jon felt, worked well.

That's exactly what this man was.

"You don't have grounds to do anything."

"And who are you?" asked Addison.

"Me?" The man motioned across Addison's office. "I'm just the one you're supposed to speak to before you speak to anyone else."

"*Lawyer*," said Addison.

"How'd you guess?" answered the man. He strolled to Addison's desk and his briefcase swayed along his thighs.

"Takes one to know one," replied Addison.

"I see."

Frankie Castellani's lawyer stood between Frankie and the officer called Merchant. This new man had yet to introduce himself. Nevertheless, the vibes he was giving made Jon remember some of the men he encoun-tered in the military. Men in suits would sometimes arrive at bases. They would come with orders from the top and then they'd give them to the men in hopes they would follow without asking questions.

On Addison's turf, this lawyer was doing his best to make his presence known. Coming dressed in a flashy suit, he spoke with a coolness that secured his place as the alpha male in the room. But there was only one alpha male here.

Some alphas were loud and obnoxious. They were the same guys who entered a room with their chins up and their dicks out. Already, they'd be looking for trou-ble. They sought the inevitable battle whereby they could prove their self-worth. Then, there was the more alternative alpha male. There was the alpha male who used his mind and his intellect. They are more strategic and passive.

Now, Addison was a man who flexed his strengths in opposing ways. He wasn't the strongest guy, but he was the most vindictive. And, while not necessarily violent, Addison was more ruthless than his cohorts. Seeing Addison standing toe-to-toe with this attorney, both stared each other down with venom and dismay. It was then Jon could see what it was like to challenge Addison at his own game. This club and this office were his and no one else's.

"You're in my office, and yet I still don't got your name," Addison looked at the lawyer with his head parallel to the floor.

"Of course. My apologies." The lawyer lent his gratitude by showing his hand. It was obvious to Jon the man was anything but sincere. "The name is

Marco Valenti. I'm the lawyer for the Castellani family."

"Don't you mean *one* of the lawyers?" Addison said.

This lawyer called Marco continued to stand before The Conquistador cooler. Arms crossed, Marco's demeanor was synonymous with his posture. He was crooked and slimy. Jon watched the lawyer snare.

"Right." When Marco sat, he dropped his briefcase next to his chair. He grinned while Jon watched Frankie inch himself closer to his attorney. "Anyway, I'm here to defend my clients against illegal search and seizure."

"Illegal?" barked Addison. "We caught them trading product right here in front of everyone, and we weren't the only ones. The police saw too."

"Yes, *we did*," confirmed the detectives.

"You might have seen it, but you have yet to recover anything, is that correct?" Marco asked.

No one said a damn thing.

Jon didn't know the law, but Addison did. He remembered Addison had a law degree from NYU. If Addison said what happened was lawful. The police were doing the same. Therefore, Jon assumed he was okay. He was safe.

"We were justified in our search. Here, at The Conquistador, security reserves the right to search and reprimand anyone who disobeys our code of conduct. I can pull you a copy of our regulations book if you'd like to take a look."

"No need," said Marco. He clicked the switches and unlocked his briefcase. He took a peek. "I have it right here."

Marco held a surprisingly detailed manifesto and

flipped through each page. Jon, as well as the rest of security, gradually crept closer.

"I am paying close attention to this section here."

"And which one is that?" Addison asked the smug attorney. He was still displaying the same level of hostility and appeared just as perturbed as before.

"*Unnecessary* violence," suggested Marco.

"What?" asked Jon. He was flabbergasted by what this slick lawyer suggested. Every part of Jon's reaction was necessary. Frankie was the one who hit first!

"Right here," said Marco. "Read it. Should a patron display uncouth behavior, security must first initiate a verbal warning before proceeding to any kind of physical reprimanding. Now, as I ask you...was such a warning given?"

"Of course it was," Jon stated.

"I didn't hear anything," said Frankie.

"Wasn't given to you," Jon replied with a glower. He was looking past Frankie and was instead focused on one of his goons. "I gave it to *him*."

"And what did you say *exactly*?"

"I think my colleague is aware of what constitutes as a warning," Addison said.

"Are you sure about that?" asked Marco, being condescending and mean.

Addison drove his knuckles hard into his neck. His scorn was so intense it practically lit a fire throughout the entire office.

"I am," said Danix. Arms folded, Danix's eyes were fixed on the attorney.

As one of the biggest and most capable bouncers here, Jon saw Danix as a living, walking wall. Tall yet also lithe and nimble, it was a struggle for Jon to imagine someone like Danix being afraid of anything.

"I heard him just the same."

"Me too," said Li. His accent made it somewhat difficult to hear. And yet, Jon heard him perfectly.

"Okay," said Marco. "So a warning was given. Was it acknowledged or did your guys just go ahead and attack?"

"There was a warning," Jon said again. "There was an order to stop. When he didn't listen, I acted because I had no choice."

"Oh, so you attacked when my client failed to listen?" asked Marco.

"Yes," answered Jon, fists clenched.

"So then, it was less a matter of him not hearing and more of a matter of him not listening to you?"

"What's the difference?" asked Jon.

"A legal one," said Marco.

"Well, we're not here to have a mediation," said Addison. "Your friend wasn't listening to a warning from our security and that's that."

"You mean my client?" corrected Marco. He spoke with the same derision as displayed earlier. He was now making it clear this meeting was professional, and yet not a single person in the room actually believed that it was. All wanted to refute it. However, everyone was silenced when Marco raised his right hand and pointed at Frankie. Addison gawked. He continued to put the guilty parties in the center of the pointless conversation.

"Whatever," said Addison. "Either way, we have full legal protection when deciding who to admit and who not to. So, in this case, I humbly request that you and your clients be marked when returning to The Conquistador."

"Marked?" asked Marco. He laughed at the word.

"You heard me right," said Addison.

"Indeed, I did," said Marco. He inched closer to Addison and squeezed the handle on his briefcase with both hands. "Indeed, I did."

"Whoa, hold up there," said Frankie, "What does marked even mean? Can I still get in or not?"

"You can," said Addison. "You're just...now being watched by us...*closely*."

"What?" Frankie begged. "What does also that mean?"

"Enough," said Marco, preventing the issue from going any further. Jon didn't know what marked was, but he had an idea. "We will sort all of this out another time," he said. "For now, I think we're about through here."

Marco placed his hands on Frankie's shoulder. He bent his body to the side and whispered into his client's ear. Jon and the other bouncers were all crowded around Addison's desk. They were there in unity to protect the man they trusted. Addison was the same man who defended all Doormen against this rising and nefarious force.

"Good night," Marco said. He stepped out of Addison's office, and the rest of Frankie's crew left too. *Good riddance and fuck you* thought Jon. Never did any conflict end that quickly or that easily.

It never did and it never would.

CHAPTER 23
WE MAKE WALLS

JON WAITED FOR THE DOORS TO CLOSE. AFTERWARD, he couldn't help but sigh. This was done not because he was out of breath or because he was relieved. It was done from sheer exhaustion and fatigue. An exchange, Jon thought, would have surely ended sooner. No, it stretched out longer than expected.

"Jesus, that was some serious—"

"Bullshit," interrupted Danix.

"I can't believe what just happened. Was that even real?" Jon faced Danix when he asked this question.

Danix also turned to see Jon before replying. "As real as it gets, right Addison?"

Jon watched as Addison's posture hadn't changed since the lawyer and Frankie left his office.

"Yes, sir."

"Well," said Jon. He pivoted to face Addison. "What does this mean?"

"What does this mean?" Addison repeated.

"Yeah," said Jon.

"It means we're about to be taken for quite a ride."

"Who?" asked Danix. "Us, the bouncers? The Doormen?"

"No," said Addison. His voice cracked as he leaned back so far he was almost falling off his chair. "It's an attack against the entire club."

What Addison said implied that everyone was now being targeted.

Now, Jon was unsure *how* to interpret or understand an act of incredible hatred. "You mean, like, what...we're going to have to close down?"

Addison was seated as he heard this question.

"No. We'll be open," he said, "but we'll just be more compromised. Now that a lawyer for the Castellani family has come here, he means business. It's all just another attempt to confront his son that could have drastic consequences."

"Hold up there," said Danix. "I thought you said we were in the right doing what we did?"

"Yeah," said Li, "he was dealing something for sure. I mean, I saw too."

"What we saw doesn't matter," said Addison. He exhaled and reached for his collar to loosen his tie. "What we can prove is all that does."

"You're saying we *can't* prove it?"

"Not in court, we can't," Addison said to Jon. "No."

"Well, will there be a lawsuit?" Jon asked, voicing his concern while giving Addison a furious stare.

"Not exactly, but we can't ban Frankie from entering our club. Given his status and his willingness to get legal, it will only make things worse. Marking him is the best we can do."

"Then, we go to the police," advised Li. "We can't arrest people, but they can."

"Which is what worries me the most," answered Addison.

"How so?" asked Danix.

"I don't think what we saw here was happening the way we thought."

Again lost, the feelings of anxiety formerly exclusive to Jon when in the military had suddenly returned. Jon just couldn't weigh the implications behind Addison's reply.

"Police would have arrested anyone else in his position, but they didn't. Why?"

"Because he's goddamn Frankie Castellani," said Danix, "that's why."

Jon could see Danix shaking his head. Jon stood back in disbelief. The situation was enough to cause such a gargantuan man like Danix to be taken back.

"Maybe, but that's only half the puzzle," said Addison.

"And the other half?" asked Li.

"That's still being formulated," said Addison, "but if you want my opinion—"

"No," said Jon. Suddenly, he interrupted Addison, which was something no one had the balls to do. "Just your honest one," Jon said again.

Addison sighed and his tongue pressed against his cheek.

"The police don't want to get mixed up with the Castellani family any more than half the badges walking around this city do," Addison said, looking only at Jon. "Their actions today were paint-by-numbers, standard protocol."

"Are you saying these cops are actually afraid to get involved with this guy?" asked Jon.

"Precisely what I'm saying," Addison replied.

"But Frankie will be back," said Danix. "I mean, he's marked, yeah, and he got away with whatever he was up to, but still...you can be damn sure he'll try to do it again. I'm no cop, but I know that much is true."

"And that much is right on the money," said Addison. He poured himself a glass of Scotch and sipped.

"So, there's *nothing* we can do?" Jon looked around the room. He observed the pensive expressions from all his colleagues. Jon imagined they were all just as conflicted as he was. "We banned him, but we can't actually stop him from coming in? Wow."

Everyone shrugged and reacted the same as Jon. What power did the Doormen really have?

"No," Addison said. "No, there's *definitely* something we can do."

Taking another sip, Addison's lips were puckered. Placing the glass down on his desk, Addison glanced at Jon. He waited for his boss's reply.

"We keep doing our jobs," Addison said. "If Frankie comes back, we'll be ready for him."

"But I thought we couldn't touch him?" asked Jon.

"We can't touch him the way we do everyone else," Addison explained. "But we might be able to arrange a way for him to fall into a trap."

"A *trap*?" asked Jon. He liked this idea.

"Get the evidence we need," Addison said, "and then handle it the way it's supposed to be handled. Police won't help us, and if they won't, then we help ourselves."

"But we're not cops," said Sam, "we don't handle things like this."

"We still *don't*," Addison stressed. He emphasized

the contraction while all the Doormen were standing around his desk. "Now we have to handle things ourselves."

"Is that really...*smart?*" asked Sam.

Now downright questioning Addison's thinking, Jon had seen through him since the beginning. He pretended to look out for everyone, acting all high and mighty, like he was speaking for the greater good. Addison ignored Sam and Jon hoped he would have more to say.

He wanted to hear him explain more.

"We'll see," said Addison, "but it's what we're going to do. This is our place, and no one comes in and corrupts it, least of all a group of wannabe criminals protected by a powerful overlord."

"So, if we can't ban him," said Danix, "then what exactly *is* our strategy going forward?"

"Same as it's always been," said Addison. "We keep our doors open, and we keep our guests happy. We keep them happy, and we continue to give them whatever they want."

"Frankie included?" asked Jon.

Addison nodded and was just as nonchalant as he had been thus far. "Frankie included."

"If we let him in, though," said Li, "we really don't know what he's going to do."

"Yeah, we do," said Addison. He turned to face Jon. He was now the center of attention. "Jon saw what was happening, what Frankie wanted, if he hadn't been stopped."

Jon nodded to consider the possibility.

Indeed, he was no cop. He was also no detective either. In fact, Jon was nothing more than an amputee

Marine trying to find his way in the world. Even still, Jon understood what Addison was saying. He understood what he meant when he said the word *trap*.

Thinking about what lay ahead, Jon's heart beat faster and his hand twitched. It was all starting to get way too real.

"A drug operation," said Jon. "One that might cause a chain reaction that might bring down the entire club."

"How?" asked Danix.

"The Conquistador is a place built on quality entertainment, class, and above all else, safety," explained Addison. "Once that is compromised, then this...all of this..." He raised his hand to gesture to everything that surrounded him, including his colleagues. "All of this goes away, and we can't let that happen."

"Sounds a lot like we are trying to be cops," Danix admitted.

"Nope," said Addison. He was being frank now. "We're just doing what we always do. Keeping things under control and expecting the unexpected."

"More people will try to move in too," said Danix. "It won't be easy to keep things under control if they're already moving."

"Not easy for other bouncers, but then they're not us," Addison said.

"Definitely not us," said Jon. He looked at Addison and joined in on this heroic moment of unity.

"So what do we do?" Li was the last to speak.

Addison curled his lip into his mouth and gawked at the Doormen. Jon let the responsibility sink in, as did the others in his company. "We get ready."

CHAPTER 24
THE PHASE ONE

AFTER THE SHITSTORM AT THE CONQUISTADOR, all Jon wanted was a good night's sleep. Back at home, Jon's body was in total agony. He was so sore and winded from the previous night's fight, he limped to his bathroom, and ran himself a cold bath. He grabbed some ice from the freezer and dumped the cubes into the tepid water. He made sure it was below zero before slipping off his clothes and squatting into the freezing liquid.

"Ah!" Like a hundred pins pricking him all at once, Jon's wounds singed as he lowered himself. Holding his breath, Jon's eyes cringed and he splayed his fingers.

Bruised and bleeding, the wounds were certain to scab.

Being in ice, Jon's body was about to experience an enhanced healing. It was an old trick learned in the Marines. Jon was assured if you're sore, you drop into a tub filled with ice. His Marine buddies assured Jon he would wake the next day a new man. Jon was skeptical about this. When Jon took this bath, the pain he once felt had dwindled. Other days may have felt only half as bad if Jon would have acted on this opportunity before.

Jon enjoyed the cold. He rested his hands on the ledge of the tub and leaned back his head. Jon felt a chill. In the water, Jon reflected on all that had happened to him so far. He didn't see his job heading in a bad direction, that is, the direction of having to make busts or face off against dangerous criminals.

The job of a bouncer is to ensure safety. It's to make sure those who make the place unsafe are taken out. And, since this was *no longer* an option, Jon's new job was to search and destroy.

A low-level thug was making a move against him and his friends.

The Conquistador was Jon Haze's home.

It was where he spent most of his time now and it was under attack. While serving overseas, Jon slept in a tent on a cot that barely fit his body. There, Jon was visited by the same excruciating thought as he was tonight. Although he was safe today, tomorrow, Jon might not be. The reality of anyone who works a dangerous job is any day could be their last.

Tomorrow was something they might never see again.

Returning home, every soldier is under the impression that their life will be easier. What's waiting for them will be euphoric and delightful. Depending on the duration of your service, what you've seen, and what you've done, life should be more tolerable.

Your days are more certain, but then they are also more contrived.

Your time is not limited, but it starts moving at a much slower pace. You might think you have everything figured out, yet there are still some surprises. The noise follows you, and seeing things you can't understand still plagues your mind. And thinking this, knowing it to be the truth, Jon's thoughts had become twisted.

The days he once believed to be unnumbered suddenly were.

"Jon?" There was a knock at the door. His eyes were shut. Behind them came a cyclone of intrusive thoughts. Jon couldn't be sure how long he'd been in the bathroom or how long he had slept.

"Jon, you in there, hon?" Gradually, Jon began to open his eyes. He looked at the door.

"Mom?"

"Yes," she said, "it's Mom. You in there?"

"Yeah," Jon replied. Her voice became higher as he began to sit straight. "It's me. Sorry. I was just taking some time to recover."

Jon's gaze shifted to his arms. He examined the many wounds scattered along his biceps and wrists. Bruises and gashes blotched his skin. With his prosthetic off, Jon's leg stayed submerged while the other sat propped along the edge. Resting on the door, Jon's bulky appendage was fashioned from titanium and layered in a durable plastic. All of this had assisted Jon well when working at the club.

"Are you sure you're alright?" Jon's mother asked him.

Jon thought about the question. It was one posed by a woman who always cared for Jon. These days, he didn't quite know if he was *alright*. Maybe he was and maybe he wasn't.

"I'm...I'm..." Jon didn't want to tell his mom the truth. About what it is that really did happen to him and the other bouncers, he wouldn't lie. From here on, Jon was going to provide the truth, and only that.

"I'll be out in a minute."

"Great," said Jon's mother. "I made some Gnocchi, if you're hungry."

"Gnocchi?"

"There's still some leftover if you want it."

Leftover.

When the word was spoken again, Jon reached up and pulled his hand out of the murky water. More melted ice cubes floated around Jon. He pressed his hand to his forehead. He was exhausted and had developed a modest headache.

"Time?" Jon asked.

"Sorry?" said Jon's mom.

Jon was positioned in the tub's center. With his legs bent, he stretched his arms.

"What time is it?"

"It's almost one," Jon's mother replied.

"*One?*"

"Yeah," said Betsy Haze.

Still rubbing his forehead, Jon struggled to accept he had only just awakened. He was going to eat because he thought he was up closer to two.

"It's not that late."

"No," said Jon. Rolling out of the tub, Jon climbed out and slipped onto the toilet so he could reattach his prosthetic. "*It's not.*"

"Well, let me know if you need anything, okay?"

"Okay," Jon said. He would have preferred to have told his mom this next part to her face. "No, I mean it, mom. Thanks. Thanks for everything."

At the time, Jon could not see his mom. Jon

preferred to think she was smiling and happy to hear what was said. Jon hoped his mom was glad to hear him being so polite and grateful.

"You're welcome," Jon's mom said. "Just...come downstairs when you're done, okay?"

"Yeah," said Jon. "Will do."

————

Jon shuffled along the stairs while the smell of fresh pasta lathered in succulent tomato sauce filled his nostrils. Jon's meals did not always include such exquisite dishes. Normally Jon had a protein shake and some grilled chicken, which he ate much later in the day. His diet was improving, but it was far from perfect. Jon didn't care what he ate or when.

He was just glad to have food.

Jon's mom stood by the counter, looking all sparkly and happy. Since Jon accepted the job at The Conquistador, his and his mother's schedules did not quite align. Therefore, they rarely saw one another or even crossed paths at all. In this case, they were here, finally together.

Always, Jon liked his mother. Always, he wanted to be with her.

He loved her.

"Coffee?" she said to her son.

"Sure," Jon said, taking a seat.

"Black?"

"Yes." Jon took his coffee black with no sugar and definitely no cream.

He swore this off all a long time ago. He was drinking more coffee now than he ever had.

Why?

Jon assumed it was because of his lack of energy and the long hours. The fact that, while working, Jon needed to be lucid and as sharp as possible. The caffeine gave Jon a boost of exhilaration. Suddenly, he was reacting to all of this like he had a B12 shot. Awakened, now at the table, Jon's senses became more attuned. It helped with his injuries.

"Here, want me to fix you a plate?"

Jon nodded. "If that's okay, yes. Thank you."

"It definitely is."

Jon was amazed to see his mother was still willing to serve him. In the end, Jon believed she was just happy to have him around and alive. Whenever a parent sends their child off to war, they embrace what few have the stomach to endure or to accept.

They *might* not make it back home.

Parents face the devastating reality of saying goodbye to their children forever. The letters, the locations, and the slight optimism do not overcome the constant thought they cannot escape.

Farewells turn to *goodbyes,* and *I'll see you again* turns into *I wish you were here now.*

With Jon's father gone, all Jon's mother had was him. No siblings, and no one there to help, Jon was exactly what his mom needed. A full plate plopped in front of Jon and he breathed in all the new scents of this healthy and balanced meals. It was all so perfect, he didn't hesitate.

Jon plunged his fork into a heap of steaming pasta. He dug deep and plowed his face full of juicy curdles. Jon swallowed the warm bits of nourishment and kept gulping until he couldn't anymore.

"So...how was work? You didn't sleep that much. Everything okay?"

While continuing to chew and swallow, Jon's session of nourishment was interrupted.

Jon didn't talk about work, not with his mother. Generally, Jon provided her with his collection of generic statements. He lent her little details, like how he was in a fight and how he handled it. For the most part, Jon's mom knew her son's job was dangerous. Then, she also knew it was nothing compared to what he faced in Iraq. She was concerned yet also somewhat relieved. She could tell her son to be careful. However, she did know the club. Jon's mom was aware of Addison Krowe and how he operated one of New York's finest establishments.

Jon wanted to tell her that none of this was true. Jon's job would not be as straightforward as it was. It wouldn't be as simple. Jon stepped into some serious shit. He looked into his mother's beady eyes. They gleamed with neediness and concern.

It was a look found only in a parent's solemn gaze. Always, the truth was far from easy.

This truth, *especially*, had no easy way of saying it.

"*Work?*"

"How was it?" Jon's mom asked.

Jon's fork clinked the plate. His wrist twitched and his body quaked.

He was not the best liar. He rarely did, if ever, *lie*. But, there was no need to lie now. In fact, this might be the first time since Jon was a teenager that he had to bury the truth.

"Work was..." Jon didn't know how to phrase it. He didn't know how to tell his mother about what happened. Eyeing his food, Jon declined to look at his mother at all.

"Normal," said Jon.

"Normal?" asked Jon's mom.

Jon nodded. He gave his mother a phony smile and tried to keep this exchange as simple as possible.

"Yep, perfectly normal." This was an outright lie, so much so Jon's voice cracked as he shared this.

"How's Addison?"

"He's good," said Jon. He didn't know for sure that Addison was.

"Oh, yeah? Did you talk to him?"

"Talk to Addison?" asked Jon.

"Yeah," said his mother.

"Sure. Sure, I talked to Addison."

"You're lying." She said this as she looked him up and down.

A mother always knows when their son or their daughter is lying. Jon was so easy to see through because he always was a horrible liar.

"What?"

"I know you're lying to me."

"I'm not lying to you," said Jon.

"And you just lied to me again," said Betsy Haze.

Jon shook his head. He thought his mom was displeased. She would reveal just how upset she was by raising her voice. Instead, she smirked. She returned to picking at her meal and was quiet as she ate.

"I suppose I could tell you more."

"Only if you want to. Sharing has never been..." Jon's mother's gaze narrowed. "Your strong suit."

At first, Jon sought to switch to being on the defensive. He didn't like how his mother would tell him he didn't share enough or talk enough. Since the war, putting one's struggles into words was a difficult task, although it wasn't impossible. Jon chose not to see himself as if he were some kind of wounded, traumatized vet.

Was war tough? *Damn right it was*.

Did Jon see some bad shit? *Most definitely*.

Counseling, conversation, sharing stories, all of this helped Jon. His chief strategy was to always keep himself preoccupied. Working nights at the club helped in this regard. Still, Jon's mother could see something was wrong. Jon wasn't himself. Sometimes, Jon's mind went awry. He reflected on what happened yesterday.

He didn't want to tell his mother the entire truth.

Doing this would only make her worry. And, at twenty-four, Jon was still living at home. He was no longer a kid, but often, his mother treated him as though he was one. There's no changing this. Once a son, always a son, and there's no breaking a mother's compassion or her constant empathy.

"I guess you're right."

Most of Jon's plate was cleaned. His appetite was no longer present, which was a good thing. "Not my best quality."

"No," said Jon's mother. She stood up and went to the sink to drop off her plate and said nothing after.

All in all, she was done talking.

CHAPTER 25
HARD THOUGHTS

JON PICKED AT WHAT WAS LEFT ON HIS PLATE AND watched his mom as she walked away.

Clearly, she didn't want to challenge Jon on anything he had said.

"Well, I guess...things have been kinda different these last few days."

"*Oh, yeah?*"

"Yeah," said Jon.

Mentioning what he did, Jon found himself drawing closer and closer to the truth. It was a truth Jon thought he would never speak to his mom. With her back turned, she was standing in front of the sink. Turning on the faucet, Jon saw an opportunity to break the trend he was once so hellbent on maintaining.

And this bothered him. Actually, it bothered him a lot.

Everything was starting to bother Jon. He was scared.

"The job, it's just—"

"Hard," said Jon's mom. Jon didn't expect her to say anything, but she did.

"Yeah." Jon licked his teeth.

"Well, what did you expect?"

Jon didn't answer. What he expected wasn't what he was seeing now.

"You work a very dangerous job and you spend time with lots of dangerous people."

"Yeah."

She was still turned and Jon glanced at her and attempted to read his mother's body language. Standing straight, Jon could see his mom lifting her coffee to her face. She took small sips like she always did.

Jon tried to study more of her posture.

If she wasn't so sad, she would have turned. She would have looked at Jon while he was there, sitting down. She refused to do this. Jon's hands stayed flat on the table. Then, he thought about something he hadn't until now. Jon worked nights as a bouncer. He accepted his job in order to not only earn money, but also to learn. What Jon wanted to do was grow. He needed something to battle his impulses and his sometimes dark and *broken thoughts*.

"Some bad things could happen," said Betsy Haze. "So, just be sure you protect yourself and stay close to your friends. Watch your back and..." Before his mother could finish, she bowed her head and frowned.

Once a mother, always a mother.

"You don't like what I do, do you?" Jon asked his mom.

A lull then surfaced and Jon could feel his mother's energy. This was a skill that he acquired while on the job. Jon recognized a hostile situation when he saw one. He was familiar with how to pinpoint certain things before they escalated into bad things. Jon's mother, in her own way, was expressing her disapproval. Jon confronted his mother about this. Given what he'd seen and faced, this was Jon's opportunity to make his mark known.

"No mother wants to see their son in harm's way, especially for no reason."

"Is that what you think I'm doing, acting without a reason?"

"You spend your nights watching drunks and fools," said Jon's mom. "You stop idiots from hurting themselves in one of the most active and volatile nightclubs in the city."

"The Conquistador *isn't* volatile, Mom."

"Call it what you want," Betsy snapped back. "You take risks you know you shouldn't. You take chances with your life, and you shouldn't have to."

"Mom, what I did before was way more dangerous than what I'm doing now. Being a Marine, away from home...you know what I did, what I had to do. How is this any different?"

Jon waited for his mother to respond. In the time he spent waiting, Jon could already determine what his mom might say. Although his question was valid, Jon's reasoning was also clear. There was nothing comparable to how it was now.

"The difference is—"

"What?" Jon asked.

"The difference is..." Jon's mom inhaled and he felt a thick air bubble in the pit of his throat. His mother was struggling to find the right words. The strain was most evident from Jon's mother's quivering lips.

"The difference is what?"

"The difference is you're *not* overseas!" Jon's mom yelled.

Jon felt like he'd been struck by lightning. His mother was so often calm. Now raising her voice, Jon understood it was because of him that she did. Jon was quiet after he was scolded. Jon hadn't been yelled at like this since he was a teenager. He looked at his mom's teary eyes. What Jon did was stabbing her in the heart. She was aching. Every son—every good son—loathes seeing their mother so upset, so disturbed, and fearful.

All of this forced Jon to return to the day when he left home. He went back to when he hoped to never see his mom sad again. Always, Jon was tepid whenever he pushed his mother's buttons. Since his time home, he refused to force her to relive the pain of watching him go away.

He refused to make her remember the things no mother should. And yet, even in spite of Jon's efforts, he had done precisely that.

"You're not overseas. You're home. You're home." Jon's mom finally revealed everything that was on her mind.

She let Jon know exactly how she felt whenever he left for work. Before, Jon had only assumed the things that changed since his time away. But then, that was Jon's problem. Jon had assumed, and he wasn't right in any of his assumptions.

"You're home now...and you're..." Jon's mom tried discussing her feelings but it was still too difficult. She could not look at her son without frowning, so Jon watched as her eyes closed. She pushed them together and what Jon's mom once held inside was still breaking her. It was still hurting, and now Jon was able to see it all as easily as he could see his enemies. He could not deny it.

And so he refused to do so.

"It's just..." Jon's mother was done.

Now able to see the state she was in, Jon walked to the kitchen counter and stayed there with her back facing Jon. He could hear his mother's gentle sobs and observed her quivering shoulders.

Was Jon a good son?

Was he the kind of person who could listen to his mother cry and then do nothing afterward? Was he this, or was he...something more?

Maybe he was and maybe he wasn't.

What Jon knew was he had upset his mother. While scrolling through the list of things Jon would never do in his life, hurting her was at the very top.

"I'm worried about you."

"I know," Jon said. "I know, but..."

Jon's mom sobbed into her folded hands. No doubt a tough woman, she had raised Jon almost entirely by herself.

"But, Mom, you know...I'm a fighter, right?"

"What?"

Betsy Haze's voice was fractured. She could barely hold a phrase together without separating her question into a string of inaudible syllables.

"I fight," said Jon. "I fight the way you fought after Dad. You didn't ask for any help, even though it was hard for you and you needed it. But this job, Mom, it's..." Suddenly, Jon found himself remembering why he was hired to work at the club. He remembered when he first made the decision to accept the job as a professional bouncer, as a Doorman, and to become something greater. "You have to trust me when I say that this is something important," Jon declared. "And I'm not just doing it for me. I know you struggle to get all that, and I know it's hard for you to accept, but remember who you raised me to be. I'm not someone who runs from danger, Mom. I mean, you taught me how to stay tough, how to keep my head in the game, and to know that there are people out there who need protecting. And that's what I do each night I walk out the front door. I'm helping people, Mom. I'm *saving* them."

Jon's mom sniffled and she wiped her nose with a tissue.

With her head down, Betsy Haze rested on her son's chest. Jon rubbed his mom tenderly along the shoulder and back. He held his mom as close as he could. He wasn't always the best comforter. In the Marines, the only comfort comes when you're welcomed home.

Generally, this is the best you can hope for. As Jon held his mother, he recalled how he had not held her this way in a long time. Boys should hug their mothers as often as they can. It's the rule of thumb growing up. At least, it was for Jon. Still, Jon hadn't hugged his mother in a long time. How much attention Jon gave to her was based on how much she gave. Nothing else.

But, at this moment, Jon considered a new question: *was he actually a bad son?*

Bad sons don't live at home with their parents, but this was only what Jon told himself. He was there, yes, yet was he present, sensitive, aware? Jon didn't even think about the effect his job would have on his mother. He didn't consider the burden she carried. Why? Now, Jon had asked himself this question many times before. Why could he not just be like the other sons and live a normal life?

A teacher, a librarian, or hell, even a garbage man would be better than what he was doing now. He compiled all the reasons why, and the results did not assemble the way he wanted them to. What Jon was saying now, he should have said before. Jon should have offered more. In the end, what he thought about his job as a bouncer didn't take effect until now.

Now, he was not just fighting himself anymore. Now, he was fighting for his mom too.

Show her that the job is more than just a job. Show her the truth.

"And no matter what happens," Jon continued, "I will come home. I made it home once before and I can do it again."

Jon could feel his mother's head resting on his chest. Jon's body was moist from tears. The reference Jon made was about how he was sent overseas to fight. He was mentioning how he had returned. Although Jon had lost a leg, he lost a friend too. He lost part of his sanity and part of his spirit. So, while Jon was correct when he told his mom he would return, he didn't come back precisely as he left.

Jon, however, kept his word then, and he would definitely keep it now.

"I will make it again. I *can* make it again."

There was nothing else to say after this.

When Jon's mother stepped back, she dabbed her

nose and Jon stared at her face. Still wet from tears, his mom still burned from all the pain she was forced to endure. What she was seeing and feeling was hurting a fraction of her heart.

And, as Jon kissed his mom's forehead, he had said all he needed to say.

CHAPTER 26
CLIMATE CHANGE

SINCE THE ALTERCATION WITH FRANKIE, whenever Jon entered The Conquistador, he was hit with a wall of near unbreakable tension. A situation was now unfolding at the club, and a serious threat was posed to everyone employed there. What bothered Jon was not so much who he could trust but only what was ahead for him.

Inside, Jon stepped past the swirling staircase and moved toward the bar. Now was the time when Jon usually saw Kya and grabbed himself a cup of coffee. At seven p.m., Jon was wide awake. He did find Kya near the bar. She was there working. Initially, Jon was hesitant to walk up to her and start a conversation. Today, his footsteps were weakened by last night's encounter. Suddenly, Jon was tingling in places he didn't care to mention.

"Kya." After being struck by a shudder and then an intrusive thought, Jon called out to Kya. She stopped and lent her eye in Jon's direction. "Jon?"

"Hey."

"You're back?" Kya said, surprised.

Head slanted, Jon's gaze was turned sideways. He thought Kya's question might be rhetorical. Why would she ask Jon if he was here?

"What do you mean?" Jon asked. "Of course, I'm back."

"It's just..."

"What?" Jon eyed Kya as if waiting for her to provide some additional clarification. "What do you mean?"

"The club is on high alert ever since..." Kya struggled to finish.

Jon's mouth peeped open and he was caught off guard after hearing a third voice a few feet behind him.

"Since the club was put on high alert."

Jon's head turned and then he felt a burning at the base of his back. He was simultaneously relieved to see that it was Danix who addressed him. He was also irked when hearing the phrase *high alert*.

Perhaps that's what he, Jon, was being offered now.

"High what?"

"High *alert*," Kya repeated.

Now turning, it was Kya who said this, not Jon.

Danix was there. He stood by the bar, arms crossed and focused. Jon could see the veins bulging in Danix's biceps. He was poised as if guarding a door, but this wasn't the case. Now, Danix was only just another bouncer standing in an empty room. However, he was alert, with his stare sharp as a razor.

"We are," said Jon, observing Danix. "We all are."

Danix marched toward Jon, who turned to face him.

"What's going on?" Jon asked.

Danix sighed, almost disappointed. Always the one to be cool and calm, Danix never looked displeased or visibly upset in any way. Yet, as Danix emerged from the shadowed dance floor, he backstepped and flicked his finger.

"Come on," Danix said to Jon. "Addison is waiting for us."

"He is."

"Meeting," said Danix. Jon could feel Danix nudging him on the shoulder. He was, in effect, urging Jon to get moving. "Let's go."

Jon accepted the invitation and his foot slid across the dance floor. He walked away from Kya. He looked back for only a second before saying goodbye.

"Yeah. Bye." A cold aura arose and Jon felt similar to when he first walked in.

He was cold and he was uncertain.

Kya returned to the menial tasks that kept her busy, and she acknowledged Jon with a slight wave. Jon then walked away.

Still, he was on high alert.

The implications of this urgency were true for all the other Doormen.

So, responding to this, as Jon was required to do, he followed Danix to a separate section. Jon trailed closely behind Danix while he was struck by a new scent. It smelled like cheap beer and sweat. When he went with Danix into the next room, which was more of a plain conference room than anything else, Jon spotted more bouncers.

He nodded at each one.

Always, he was polite. This morning, he was tired. There, he crossed in front of Addison. For the first time since being hired, Addison was not wearing a suit. This altered the tone of the orientation more than Danix's behavior did. Addison not wearing a suit was like The Conquistador without its booths, music, and booze. It was what the club would be if it didn't have cheering faces or loud music.

"Welcome, Danix, Jon..." Addison said, casually playing the role.

"Hey," Jon replied. He looked around the room and everyone was now sitting there.

Spread out, no one was engaged in conversation or appeared captivated in any capacity. They behaved as though all of this was routine. There was no enthusiasm or desire to actually be present.

Jon sat in the closest chair he could find and stayed quiet.

"Have a seat. Nice to see you."

"Thanks." With Addison extending the greeting, Jon was comfortable assuming that he actually was *happy to see him*. In the end, it was difficult to tell.

"Thanks."

"Everyone here?" Addison looked around the room. "Good," he said. "Let's get started."

The room went deathly quiet. From where Jon was sitting, he sensed a foreshadowing aura, but this wasn't coming from Addison or from Danix. Larry Thomas was missing, and so was Sam. Jon took a deep breath. He felt like he was losing oxygen, even in spite of the fact there was really no reason for him to have lost it.

Either way, he felt strong. He felt ready. If this was the club on high alert, then that's precisely what Jon was going to be.

"Okay, welcome everyone," Addison continued.

"Nice of all of you to be here today. As you all know, something serious happened at The Conquistador and well, it needs to be addressed as soon as possible."

While no one said anything, there really was nothing to say. They knew what was happening, what occurred, and what needed to be done now.

"First things first, we have a problem," said Addison. "The problem is...we're no longer the safest club to be in right now."

"Come on," said Danix. "The Conquistador will endure. People know that we don't tolerate any bad shit happening here. We're equipped to handle it. We're prepared."

"The Conquistador has more at stake than its reputation," said Addison, standing at the head of the room. "We're losing ground, and we are, nonetheless, up against something real now."

"Real?" asked Li. "What do you mean?"

No response, and Jon overheard Addison sniffling. His hands slipped down to his hips.

"Real meaning..." Addison continued and Jon took the liberty after a new word abruptly entered his mind.

"Criminal."

All eyes were on Jon, who had garnered the attention of nearly everyone in sight, including Addison.

"Exactly," said Addison.

"Why can't we just talk to the cops? Why not tell them everything we know?" The question was posed by Jamal. Jon remembered he was not in the room when everything happened. He was not present when the police *were* called or when they did come in to *help*.

"Been there," said Danix. "Done that."

Speaking with disappointment as well as some self-loathing, Danix rolled his hand up to his face and began rubbing his neck.

"The police want nothing to do with this," Addison said, "as you have all come to learn."

Addison frowned. Jon could see it, but he was not used to it. Jon watched as his boss and friend pivoted. He slipped his hands down to his hips again.

"We did, and nothing happened."

"Well, if word gets out that some low-level mobsters are moving in and there are no cops who can stop them, then this place will turn into Ruby fuckin' Ridge."

Jon didn't get the reference. From what he could infer, it sounded bad.

"Whatever that means," said Jamal.

"It means," said Addison, "this could be a land rush. Everyone will think we've gone soft and they'll come for this place, and so they'll come for us too."

"Maybe we can add a few men on the door," said Li. "We could double up, work longer shifts if we need to."

While this did sound like a plan to Jon, he didn't want it to be their chief strategy when fixing the current problem. In Jon's opinion, he was working long enough as is.

"Not interested in bringing in any reinforcements," said Addison. He looked around the room. "We have everything and everyone we need right here."

Hands on his hips, Jon did nothing but watch. Jon could see a wiggle at the side of his mouth. He seemed like he wanted to smile. What was said was actually very flattering considering everything the security had faced so far.

"We will handle all of this in-house, by ourselves," Addison confirmed again.

"We're not the police," said Jamal. "We do all of this already by ourselves, and if we keep doing it, then we're going to have to get more...*formidable*."

Jon knew what Jamal meant, and he liked it.

"Formidable, yes, but also smart," said Addison.

"So we are going to do what exactly?" asked Danix.

"We just have to stay smart, stay wise," said Addison. "Just like the old days."

Old days.

Other than a few weird sayings and phrases, Jon had no idea what it all meant. He asked himself: *how old were the days Addison was now referring to?*

"Old days?" Jon was speaking only to himself. He thought he had whispered it. He eventually realized he said it louder than intended. Eyes down, Jon looked at the floor. He didn't care people heard him. Jon wanted everyone to know he had no idea what the old days were.

But he wanted to know. "What does that mean?"

"Few know."

Larry Thomas entered the room wearing a suit, jacket, and tie. His hair was slick as he roamed around the table. He walked toward Addison and stood next to him.

"But the one who knows it the most..." Addison stepped aside. He let the one who owned The Conquistador take over the meeting. "Is standing right here."

A lull coursed throughout the room. Jon gawked, as did everyone else in attendance. The arrival of Larry Thomas shed new light on the situation. Jon could grasp the urgency of it well before his boss had arrived.

"Whether we want to admit it or not, we are under attack, and that has not happened since..." Stopping in mid-sentence, Jon's chin perched. He found himself feeling both curious and scared after hearing what Larry said.

Since...when?

"That's neither here nor there," said Larry. He axed the notion of pushing this topic of conversation. He was not here to talk about the past, and so, when Larry walked to Addison, he stood beside him like he was his shadow. He was Addison's shadow and no one else's.

"So...we decide how best to combat the threats that are finding their way into our place of work," said Larry. "We find them and we take care of them, just like we always have."

Larry sounded weak. He looked brittle. He was hunched and his hand twitched as he talked to the Doormen.

"But, of course," said Addison, "this does change things a little bit."

Addison was seemingly overriding Larry's authority. While it was clear it still remained Mr. Thomas's club, in the end, the Doormen were Addison's bouncers.

"Change things...*how*?" The inquiry came from Li, who sounded uncertain.

"Well, we're going to have to do more than what we've done," said Addison, "because it's not just about keeping the club secure, not anymore."

"Throwing out the playbook, are we?" asked Danix.

Jon glanced at his friend. What Danix said was exactly what he was thinking.

"Yeah, you could say that," said Addison.

"And...what's it going to entail?" asked Li.

"We're going to...*trap*. *Ensnare*."

"What?" Although Jon didn't ask about this, his eyebrows furrowed. The question came from Larry Thomas. Addison did technically work for him. He was the one giving orders and was evidently overriding his boss's authority.

Noting this, Jon didn't care.

"We need to show Frankie and his father that, while the power might lie with his family, his son will not be setting up any operations here at our club." As Larry made this declaration, Jon felt warm and bubbly. It was like something had awakened inside of him that, until now, he was unaware of.

"But won't making a move against Frankie be the same as making it against his dad?"

Jon was now the one asking questions. He believed his question was better than the others. He didn't know for sure.

"No." The response came from Larry.

Now standing at the head of the room, Mr. Thomas was looking only at Jon, who was worried. Maybe, he thought, he was challenging his boss's authority. He didn't know for sure. When Jon asked his question, everyone in the room declined to speak.

"It won't. It'd never."

Never, thought Jon. This was a harsh word to use. How often do people use it to describe possible realities?

Like the old saying goes, *Never say never*.

Yet Larry said it quite clearly. Why he was so certain, Jon didn't know.

"We take all the steps we need to in order to put an

end to whatever Frankie is trying to build. We operate strictly within our own boundaries, our own rules. We work together and do whatever we can to keep him and the others like him out of our club. We prey, we watch, we observe, and we don't hold back, not this time."

Larry outlined these new rules of The Conquistador but it all turned out to be less of a meeting and more of a call to action, to power.

"So...we fight?" asked Jon.

"Yes," said Addison. "We fight."

CHAPTER 27
A NEW DAWN

THE DAY AFTER, JON HAD SLEPT NEARLY THE WHOLE day. When he opened his eyes, he rolled out of bed and dropped down to the floor. After landing on his hands, Jon commenced with his daily push-ups. He did this and then he moved into some sit-ups and pull-ups. He used a rig he set up near his closet.

"Jon, are you up, sweetie?!" Jon heard his mom say from the floor below. He never went down to the first level until he was done with his exercises.

"Yes!" replied Jon. He wrapped up his push-ups and then turned over. He was about to jump into his sit-ups but yelled to his mom down the floor below. "Be down soon!"

"Okay!" Now on a plastic puzzle mat Jon kept stashed under his bed, he slid the rubber square out from underneath. Then, Jon began to move along them. Going up and down in perfect unison, the mat was sweaty and slick. Jon grabbed his phone and scratched his neck. It was still tender. With his phone pressed to his face, there was a message waiting for him. When

Jon saw Kya's name, his heart sank. Seeing her making contact with him only made him want more. Throughout all of yesterday's meeting, not once did Jon stop to look in her direction.

Not once did he notice her.

For him, that was the first time in which he neglected to acknowledge Kya. This was strange considering some nights Kya was all Jon could think of. She was often the only person he wanted to see.

> Hey, are you there?

This was a question. It was not a greeting or a casual extension of any kind. It was just a reach-out. Kya was contacting Jon because she really *did* want to talk to him. Quite possibly, Kya wanted to do more than that.

> Just woke up. Why? What's up?

> Nothing. I wanted to know if you're free.

Jon felt a flutter in his hands. It disrupted the grip he had on his phone. It almost fell, but Jon seized it by the corners and squeezed it hard into his hand.

> I will be.

He watched the ellipses and waited for words to come. Eventually, Jon saw another green balloon pop up along with a few others.

> Great.

> Let's get together.

> Talk. Down?

For Jon, he yearned for Kya to reach out and connect with him. It felt like it wasn't real. No, it was all something he had imagined. Jon wanted to see her, but how and where, he was going to leave in her court, so to speak.

> Sure. When? Where?

He could see the same ellipses again. Jon stopped and waited.

> Bill's coffee shop. Know it?

Jon grinned.
Hell yeah, he knew it.

> I do.

> Great. Be there around 2. We can have some food too.

Jon hustled down the steps. His mother called out to him. She urged Jon to come to the table and have a quick bite before taking off. Jon often rejected his mother's offer at such times. He exercised as soon as he was awake. He'd ride the subway and eat. Today, he had somewhere to be and someone to see. In a hurry, Jon didn't go without first saying goodbye to his mom.

"I gotta go. Bye. Love you."

"Wait, wait," Jon's mom begged her son to stay. "Have something to eat. Come on now."

Before Jon left, he did as his mother asked him to do. With a plate filled with brown rice, Jon grabbed the dish and the fork. He stuffed his face and, on the final swallow, Jon leaned in and gave his mother a quick peck on her cheek.

"Thanks, Mom. Love you. Love you lots."

"Okay." Jon was about to step through the door. He remembered the conversation he had with his mom two nights ago.

Open up. Share. Speak. Honor.

"Do you want to tell me—"

"Yes," Jon said. He answered without skipping a syllable and then looked at his mother. He could sense she was concerned.

"Who? Which friend?" Jon's mom asked.

"No one you know," said Jon. "Someone I met, you know, at work."

"Another bouncer?"

"No, she's a waitress, actually," said Jon. He was careful about how he revealed this special person to his mom. As soon as Jon mentioned Kya, he looked away. He knew the response he was going to get. He decided to avoid it while he could.

"Oh...so...she's a—"

"A girl, Mom," said Jon. "Yes, a girl."

"Oh," she said, gasping with relief. "Good."

"Yeah." Jon nodded.

He hated when his mother discussed these topics, but she only did because she cared for Jon, and that was something. Actually, that was good. It was good because she was good.

In fact, Jon's was wonderful.

———

Jon didn't think much about relationships.

In the Marines, there isn't much fornicating going on, except for the nights when the mood strikes and a person find themselves with the only thing they can get their hands on. Often, Jon would rub out a quick one before his bunkmate noticed. Sometimes Jon would indulge in this while his brothers would travel to the nearest village and get their fix there.

Most often, Jon's only goal was to live to see another day, not to get laid.

Jon had sex with only one girl in his entire life. He went years without feeling the touch of another person. Some nights, Jon would masturbate before falling asleep. As far as engaging in the same material he once did back in high school, porn was now something that made Jon sick to his stomach. To combat this, Jon would summon all the faces of the women he was attracted to. He thought about mostly *real* women. Sometimes it would work and sometimes it wouldn't. What Jon desired most was the touch, the feeling of being wanted. It was the conversation and the opportunity to be desired. He wanted to feel like he was attractive, handsome, and a man who was well suited to someday obtain the perfect girl.

This was all he ever wanted.

———

On the subway, Jon rode to the location selected by Kya. He was dressed in a leather coat, jeans, and his favorite pair of Jordans. He wanted to look presentable even outside The Conquistador. This was the only other look that fell within his budget, so hopefully, Kya wouldn't pass any judgment. Jon hoped she might see him differently. Later, Jon exited the subway and walked down the crowded streets. Today, he would come to know for certain whether there was something there. If it was something that he could hold on to after it was offered to him so generously.

And yes, he wanted Kya.

On his way to the cafe, Jon sent another text. He hopped onto the sidewalk and began to jog.

> On my way. Be there soon.

K.

Kya's response was only one letter. Jon hoped to get more.

In the cafe, Jon heard the chiming of a bell. He was greeted with booths, tables, and a long countertop with baristas. Christmas décor was scattered around the inside of the café.

Already? Jon thought.

Spending so much time working, Jon's days and weekends began to all blend together. He had grown immune to just how time had passed or how the seasons had changed. What Jon wanted before accepting the job was to come back and regain everything lost. As of now, Jon was enjoying the sound of the cool Christmas music heard inside this café.

Everyone there looked at Jon.

He was scarred and bruised. In fact, Jon looked like Brock Lesnar after his fight with Cain Velasquez. It didn't take long for Jon to spot Kya. She was at a booth, yet Jon watched her from the farther away. Her hair was down, and her lipstick was diligently applied. Kya was the someone who, for Jon, had her own unique shine.

"Hey," said Jon, and he made his way over to her.

He watched Kya put her phone down. Pulling out a chair, Jon took a seat directly in front of her.

"Hey," Kya replied. "Thanks for coming."

"Yeah, no worries," replied Jon. He was only somewhat comfortable. This was their first one on one. It was not going to be easy. "Hope you weren't waiting too long."

"No, I wasn't."

"Oh, well, good then."

"Yes. Did you just get up?" asked Kya.

"Uh," said Jon. He thought about his daily routine and then remembered the time.

In fact, he did. He did just get up.

"Not really," Jon pretended like he hadn't. "I usually get up early so I can go to the gym, get a jumpstart on the day. Been training a lot lately."

"Really?" asked Kya. "With the guys?"

The guys.

Is that how Kya knew them as? Was Jon officially one of them?

Was he one of the guys?

"Sometimes," Jon said with a slick smile and trying to come across as confident. "Not often, though."

"You should," said Kya. "They like you. They think you're doing really good, actually."

"They do?" Jon said as he tried to hide his excitement. He placed his hand in front of his face to cover up his smile. Jon had no idea if this was the right move to make.

"Yeah. I mean, especially the other day with Frankie."

"Oh," said Jon. He recalled the day. "Right."

"Which is why I asked you to come here, actually."

"Really?"

"Yeah," said Kya. She stopped making eye contact with Jon.

She looked down because she seemed embarrassed. Her cheeks were rosy as Kya licked her lips. Why she appeared this way, Jon hadn't a clue. He was, however, feeling curious as to why she was.

"Sorry for the last-minute call, it's just..." Kya's lips curled into her mouth.

"What?" asked Jon. "What is it?"

"Do you know what you're doing?" Kya asked after a beat.

Head slanted, Jon was confused and uncertain. "What do you mean?"

"What you're doing, with what lies ahead?"

"Like...with our new policies, what it is we're doing?"

"Yeah. I mean, you're not concerned?"

Jon shrugged. To be honest, he saw what was happening like he did on a mission overseas. He was adapting to new threats and fighting to survive. You don't think about it too much, because thinking about this isn't your job. You react and you asses, and that's the name of the game for any soldier. Jon believed the same applied here too.

Both his duties as a Doorman and as a Marine were starting to intersect.

"Well, I don't really know," said Jon. "I just assumed..."

He examined Kya. Head down, Kya's hands were latched around her steaming cup of coffee.

"What?" Jon asked. "What do you know about it?"

"How much do you actually know about the place you work?" Kya asked.

"What do you mean?"

Kya grunted. Jon thought she looked bothered. He was starting to doubt his next few words.

"Nothing," said Kya. "Just, when you try to take care of Frankie, just be careful, all right?"

"Careful?" asked Jon. He couldn't help asking this.

Since when did Kya care about Jon's safety? He was a bouncer. He was never safe.

"Careful, yes," said Kya. "It's not going to be easy."

"It never is."

"You know what I mean," said Kya. "Trust me. It's about to get a whole lot worse."

CHAPTER 28
SPOKEN AND UNSPOKEN

When Frankie Castellani returned to The Conquistador despite being banned, Jon Haze was feeling something he hadn't felt since the war.

He was now bombarded with new thoughts, with each one being the same. Jon thought every day could be his last and home might be a place too far away. Jon fought hard to stop thinking this way. Then, as he stood in front of the mirror, Jon knew he had quite a big night ahead of him. The son of a very dangerous man was making a move against The Conquistador. Now Jon had his orders. Despite all the impending consequences, Jon recalled the oath he'd taken since the day he was hired.

He was to keep the club secured and safe, to monitor, assess, and protect.

No matter what.

Why Larry Thomas and Addison were so insistent on putting the bouncers in harm's way might point to other intentions. Jon believed this was something linked to what Kya said back at the café. Now, Jon didn't know for sure if this was true. He reviewed the interaction he had with Kya and considered the implications.

"*How much do you know about the place you work?*"

It was a good question. It was so good Jon asked it again.

How much *did* he know? How much did Kya know?

Kya implied she knew things. They were things Jon didn't know about The Conquistador.

The Doormen were about to engage with a wannabe gangster. Jon suspected someone at the club was working against them. He suspected Sam from the beginning. Jon couldn't prove it, but he did trust his instincts.

The Marines taught him well. Then, Jon remembered one's instincts count for a lot in this trade. In war, Jon had his instincts too. He trusted them until they proved him wrong.

So, what were his instincts telling him now?

What Jon imagined was an outcome whereby no one won.

He thought about the night ahead.

Jon considered what he and the other Doormen were planning to do. He thought about how they planned to provoke and upend the son of this very dangerous man. They were going to strip Frankie Castellani of all the people who were enabling and protecting him.

In the process, the Doormen were going to risk their lives to protect the club.

Despite the fact that no police or outside authorities would be able to support them.

Frankie Castellani wanted to move his father's products in through The Conquistador. He would use this as a breeding ground for his new operation. So long as the police refused to get involved, then no one could stop them. After all, the Doormen weren't police.

And Frankie was going to do his thing only because he wanted to do his thing. As long as drugs and crime are happening in a place that allows it, if it's a country or a club, it doesn't matter.

The soldiers fight and they protect. They guard and they attack.

If necessary, they do whatever they have to do to get the job done.

It was in this way that Jon came to fully embrace what he was about to do. He was going to war, just not the war he was used to. Jon gazed at his leg. Once whole, he could once wiggle his toes, even touch them. There was a time when Jon could rotate his ankle. He could trim his nails and move. Funny, Jon hadn't touched any part of his missing leg since he started working at the club.

Back in the hospital, Jon thought about his absent leg all the time. Whenever he did, he'd shove the thought back where it came from. He didn't want to think about what he didn't have. Yes, of course he missed his leg. However, Jon didn't want to miss something he knew he would never get back. In the end, it was nothing compared to what James's family had lost. And so Jon couldn't mourn for what the war had taken from him. No matter what he did, it would always be so much less.

Strange how losing something was only for certain people, people like Jon.

A person can lose a lot. When you're standing next to people who have lost everything, it almost feels like you shouldn't complain or mention your own struggles. When you do, you're automatically compared to how someone else feels. You're compared to the others who have it so much worse than you.

It's an ugly fact, but a fact it is, no less.

There was so much Jon didn't discuss upon his return.

There was so much he should have talked about but didn't.

His mother encouraged Jon to share more. Sometimes, she demanded he share more. Whenever she tried to get Jon talking, he resisted. Jon would walk out the door and would say nothing to no one. All Jon's mother ever wanted was for her son to be happy. It's all parents ever want for their children.

Jon's mom wanted her son to be happy. She wanted this despite everything Jon did that made his mother completely miserable. He went into the Marine Corps because he wanted to serve his country. He enlisted, not thinking about the impact it might have. Jon went to war without once considering the weight it would put on his mother's shoulders. He didn't think about the heartache she'd endure. Jon didn't consider what she felt when she saw her son step off the plane missing his leg.

Jon was often oblivious to the truth.

He survived, yes, but he had come *close* to death. Jon had grazed the worst outcome and this was enough to give his mother nightmares. Some nights, Jon could hear her sobbing in her sleep. He considered what he was going through and didn't think it needed any attention. Jon had lost a brother in the war. He lost his leg, which was something valuable and irreplaceable.

By doing this, Jon was perpetuating a cycle he was already very much a part of.

He had become part of the problem and he didn't even realize it.

Jon didn't communicate and he didn't discuss. He didn't talk and he did not listen.

And, if that was not enough to hurt his mother, he traded one dangerous job for another.

Jon went headfirst into violence and was working too many late hours. Sometimes, he would come home only to find his mother asleep in the living room. She'd wait all night for him to come home. Jon would sometimes put a blanket on her. He needed her to stay warm. Jon would kiss her cheek just to let her know he was home safe. He would do all of this, yet Jon hadn't considered what his mom was thinking about when he was out. He didn't imagine her pacing through the living room or praying for his safe return.

Jon's mom would cook for him and she would clean for him too. Still, Jon hadn't considered the pain she was carrying, the hardship. She was a woman with so much to say and no one to listen, least of all Jon. So absorbed by his own life, Jon didn't think about her. At least, he didn't think *enough* about her. He was always too wrapped up in himself. He was too focused on the job. He didn't consider the impact or the aftermath.

Tonight, for the first time, Jon did.

Jon stood in front of the mirror and looked himself up and down.

He wasn't wearing his prosthetic, so he was using a walking stick to keep himself upright. He did this despite having not done it since before he could remember. Jon was a man without a leg. He was someone who used to be a soldier, but now he had become a bouncer. He was a man who lost someone and so many other things. Jon was now trying to pretend he had lost nothing. He lost himself in the war. For him, this job Jon thought was a way to distract him. It was a way to keep his mind out of his body. By doing this, Jon could find his own way and no one could stop him.

This was what Jon thought he was doing, but now he knew differently.

Of all the questions he thought he was answering, there was one Jon hadn't yet.

What did he now fight for?

The Conquistador was just a place for work. Jon treated it like this. Now, he saw everything differently. He went to work every day and not once did he consider those in his company as the men he was serving. They were friends, but so were Jon's fellow Marines. Jon didn't offer this title to them because, until now, he didn't see them as soldiers.

But they were.

Jon went to The Conquistador every day, and every day, he was going to a war.

The difference was here, Jon's enemies had taken on a new form. They were different from those he fought overseas. What made war different from so many other conflicts was its lack of predictability.

The Conquistador was not what it seemed. These words came from Kya, not Jon.

To him, this could only mean that what lay ahead was not different from a war.

Nothing was as it seemed and yet everything

seemed exactly the same. Jon could fight, but he didn't know what would happen if he did. It was because of this that Jon lost someone very close to him. After that, he couldn't shake the feeling. Whenever it emerged, he would fight it. Jon would go to the gym or ask Addison for longer shifts. He would spar at Danix's dojo and train with him or he would simply go to his room and sleep.

Jon now vowed to be nicer to his mother. He swore he would share more with her when he could. And, most importantly, Jon would always tell her the truth. He would be more sensitive to her struggles. He said he would do this, but how long would it take for him to understand the challenges that lay ahead?

Jon wanted all of this.

But then, here he was, about to embark on yet another dangerous mission.

As he vowed to tell his mother everything, so far, Jon hadn't said a word.

CHAPTER 29
WHAT IS NEEDED

THE DOOR OPENED AND JON HEARD TWISTING OF locks and screeching hinges. Jon could also hear the footsteps, but was still in his bedroom staring at his reflection. He didn't do anything. No, he just stared.

How was he going to take Frankie down tonight?

He wanted to tell all the other Doormen he had a plan.

And yet, Jon knew things. Often, he found himself feeling more aware. He thought about it constantly. No matter how much he tried not to, the worse it was. So, because Jon's mind was often overwhelmed by possibilities and strange ideas, his hand would tremble. His heart would race. Sometimes, he would find it difficult to move.

"Mom?" Jon had not called out to his mother.

When he called her now, Jon shuffled toward the door. He listened to his mom's feet dragging across the floor. Jon never heard this sound before. He studied the sounds of his mother, so healthy and beautiful. He never told her this. For Jon, he felt like he was waiting for the right time. There was no other right time than right now.

"Yes?"

"Can you come in here for a second, please?"

Jon was hardly wearing any clothing. He slipped on a random shirt and sweatpants. He didn't attach his prosthetic, and he refused to because this woman was his mother.

There was nothing to hide.

Even if there was, Jon was *not* ashamed. He crept into the space and turned to face his mom. She trembled and nibbled on her tongue. She was clearly worried, and the thing she worried about most was Jon.

He did not call her unless he had to.

And, should Jon call his mother, it was only because it was an emergency.

This made her feel even more worried. However, this was not the case here.

Jon just wanted to tell her the truth. It was a truth that Jon should have said a long time ago but didn't. He didn't because he was afraid, because he was a coward, because, in many ways, Jon was also too weak. He waited for his mom to come into his bedroom. Jon heard footsteps. He detected the pitter-pattering of slippers sliding across the carpet.

"Jon, are you in here?"

"Yeah, Mom, I'm in here."

Jon struggled. It felt like every time Jon wanted to say something, the words got sucked back into his mouth. He was here to tell his mom the truth and nothing else. She opened the door and peeked in with her head. Like all wise mothers, Betsy Haze respected her son's privacy. She didn't step into his room until she had permission. Jon once thought this was good practice. He appreciated the fact that his mother respected boundaries and chose not to cross them. Now that he'd been working late, he liked when his mother knocked.

In fact, part of Jon hoped she never would stop.

"Can I come in?" she asked.

"Yeah," said Jon. He moved his head to give a slight nod. He allowed his mother to come into his room. For once, Jon was going to be completely honest with her. He had some things to say, no doubt.

"Today, I'm going to work. I just wanted to tell you that."

"To work?" she said. She was surprised to hear that this was Jon's news. Jon's mom's eyes opened wider.

"Yes, and it's going to be a different day."

"Different?" Jon's mom snapped. "Different how?"

Jon's mother could suddenly detect an obvious change in her son's tone. She could tell from how Jon phrased his words. Yes, Jon was going to The Conquistador to be a bouncer, but tonight was different from all the others.

No. Where Jon was going was to war.

"It's just...I don't know when I'll be home, that's all, so you know...don't..."

"Don't what?" asked Jon's mom. Fear clung to her voice and spread out all her words.

Nervous as she was, Jon didn't want her to be.

"Don't wait up," said Jon. "Don't wait up for me, okay?"

Jon listened to his mother gulp anxiously. He took another look at his prosthetic. It was a newer model, supposedly more durable. Jon was looking forward to seeing if it would prove useful.

"Okay. I won't," said Jon's mother.

Now Jon could sense her fear as his hand slipped to her knee and rested there.

"It's going to be okay, Mom."

Jon's mom nodded and looked sullenly at her son. It was clear how she felt. At the same time, it was also clear how Jon felt too. He was about to embark on his most dangerous job yet, and he didn't want to leave in a hurry.

Like before, what Jon desired was time. He just needed time.

"Don't go just yet," said Jon's mom. "Stay a little."

Her lip trembled, and Jon rubbed his mother's knuckles. He felt the softness of his mom's skin. He liked her touch. Always did and always would. As the two sat together, her head rested on his shoulder.

They sat together for as long as they could.

In four hours, Jon would be at the club, and he'd go head-to-head with the son of a notorious mobster. Like when he left overseas, Jon did whatever he could to make a moment last. He tried to turn a minute into an hour, and the only way to do that was to just be silent and enjoy the peace and quiet.

Jon held his mother and listened to her soft breathing.

"Okay, Mom. I'll stay."

CHAPTER 30
SET UP AND DIVERSIONS

"Take your positions."

The order came from Addison as soon as all the Doormen arrived. Addison had requested to meet all the security in his office before the evening began. All the bouncers were lined up and ready. Jon was there early, as was Jamal. Sam, Li, and Danix were present while Addison stood behind his desk. His hands were firmly planted as he leaned forward and gawked at his employees.

By asking all to take their positions, Addison was, in effect, asking them if they all knew their role. Frankie was not banned, he was only marked. Jon knew this to be a different classification.

All of them did. Everyone was there on time, but not Sam.

Apparently, he thought the meeting was at a later hour. Addison told him just to follow Danix's lead. He continuously asked questions and begged for more details. Addison was the one who said what they were doing plainly as he could: *We're just going to work.*

Frankie Castellani had signed up for a premium experience at The Conquistador despite his marking. This meant he'd not only get early access, he'd also get his own booth and free bottle service too. He was to have the best of the best shit, including and especially any alcohol and his choice of the waitress staff.

As it turns out, he made a request. Frankie wanted Kya to be his server. Since the club was already in hot water, the son of the mobster was paying upward of ten grand for his new experience.

"No mark will stop me," Jon overheard Frankie say while leaving the club the night he was confronted. Therefore, saying no to him just wasn't in the cards, not when he paid big money, and definitely not right now.

"You all good with this?" Addison asked Kya before she began her work too.

She was going to be out from behind the bar tonight. Out on the floor, where the going was tough, the expectations were even worse for someone like herself.

"Yeah," said Kya. "It's the job, right?"

Jon watched as Kya stood primly in front of Addison. Always a calm and consummate professional, Addison placed his hand on Kya's shoulder. The gesture was only an extension of her kindness. It was this and nothing else. Addison was more than just the cooler at The Conquistador. No, he was a good man with a good heart. He was also quite paternal. He was someone who wanted what was best for his employees.

Jon was far away and could only see part of Kya's expression. Her forehead was wrinkled and she was moving fast. To Jon, she seemed anxious and worried. Jon believed Addison was aware of this. He understood why Kya was so nervous. She was going to serve someone dangerous. Jon was worried about Kya and on her way out, she passed Jon by. When he gave Kya an enamored look, Jon had a rush of new thoughts and ideas. Right now, there was a lot to say and even more for him to do. He wanted to reach out and tell Kya to be careful. He wanted to tell her he would be there for her. He wanted to assure her that he was going to stay close. When Kya left, Jon stayed. He felt his prosthetic rubbing his skin. The newest model was more comfortable, no doubt. It gave Jon much more stability and he felt far more secured. With this, Jon felt not only indestructible but also versatile.

Jon was about to exit Addison's office when the cooler called out to him.

"Hold up a minute." When Kya passed Jon, Addison reached for the Marine's hand. Jon didn't want Kya to go before he told her everything was going to be all right. And yet, Addison ordered the Jon to stay.

Jon sighed as he turned. "Yes."

"Whatever happens today," said Addison. "Just do your job, yeah?"

Jon nodded.

"Stay focused and sharp. Trust me," said Addison. "You do that...everything else will fall into place."

He knew what Addison was asking Jon to do.

"It's just...it could be hairy, could get dangerous."

"I knew the risks when I took this job, Addison," said Jon.

Until now, Jon mostly referred to Addison as Mr. Krowe. Today, Jon decided to refer to Addison by his first name. When Jon said this to his boss, Addison looked on with a stern, cold expression.

"I knew it then," said Jon. "I know it now."

Addison peered over his shoulder and nodded. Jon's hand rested on the door handle. He hadn't walked through yet, though he wanted to.

"Good," said Addison. "I just want you to be sure."

"I am," said Jon.

"Okay. Get out on the floor and take your position like the rest. Soon, I'll take mine."

"All right," said Jon, "but just remember that—"

Before Jon could finish, Addison lifted his hand and showed his palm.

"Don't," he said. He stopped Jon from saying more.

While the Marine could have interpreted this as offensive, he didn't. In Jon's opinion, he had spoken long enough. He was now ready to execute his plan exactly as intended.

"I know my role," said Addison. "Trust me."

Jon didn't reply. He just nodded and walked.

He left Addison's office and stepped along the balcony above the dance floor. The time was now ten o'clock, the prime hour for any nightclub. The line was extended all the way to the end of the sidewalk. Jon turned to face the crowd. He held a cup of coffee and stood next to Jamal. He was guarding the door like he was supposed to. Tonight, Jon was in charge of admittance. He was given a list of everyone who was allowed in early. Jon knew some of these guests, but he didn't know all of them.

The only one that caught Jon's attention was the same person he was here to bring down.

"Is *he* here yet?" Jon didn't need to specify the name of the person he was referring to.

"No," said Jamal. "Not yet. But I suspect he'll be here soon."

"Good."

"Are you feeling good?" When Jamal asked this, Jon nodded. But when Jon moved his head to nod, it was only a reflex. Should another bouncer ask if you're *feeling good*, it usually meant *are you ready?*

In essence, they are asking you if *you're prepared for what lies ahead?*

Jon answered the question without thinking about it. He thought he was prepared. He thought he was ready. Then, Jon saw a white limousine starting to approach. Jon heard music blaring from inside.

As the vehicle drew nearer, Jon stepped back.

His job was to let Frankie Castellani despite the order. Jon would do this so all the Doormen could finally expose this asshole and send a strong statement to his crew.

Don't. Fuck. With. The. Doormen.

Jon hung back and stared at the long car. It stopped by the curb. Its doors opened, and from inside, a man in a white suit stepped out. There were very few people who looked good in white suits.

They were either rich fucks or rap stars and Frankie was neither.

His parents were rich and yet, Frankie presented himself like the dollar bills in his pocket were actually his to hold. When Frankie vacated his limo, two more men people emerged. Jon reviewed the men as they came forward.

The first one was big, no doubt.

Jon studied his appearance and then gave him his name.

It was easy to remember.

Big Guy.

Big Guy moved on and held the door open for the next guy. Jon stayed right where he was. This was next to Jamal. After *Big Guy*, the one who came next was shorter. He was almost the same size as Frankie. He had a very specific hairstyle. He was slick and he was clean. He was wearing a yellow suit and brown dress shoes.

After Jon saw him, he gave him a name like he did to the last one.

Slick.

With three people now exiting the car, Jon waited for the train to stop moving. However, as they continued to roll out, from behind *Slick* came a towering mammoth of a human being.

"Shit," Jamal uttered the word. Jon's thoughts were the same.

The next guy could not be called big or slick. Although he acquired some of the same characteristics, he was very different. There were few people whom Jon found terrifying. The Marine Corps helped him fight through many of his fears. It narrowed Jon's list of who he was intimidated by.

In this case, he had come across someone he still found to be quite scary.

The best fighter Jon knew was Danix. He was the most gifted and the deadliest by far. He was also a strong and ferocious combatant, having mastered more than a few martial arts. Offhand, Jon couldn't recall anyone in the same league as Mr. Slade. Still, there was something about this third man.

He looked a lot like Danix.

He was just as tall, and his shoulders were wide and his back was loaded with muscle.

What Jon noticed first was not this man's size. No, what Jon saw initially were all the scars he was carrying. Jon spotted all the marks. He knew all the etches and all the cuts as he looked at the slits on this man's flesh.

This one Jon called *Giant*.

Whoever Giant was, Jon had a few ideas of who he could be.

Based on Jon's assessment, Giant had to be Frankie's muscle. And all of this was odd, considering that the other guys were already his muscle. With the addition of a third guy, the Doormen would have their hands completely filled, no doubt. Jon wasn't surprised. He knew the plan wouldn't be easy and he was definitely prepared for whatever lay ahead.

"Yeah," said Jon. He acknowledged the comment Jamal made earlier. "Big time."

"Right."

Jon glanced at Jamal, who stepped aside and unhooked the velvet rope.

"Time starts now," Jon whispered to Jamal. And Jamal gave his fellow Doorman a humble nod. Although the plan was already in motion, before it could commence, Frankie needed to be let into the club. Jon held on tightly to this list. He looked until he saw Frankie's name.

"Right," said Jamal. "He's all yours."

"Yes, he is. Name?" Frankie was wearing sunglasses. Like he didn't care, it was night, and Frankie was wearing fucking sunglasses. "You know my name," Frankie said.

Jon scanned the list like he pretended not to know.

As far as Frankie Castellani was aware, Jon was just another Doorman doing his job. He was checking to see who was on the list and who wasn't. While Jon perused, Frankie and his entourage were huddled together, laughing. The girls in their company wore heels and miniskirts. Their outfits sparkled among the flashing lights outside The Conquistador's main doors.

Jon didn't move a muscle. He lifted his head and looked at Frankie.

"You're all set, Mr. Castellani," Jon said. He was smug. He was communicating to Frankie a clear message. He shouldn't be here and yet, he was. "After you."

"Right," said Frankie. Strutting his stuff, he made his way inside. "You're goddamn right, I'm in. Come on, fellas." Frankie lifted his hand and gestured to those in his company. "Let's roll."

He was providing them with an invitation. The three gangsters and the three eye-candy girls walked straight toward the entrance. Soon as Frankie passed, Jon pushed his ear and called his fellow Doormen through his mic.

"Castellani is on the move. He should be your way soon."

————————

The first to answer was Danix. He was inside the club with eyes on the dance floor. "Yep, this is Danix. I see him." Danix turned and watched as Frankie Castellani strolled through The Conquistador. "He's coming to you now, Li."

When Frankie approached the booth, Li was there. Like Danix and Jon, he pushed his mic into his ear.

"Got 'em," said Li.

When Frankie drew closer, Li shuffled in the other direction. He moved aside to give the son of New York's most powerful mobsters room to move in.

Li addressed Frankie with a slight dip of his head.

Soon after, Frankie was taken to his booth. There, he sauntered toward the leather sofa and plopped himself down while Kya stood there and waited. Along with his own place to sit, Frankie was gifted with all the prizes one might receive when purchasing this package. He had a fat bottle of Grey Goose, ten shot glasses, loads of cash and a beautiful waitress ready to meet his every need.

———

Jon wasn't in the club at the moment. He was still with Jamal guarding the door.

"Okay," Jon said to Jamal. "That's my cue. Time to start making my move."

"Right," said Jamal. "Go get it."

Just like that, Jon was back inside The Conquistador. Jon ambled and, once he was in, looked at the stage. The DJ tonight was called Quickness. A dumb name, truthfully. Jon didn't know what constituted a good DJ title, but he didn't like this one at all.

"Hit the music hard," Jon said through his mic. "Remember, we need to split Frankie up from his cronies. We need him interrupted, rattled, and compromised."

"*Right.*"

"*Right.*"

"*Right.*" Danix, Li, and Addison replied at the same time like Power Rangers.

Jon remembered the war. Some of the Doormen had served too. Therefore, they were all well-versed in certain tactics. Again, it was mostly about disruption, distraction, and misdirection.

"*Let's do it,*" Jon heard Addison through the mic.

"DJ Quickness is just getting started. Li, give one of those lucky patrons a nudge, yeah?"

"*On it,*" Li said to Jon.

The nudge he was speaking of was known as a "King" tactic. It was one way they controlled their guests. They'd gently bump their shoulders and move them like they were part of a herd. In more ways than one, they were.

"First one is the biggest. We need him out right away, so we have to get him provoked."

"No problem," said Li. "I know just who to send his way."

Jon smirked. His eyes were on the dance floor. He spotted Li in the crowd. He moved in between a group and glanced at Danix and Addison.

With eyes on Li, the name of the game—at least the first phase of the game—was disruption. It was time to knock Frankie down a peg. He was marked, which meant he was a person of interest essentially, among the Doormen.

When Li cut across the dance floor, he walked up to the group of boisterous fellows. They were now facing the stage. Li noticed this group wasn't far from Frankie and his cronies.

The Chinese American bouncer marched forward.

He passed in between a group of girls. Li was so agile he moved like his feet weren't even touching the ground. Jon stared from the opposite end of the stage. He watched Kya and Li at the same time. In a flash, Li kicked someone inside the crowd. It was a quick kick and was followed by an even quicker nudge. This was the technique since the onset of their plan.

In a second, one guy tumbled and he slipped into Frankie's booth.

"What the fuck?!" Giant abruptly stood.

Jon watched as this fool looked around at the one who bumped him. Frankie, Big Guy, and Slick all sprung to attention too. They turned and the girls backed away. Although they were all glaring at the nearby bystander, upon hitting the nameless patron, Li disappeared into the crowd.

"Get outta here, man! Just get outta here!" Giant began to push the bystander away.

Kya was huddled in the corner. Jon watched her very closely. She had a role in this too. Holding a half-filled glass, Frankie and his boys tried to calm Giant down. However, Kya spilled her drink onto his jacket. It was a purposeful and solid tactic. After this, Jon smirked at Kya.

"Shit! She just spilled a drink on me!" Giant yelled. Frankie glimpsed at the wet mark on his friend's shirt.

"Son of a bitch. This shit's expensive! God fucking damn it!"

No one saw what Kya could see. No one realized she had intentionally spilled her drink on another customer. Still, Frankie kicked his feet to express just how fucking angry he really was.

What the Doormen were doing was working.

Frankie's group was being hit by some serious disruption! Giant pushed back into the crowd. He made his move, and Danix eyed the altercation from the floor. *Soon it would be his turn to move in.*

"Hold it!" shouted Frankie. Jon could hear him through the music. "We can't be fighting. We gotta lay low, man."

Frankie warned Giant to stay back and everyone else eased away just the same. Jon marched to Frankie's booth. They had settled, which was fine, since Jon had planned for this.

"Hit 'em harder," he said into his mic.

―――

Danix stepped forward and moved after Giant, whose back was now turned. He wasn't looking and therefore, couldn't see what was coming. This was what Jon wanted!

Danix was big and he mastered the role of being a big guy. He knew how to manipulate the guests if a situation called for it, and it absolutely called for it now. He reached out and grabbed Giant's shoulders. A guy this big didn't like being touched. Danix didn't care. He was often the biggest guys in almost any room.

All of that changed here. Sure to Jon's prediction, emotions ran high. Their aggression was palpable. Once Danix made contact, Giant reacted. He hit with a jab and Danix took a solid hit to the mouth.

"Don't touch me!"

"Rico!" Frankie shouted to his friend, but by then, Rico—Giant—was facing down someone as big as he was. The rivalry between Rico and Danix was obvious. Danix glared, and so did this goon who hit him.

Jon assumed that, in the back of Danix's mind, he was waiting for a fight like this to happen. Two heavy-weights were now facing one another and both were clearly ready to get down. Yet Rico's orders were *not* to fight. Jon's plan was clear.

He wasn't trying to stop Frankie from starting the operation. No, Jon was thinking smarter and bigger than that. He wanted to bust Frankie clean. He wanted him cornered and he wanted him isolated. He wanted him like he should have done back in the Marines.

He knew how to pin people down and how to lock them up.

Jon knew how to do this better than anyone. And that's what he was going to do now.

Danix and Rico waited and both refused to make the first move. He waited as the two gargantuan dudes began to circle. Furious from the altercation, Rico just reacted as Frankie yelled, "don't!"

The first fist was thrown. Danix and the other Doormen were well within their rights to bounce this guy. Yet, this was only just the first step in the grander scheme of things. It was just the beginning of Jon's unfolding plan.

───────

When Danix threw down with Rico, Jon began to move to an entirely new location. For now, he needed to get to the booth. Now that one of Frankie's cronies were set loose, the next phase needed to be set in motion.

"Bring out the bottles!" Jon screamed into his radio.

Currently Frankie, Big Guy, and Slick were all watching Rico going toe-to-toe with Danix. The fight was unfolding but it was now happening in a closed space. The two men swapped blows as the DJ continued to play more music. The other Doormen began to close in. So long as the fight persisted, Frankie and his boys would be crippled.

This was something Jon didn't expect at all. Damn well, it's what he wanted.

Jon radioed for the bottle service to come now. Frankie still had two boys with him and it couldn't stay this way. After he shouted, Addison pressed his finger to his walkie and answered.

"Got it," said Addison. "Ladies."

A row of five girls marched from behind the booth. In their hands were bottles filled with sparklers that they held high as they strutted along. Despite the altercation, the girls moved like they were supposed to be there.

This didn't matter. Jon could see that Frankie was preoccupied. He was trying to stop the fight between his friend Rico and the biggest, baddest bouncer at The Conquistador. Although Jon's plan was working nicely, the Marine stayed on Danix.

His fight had to be seen to be believed.

Danix's hands were like two solid bricks. Seeing them move was like the fat head of a sledgehammer slamming into a tire. Now, the one he was up against, Rico, was also big. He and Danix were like two bulls at a rodeo. They were about to go head-to-head for all to see. As they collided, Danix relied on the straight hits. Rico was definitely more of a bruiser. The DJ kept the crowd entertained, but some did notice.

Frankie and his boys were all up in arms, and their biggest bruiser was now occupied.

Danix kicked left and right. Rico tried blocking. He shot his arms up and then around.

Jon couldn't judge Rico's fighting style. He did know Danix's. Jon had trained with Danix before. He was a Muay Thai fighter and was a big karate guy also. He also taught Krav Maga. In the end, Danix's skills were too great in the presence of this amateur fighter. Rico was strong, yes, but he was sloppy. He was trying to land big blows on Danix and the elite Doorman knew exactly where to go and what to do.

Danix popped Rico's shins and then in the shoulders. He locked his wrists and pounded his chin with hard, fierce elbows. When Danix nudged Rico out of the fight, Frankie's other cronies were now getting in too. Slick and Big Guy were both interested in fighting, which Jon predicted well before any of the others did. He knew what was about to happen.

This was Li's cue. It was his moment to do what was necessary.

When Li stepped in, he saw the second man and was instantly ignited.

Jon's goal had always been to force Frankie Castellani to do something reckless. Though not a concerted attack, it was a setup. It was an attempt to get Frankie to move against his friends and to get his friends to move against him and expose himself completely in the process. The Doormen were, in their own way, assessing a man's loyalty. They were gauging Frankie's ability to stay calm and collected. This was all part of their concerted attack. It was for this reason they were different than those they were trying to defeat.

Resorting to violence was never the Doormen's first choice. Here, however, it was.

"Get back!" Slick yelled at Li. He stood in front of the booth. Rico was now in a chokehold delivered by Danix. As a result, the big Doorman was now starting to pull an even bigger dude away.

"Rico!" Frankie shouted his friend's name. By the time he did, Rico/Giant was out like a fucking light. And Danix's part was done. He won.

CHAPTER 31
LET IT RIDE

"Fᴜᴄᴋ ʏᴏᴜ, ʏᴏᴜ Aꜱɪᴀɴ ꜰᴜᴄᴋ!" Sʟɪᴄᴋ ʏᴇʟʟᴇᴅ at Li.

He backed away shortly after. Opening his hands, Jon watched from the side like he did before. Still assessing the situation like he was trained to do, Jon sensed tension. Usually, that was the moment whereby the Doormen would step in.

This was not the plan, not now.

"Leo!" And Jon had Slick's name too. He was Leo.

Leo stepped toward Li, who cocked his fist back and attacked. Time for Frankie to lose yet another friend!

Now, Li was a fast fighter. Lightning quick, he was also agile. His fighting style was known as Wing Chun Kung Fu. Here, the style worked spectacularly well. Li struck with a lot of rapid, open-palm strikes. He hit repeatedly and took Slick out of the picture. Slick broke himself away from Frankie, and it was then that Jon came forward.

Li wanted to provoke Frankie into reacting. This wasn't too difficult for a man such as himself. He had essentially set up his entire operation without thinking of any of the consequences.

And yet, what Jon was seeing now appeared specific and clear.

Li knew his role.

As Slick, a.k.a. Leo, came in for another strike, Li caught his fist. Then, he twisted his arm and kicked in the knee. The music continued to play loudly as Li delivered another solid hit to his opponent's legs. Li wrapped up Leo's neck.

He did this before he began to drag Leo away.

"Shit!" Frankie screamed with his hands pressing his skull. In distress, he watched as all his friends were taken from him.

Li's exit strategy was key to the plan's success. With Rico out, Leo was next, but where could he go? In the corner of the dance floor, right between the second bar and another booth. Li dragged Leo by his neck toward a new door. After it opened, Li slipped under Frankie's arm, and then he was gone.

"Shit! Leo!" Jon heard Frankie shout.

Frankie Castellani was furious. More than this, Frankie Castellani was confused. The best part of the plan was the primary shift in criminal responsibility. Frankie thought he was doing something wrong. In reality, he was being set up, foiled, and made to look like a fool. Frankie watched as his second-to-last friend was taken by one of the bouncers. Frankie stepped out of the booth. He stood and slipped down on the last stair.

"Leo! Leo, where are you? Where?" In the midst of calling out to his lost cohort, Jon moved closer to the booth.

"What are we gonna do?"

This question had come from Big Guy, who was the last of Frankie Castellani's cronies. Li nodded to the other team of bouncers. They were tier two, and they swarmed the last guy from out of nowhere.

"Adriano!" Evidently, this last guy had a name, and he had a place too.

It was out the goddamn door.

————

Jon watched Frankie's grimy hand run down his cheek and graze his chin. "I..."

"Excuse me?" Jon snuck up behind Frankie and addressed him while standing next to Kya.

"What?!" Frankie turned. "You!"

His tone spiked as he came to see Jon. The Marine knew Frankie recognized him. Their previous encounters were memorable to say the least. When Frankie shouted at Jon, the Marine backed off and showed his hands.

"Look, things are getting intense over here," Jon said to Frankie. He was being overly polite. He acted like he truly had no idea what was happening.

But he knew. Jon knew damn well what was happening. "I just came by to see how everything is going."

"Well, it ain't goin' well!" Frankie screamed like a spoiled teenager. Jon observed all his distress and his anger. He knew then that his plan was working, and working well.

"We noticed an altercation. One of your own did hit one of our guys. I saw it from farther away."

"No!" snapped Frankie. Barking at Jon, the Marine

could smell Frankie's fucking wretched breath. It rank of alcohol and shit. "He was provoked! We were provoked!"

"Okay," said Jon. He was calm, remembered his training.

Be nice.

"Do you want to step out of the booth so we can talk more about it?"

"No!" yelled Frankie. "I'm not leaving because I did nothing wrong!"

Jon scanned the dance floor. No Danix and no Li.

The DJ continued to play on. Everyone danced to the techno beats. As a result, all were unaware of the altercation. Frankie's location was beneficial. His booth was far from the floor. As a result, none of this interfered with the plot to provoke Frankie.

Actually, the plan was working. It was working well.

"I think you should step out of the booth," Jon said to Frankie Castellani, knowing damn well the boy would refuse. He wasn't leaving. Truly, he hadn't done anything wrong. This is good, thought Jon. Keep talking.

"Fuck you, man!" Frankie pointed his finger at Jon like they were equals.

They most assuredly were not.

Right now, Jon and the Doormen were well within their privileges to own his ass. At this moment, Jon knew exactly what needed to be done. Some clients didn't care to hear the truth. Jon, however, was damn well counting on the fact that Frankie wasn't.

"Come on!" Jon yelled. He raised his voice so he could be heard over the music. It was not to be invasive or threatening. At least, this was what Jon could claim. As every other bouncer knew, this was most assuredly *not* his intention. Jon stood with Frankie and waited for him to react. With the third and final one in Frankie's party, Jon wanted him out so Frankie would retreat. They could reach out to someone at the club for *assistance.*

"I just want to talk."

Soon after Jon acknowledged Frankie's last friend, he looked at Kya. Before executing this plan, Jon relied on Kya and the other waitresses to "tip" the scale. If he signaled to her—or any of the other waitresses to react—then they would.

Kya nodded at Jon.

In that moment, she knew exactly what she needed to do. Kya grabbed the bottle of champagne. Then, with the flick of her wrist, knocked it over. Frankie was preoccupied. None could see who was really responsible for the act. Yet, it was Frankie who responded first. Jon knew he was still furious. All it would take was the right push at the right time to set him off.

"Jesus!"

Kya doused Frankie's hand. While Frankie was about to turn to face Kya, Jon stepped in. As he suddenly moved in, Jon noticed Frankie's arm was cocked. Hot-headed and so poorly composed, Frankie was everything the Doormen were not. More than this, he was everything notorious criminals were not. He didn't think or consider the nature of his actions or, for that matter, the consequences. Always, he let his environment get the better of them. All of this was exploited by Jon and the Doormen.

So, with another trap set, Frankie reacted. Seeing

his hand wet, his fist flew forward. "God fucking damn it."

Jon saw the punch coming before it landed.

The Marine crisscrossed his wrists and cross-blocked. Doing this, Jon deflected Frankie's pitiful excuse for a punch. He grabbed Frankie's arm, pulled it to his chest, and pressed the elbow. From here, Jon completed a straight-arm lock and brought Frankie to the ground. "Cool it!"

"Shit!" Frankie stomped, all pissed off and brooding.

Right now, while in this state of utter duress, Frankie was turning to the only person who could relieve him. Thankfully, it was another bouncer. A tremor suddenly crept through Jon's once steady hand. The last time this happened was back in Iraq. Jon remembered the day perfectly. The more he did, the more his hand continued to shake, and then he recalled a moment he shared with Addison way back when.

"*Be careful,*" Addison said then. "*In this business, nothing ever goes the way you want it to. I think you would know that.*"

"*I do,*" Jon replied. "*And sometimes...I count on it.*"

CHAPTER 32
CURTAIN CALLS

JON SAID NOTHING TO ADDISON NOW BECAUSE NOW he was counting on Frankie Castellani to lose all his friends, which was exactly what happened. Jon wanted Frankie cornered and desperate. This was what Frankie was facing now! He was being toyed with—trapped!

And right now, Jon was slowly getting to the final act. With Frankie's cronies out of the picture, Frankie was now alone. Jon gawked and saw the young fool reaching for his phone. Who he was calling, Jon didn't know. At this point, he could only suspect who it might be.

Jon had his ideas, sure. So far, all of these ideas had come to fruition.

He was a soldier. He knew how to plan for war.

"He's still not moving." Jon heard this through his radio.

All the Doormen were back. Then again, Jon couldn't see it all too well. He peered over his shoulder to see if there was anyone behind him. Li was gone, as was Danix.

But where was Sam?

He should be on the floor the same as everyone else, but he wasn't. Jon shook his head to rid himself of all the distractions. He cleared his consciousness as best he could.

Yes, Frankie was *not* moving. Still on his phone, Frankie kicked the table and tossed away a few of the bottles. He threw whatever he could find in his booth and further expressed his rage. With his night now ruined, Frankie's plan to continue this operation within The Conquistador was no more. Frankie was thwarted. He was done for. He just didn't know it yet.

"He'll move," said Jon.

Jon waited for Frankie to make his move. And yet, Danix, or Li, or whoever was on the mic now, they were not moving. So, Jon needed to make moves of his own.

"Kya," Jon said, hand gripping his walkie.

"*Yeah.*"

"I need you to help me get Frankie through the door."

"Through the door?"

"Yeah," said Jon.

"But that's..." Kya was hesitant to answer. More static rang in Jon's ear and he was forced to turn. His finger was pressed so hard against his ear it was almost inside.

"Yeah," Jon said. He stepped back. "Curtain call."

Through the door had only one meaning.

What lay beyond, Jon thought, was likely a hallway. Jon had never ventured into this space to know for sure. He never did because he never had access. He was told *never* to go there. This door led to a room that was accessed only by Larry and Addison.

No one else.

It was called a *secret* for a reason. Constantly under surveillance, should someone stumble there, then there would be dire consequences, allegedly.

"Strictly forbidden." Jon inquired about this back when he was first hired. The response from Addison was clear. After, Jon refused to make inquiries or claims of any kind. Yet, when he shared the plan with some of his other bouncers, such a location was suggested by Addison himself.

Jon found this suggestion askew. Why Frankie would choose to go there was both confusing and suspicious. At the time, Jon didn't challenge Addison on the truth about this passage. He didn't care what was in this room, only whether or not Frankie would go through it. Jon had been forced into moving off the dance floor and heading into this very secret room. Jon could see Frankie clutching his phone and frantically turning side to side.

Jon gradually stepped but Frankie turned and kept turning. Now lost, Frankie remained in a state of duress, but Jon didn't break focus. He refused to look away for even a second. After spinning for three minutes, Jon saw an outline of Frankie motioning through the blacked-out section of the club.

"Son of a bitch."

"What?" Addison's voice crackled in Jon's ear.

"He's going for it," said Jon. "He's going for that *door!*"

Frankie shuffled and Jon observed the flashing lights reflecting off Castellani's frightened face. It was then that Jon tried to read his lips. He had become increasingly good at this. In this job, one could rarely hear or see much of anything. So, reading lips and facial expressions was a bona fide occupational requirement. And as Jon could read, it was enough for the Doormen to get the job done. It was a skill not foreign to Jon anymore. And now, he could grasp some words based on observing only how their lips moved at the same time. Sometimes it served Jon well, but he was never completely confident in this practice.

He thought he could do it. Frequently, Jon didn't know for sure that he could.

When he looked at Frankie, Jon's vision sharpened.

He stared at his flapping mouth. *I know what he's saying.*

Sam. Frankie was saying Sam!

Jon could only barely detect this one word. Frankie's lips seemed to be forming the right consonants. He was calling Sam, but where was Sam now? Jon had no idea. He assumed Sam was on the floor, guarding and observing like the rest of the Doormen were expected to do. In all likelihood, Sam probably was guarding a section somewhere.

And yet, Jon had not seen him once tonight.

He was missing!

Addison was the one who assigned the bouncers to the floor. This plan was discussed. And, based on how to trap Frankie Castellani, Sam was there for the entire briefing. He was there, but he was not given an *assignment*. At least, Sam didn't get one from Jon. This was his plan, after all.

When Frankie pushed through the door, Jon's hand dropped down to his radio.

He marched. "I'm going in."

"No...don't." The voice sounded a lot like Addison's. However, it was compromised by the same irritating static.

Interference only happened if a person was isolated. This indicated that Addison was not on the floor anymore. Wherever he was, it was a hidden space. Jon peered over his shoulder again. There were no more Doormen.

At this point, Jon could only assume they were occupied, either with Frankie's cronies or some new challenges. Whatever the reason, it was up to Jon to finish the plan. As soon as he went through that door, he was out of the club. This was what Addison warned Jon about. *"If he does go through, then that's the place we have to stop him."*

Jon didn't know what this meant. He could sense the seriousness in his boss's tone. Jon's prosthetic felt lighter. Unlike the last one he depended on, this piece was snug and tight. He felt exceptionally mobile, agile, and rapid. He cut through a group of people without once ever feeling like he was being held back.

Jon's mobility was difficult to explain.

It was as though Jon's prosthesis was responsive, maybe even a little reactive. With a little extra effort and pressure added to Jon's leg, he could spring faster and forward easier. All of this was immensely helpful as the Marine made his way to the mysterious door. Right now, Frankie was moving toward it. His phone was no longer in Frankie's hand. Instead, Frankie moved while looking back to make sure not a single person was following him. It was obvious Frankie was going somewhere he shouldn't.

It had to be Sam who told Frankie to retreat to this area. Yet, it was Addison who refused to stop him. Jon didn't want Frankie to go there. On the contrary, he most definitely needed to be stopped. Jon followed the son of the mobster, cutting through the gyrating people sprawled across the dance floor. Honestly, the altercation with Frankie and his boys hadn't disrupted any part of DJ Quickness's performance.

And that was damn impressive.

Jon scurried up to the door, stopped, and looked back. Now unsure if he was alone or if someone was following him too, Jon walked on. Now inside, he was suddenly in a hidden hallway. Specifically, he was in a section of The Conquistador no one was allowed to be. But this was the plan, and it wasn't over, not yet.

There was still time.

After passing through this unknown passage, Jon found himself in a stark hallway. It was a quiet place made all the more quiet by the lack of activity or no one else.

Everything about The Conquistador was well-placed and well-suited. Its décor was tasteful, and every room that Jon stepped into was full of character and life. Jon couldn't say the same for this room now. No, this new hallway was absent of any décor whatsoever. It looked like a corridor that belonged to a fancy, expensive office building. It had no part in any club. After Jon walked through, the door itself shut differently than the others. It didn't make a sound as it tapped the frame. And, when Jon turned, he was struck immediately with burning waves of fear.

It was as if the Marine had passed into another dimension.

Jon was ordered never to step foot into this location. Now he was beginning to understand why. Such a place was forbidden, so what it contained had to be either valuable, a secret, or both.

Whatever the reason, Frankie was here, somewhere.

Jon could see him now. He was still lost and still wandering through such unseen territory as if he were supposed to be here. He most absolutely was not. On his guard, Jon steadied. On either side of him were three doors fashioned with chrome door handles and painted silver. Jon minded his footsteps as he walked.

With both hands by his side, Jon's head was up, and his mind was sharp and steady. He didn't call Frankie's name. For some reason, Jon felt like he should be more reserved. He had to be careful when in here. Again, there was something ominous about this place. The corridor was silent. A shudder ripped through Jon's hands. While he was hot on Frankie's tail, right now, it seemed as though Jon was stumbling on something new. He carefully placed his feet down. One after the other, Jon watched his six. Always, Jon watched his six.

Approaching the center, Jon saw a shadow six feet in front of him. Jon observed this silhouette. He studied its shape, and while it was clear he was not alone, Jon rolled his fingers into fists.

"Where do I go now?" This was the first question Frankie asked when inside this secret space. Clearly, he was looking for someone, someone important.

But right now, Jon didn't know who.

"I'm in through the door. It was the only place I could go. Plus, I couldn't find you anywhere." Frankie continued to exclaim as he fell into a panic.

Jon could hear him skipping along like he belonged here. Jon stayed covered in the doors. He pressed himself hard against the passage. He did his best to blend in, though there wasn't a lot to work with. He could only keep himself hidden based on his surroundings, though there weren't many.

"What do you mean I wasn't supposed to go through? Where else was I supposed to go?" Frankie asked fiercely as he stood in the dark. "Did you not see what happened to me on the floor, how they got rid of everyone around me like some fucking police? I told you what was going to happen! They're trapping me, dude! They're fucking trapping me!"

Jon's gaze stayed as unbreakable as he could make it. With Frankie now at the end of the hall, Jon walked closer so he could see almost perfectly. Frankie stood with his hair disheveled and continued to hold the phone. Now Jon had assumed Frankie was alone. He thought it was only him and Frankie in this secret, forbidden corridor. Seconds later, Jon came to understand the truth. He was not the only one there. Someone else was there too.

"You shouldn't be here."

Jon watched Frankie lower his phone. The Marine was still standing in the doorway. He was there, but he wasn't moving. Jon couldn't because, at the moment, he was captivated. Frankie was not alone, and the person Jon initially thought was there was not.

Frankie was not with Sam!

"Fuck me." Jon's hand trembled. His spine tingled like it always did when things became too real too fast. Suddenly, Jon felt a strain. Still, he was healthy and limber.

He was hurting because someone was waiting for Frankie to arrive in this location.

Not Sam. Not Sam. Not fucking Sam!

Jon couldn't stop saying these words in a state of duress. It wasn't Sam who was working with Frankie. At least, it wasn't *just* Sam. Jon glared at the one working with Frankie since the beginning.

"Addison?" said Frankie.

It was Addison fucking Krowe.

No. Please, God...no.

CHAPTER 33
ALL THE THINGS UNSEEN

IT WENT WITHOUT SAYING JON COULDN'T BELIEVE his eyes.

What he needed was time—time to think and time to question.

But there was no time now. With Addison in this *secret* hallway with Frankie, Jon nudged himself back and continued to hide. Still, Jon was ogling both men while staying hidden as best he could. The entire time, Jon was asking himself:

What the hell was Addison doing here?

How did he get here as fast as he did, and what was the reason for his arrival?

Jon stared, and two seconds later, the Marine had his answer.

"You entered the room. Figured you would," Frankie said. "And you didn't stop me? Why?"

"You wanted to start an operation, right?" Addison replied. "You want to work at The Conquistador, move product without anyone knowing about it?"

Frankie nodded, and Jon continued to stare at the man he once trusted and called a friend.

"Yeah," Frankie said.

"Well," replied Addison, "I'm the only one who can get you all of that."

"You're saying you want to help me?" asked Frankie.

Jon shook his head. This hurt him more than anything. For so long, Jon looked up to Addison. He respected and he admired him. More than that, Jon idolized Addison Krowe.

In so many ways, Jon wanted to be Addison.

Now, Jon saw Addison as someone completely different. Right now, Jon could only see Addison as a traitor because that's exactly what he was. And, even believing this for a second had pained Jon so deeply he had to look away. Once he accepted this cold, hard truth that was his reality, Jon noticed Addison by the door. In fact, he was standing *right* by the door. Seeming as though he was guarding it, almost like Addison was there to protect it. From here, they could get Frankie to confess and reveal the traitor at The Conquistador.

"I want to show you the way to help."

Jon observed Frankie's expression.

After Addison said this, Frankie's eye went down and then up, almost crossing in the middle like a dimwitted fool. Jon couldn't understand what Addison was doing. He continued to watch the scene, and right before Jon was set to reveal himself, another door opened, and another person entered.

Not even Jon expected who came next.

Well, Jon once expected this new visitor. He just didn't expect him to be here now.

"Frankie, where are you?" Sam stepped in and joined Addison and Frankie Castellani at what was now a secret meeting.

And so the plot thickened, and Jon was struck with a new and haunting thought.

Sam was the traitor Jon predicted, but now he and Addison were both helping Frankie!

Sons of bitches.

Jon flinched. He grimaced like he had just swallowed something sour. In a way, that was exactly what happened. Again, Jon didn't want to believe Addison was betraying the club. Then again, what he said to Frankie did sound disturbing. Therefore, Jon was now the one lost and confused. Seeing Sam only proved to Jon that the Doorman's plan to catch Frankie was flawed from the beginning.

What was he thinking? Jon asked himself. How could he have let this happen?

"Frankie?"

"Sam," Frankie Castellani said. He looked at Sam. In Jon's opinion, he sounded relieved. He also appeared quite happy to see Sam.

"I got your call," said Sam. He walked toward Frankie.

It was at this moment Addison stepped back. Jon continued to watch from afar. He found it strange how Addison was moving. As soon as Sam entered the picture, Addison motioned back to the door. He began to slip behind Frankie. It was the same door Frankie was trying to get to. Frankie stopped when Addison came forth.

And, as Addison moved in front of this door, the cooler's gaze suddenly shifted.

He was looking not at Sam or at Frankie.

No, now he was looking at Jon. He was staring directly at the Marine like he knew he was there. Addison winked. He gave him the thumbs up.

The signal!

It was the same one the Doormen gave to each other.

And it only had one meaning: *don't worry. I got this*.

After giving Jon the classic thumb, Addison's hand moved again. He was now waving. In this way, Addison was inviting Jon to come out. For what reason? Jon couldn't be sure.

Addison was now trying to show Jon something because now he was able to.

"What are you doing back here?" Sam yelped at Frankie. "No one is allowed back here," Sam ranted like he actually wielded power and authority.

"I thought you said meet at the back," Frankie snapped back. "When everyone got tossed, I just went to the back as quickly as I could. This is where I ended up. I didn't actually know what the fuck was behind that door. I just decided to walk through it."

"Yeah, well, I know," replied Sam. "But this isn't... this is *not*..." Jon could see Sam was flummoxed. His head turned and he looked in multiple directions as he finished his thought. "It doesn't matter. You're here now," Sam said. "And it's fine, it's just..."

Sam abruptly turned to face Addison. "What are you doing here?"

"What do you mean?" asked Frankie. "Isn't he with you, with us?"

Jon stared at Sam's expression. Now he was the one confused.

Jon gulped.

Now he was aware of Addison's *true* intentions. He was here to set up not one but two guilty parties! His plan to move into the room was orchestrated and clear. He wanted Frankie to step into this hidden section of the club. Addison wanted Frankie to call Sam.

Jon thought the plan was to bust Frankie Castellani, but it was also to find Sam.

Jesus Christ, Jon thought. *Addison Krowe was a fucking genius!*

"Uh, no..." said Sam. He was glib.

Obviously, Jon understood he didn't expect Addison to be here now. The fact that he was revealed Addison Krowe's true intentions. Addison was smarter than Sam and a lot smarter than Frankie. And now Addison had them both right where he wanted!

"He was never with you," said Jon. "Always, he was with me."

"With you?" barked Sam.

Jon stood next to Addison. "With *us*."

"*Us?*" asked Frankie. He looked Jon up and down and scowled.

"I know you," he said. "You're the one who was on the floor, the one who's been fucking with me since the start!"

Jon had nothing to say about Frankie Castellani's accusation. Even if Frankie did recognize Jon, it didn't change the real reason why he was there or what he wanted to do.

"You're the one who started everything!"

Jon continued to stay silent. His presence had only

initiated the second part of his plan. The reason why he had come here was to push Frankie just a little farther than before.

"You pushed me. You pushed my friends, and you pushed me out," Frankie said while pointing at Jon. The Marine stayed exactly where he was. There were no words and no comments other than to continue to stand his ground. "You're the reason I'm here now."

"Nah," said Sam. He took a step forward. "He's not anyone. He's just a rookie. He's a rookie who doesn't understand how things work around here. He doesn't know the truth."

Sam glowered at Jon, and the Marine returned the look of scorn with one of his own. Jon was just as cutting and venomous.

"He still has a lot to learn."

"I know what you're doing is wrong, and it's not going to happen, not as long as I'm still working here and standing in front of you like all good employees should."

Jon was aware of his choice of words. All of them were ridiculous. Jon sounded like he was in one of those cheap action films delivering a cheesy line that was not intimidating in any way.

It did, however, capture exactly what Jon was feeling now.

Sam marched into Jon's space. The rival bouncer's chest was flexed, and both his fists were clenched.

"So long as you're working here." Sam chortled. He glanced at Addison.

Since Jon decided to emerge from his hiding place, Addison was silent.

It felt eerie for him to be so quiet. It was even

weirder how Sam was looking at Addison. Still, Jon stayed on his boss. The Marine's assumptions were not brought into complete perspective until Sam decided to speak again.

"You really have no idea, do you?" Sam asked Jon.

A pinch stung Jon's hand. He felt like he was being burned with a cigarette.

"You don't know anything at all."

Jon gazed at Sam for a second time. Jon's eyes were wandering yet again. Jon could read Addison's expression. He was hiding something, and he wanted to ask what the hell Sam was talking about?

What did he mean?

Addison. The Conquistador. *You don't know anything at all.*

What the fuck?

"Yeah!" Frankie exclaimed, still in the hallway. "Do you really think you can stop this? This club will be mine, and there's nothing you can do to stop that from happening! There's nothing you can do to stop me!"

"That's enough, Frankie," Addison's voice was beckoning. He sounded more like a parent than a boss. At last, he decided to say something. "And it's over, Sam." Addison addressed his fellow Doorman with a firm tone, like a teacher reprimanding a student. It's another reason why he sounded so disappointed.

"This is where it ends. You can't do what you wanted to because you know what will happen if you do. The Conquistador has rules," said Addison. "Always has, always will. And those rules are what's kept it going for so long. You know this to be true."

"I know it has secrets," said Sam. His need to

disrupt provoked a glower from Addison. Jon stood back and watched. "But not more," Sam said again.

And once again, Jon was lost. The secrets Sam was referring to now might be the same ones Kya mentioned to Jon before. This happened when she and Jon were together in the coffee shop. Instead of elaborating on what these secrets actually were, Addison refused to comment.

"The old ways are done," said Sam. "It's time for something new to take over."

"No," Addison said, and he finally turned to face Jon.

He didn't look at him the way he did Sam and Frankie. Addison stared at Jon so the Marine could see the determination in his boss's eyes. Until now, he was only pretending to be.

He was *playing* like he was on Frankie's side, like he was a*ctually* willing to work with them.

But no.

Addison's attitude was only a ploy. It was something done so he could get in front of that door and protect what was on the other side.

But what was on the other side?

Jon wanted to know, desperately. He searched for ideas while his hand began to quake. Then Jon remembered what he was really doing here.

Set up. Foil. *Win*.

Jon's head shook again and he regained his former mindset.

"No one takes over," said Jon. "The only thing that's ending tonight is...*you*."

"Is that what you think?" Sam replied to Jon.

"It is," Jon said.

"Ha!" Sam guffawed while Frankie was anything but afraid.

"We have big plans for this place," said Frankie. "What do you think my operation was going to be? You think I was planning to just move drugs into a club, or did you think I wanted something else, something bigger, *better*?"

Jon felt like he'd been struck by lightning. He could feel a surge of energy coursing through him now. He believed that Frankie Castellani had selected The Conquistador to open a drug operation. Until now, this was just Jon's assumption. He wanted to make money without the help of his father. Jon thought Frankie's goal was to become a run-of-the-mill gangster—a low-level fool. And yet, according to Frankie's statement, he was planning something different, something much, *much* worse.

"I'm for a revolution, baby!" Frankie yelled. "That's what this has always been about! It's about the future of this industry, the club industry! It's about saying no to the old ways and saying yes to the new, better ways! I have my own ideas, sure, and I have my ideas now too, but Sam over here..." Frankie nudged Sam's shoulder. He gave him a playful snap, yet Sam did not move. Sam and Addison were locked in an intense stare-down. "He's gonna help me get there. All we need is a little, how you say...*gold, a key to let us in*?"

"Sam's not going to help you to get anything like that," Addison said to Frankie. Jon was irked by the use of the word *gold*. He had no idea what that meant. Still, he watched his boss with fury filling his eyes. Jon could read Addison's perturbed expression as he said those words with ominous intent.

"He can't help you because he's not going to be here anymore. He won't be, and neither will you."

"Is that so?" asked Frankie.

The spark Jon once felt continued to burn inside, and he took it all in. Then he stepped closer to make sure he was as close to Sam as he could get.

"Yes, it is." Filled with pride and joy, Jon had sworn an oath to defend The Conquistador.

In the end, he was more than just a bouncer and a Doorman. Jon was not just someone who cracked skulls and asked people to leave whenever they disobeyed the rules. No, Jon was a watcher. He was a guardian. He was someone who cared about safety, rules, and ethics.

Above all else, Jon was kind. Always, he was kind.

Whatever Frankie was planning and whatever he wanted to do, Jon didn't care. He didn't care about his ideas or his opinions about the club's future. In the end, Jon only cared about one outcome. He wanted to fight and he wanted to protect.

"So you think you can stop the future?" Sam asked. He was speaking to Addison, not to Jon.

"No," Addison replied, "I'm just here to stand in *your* way."

Jon stared his colleague up and down and kept Frankie in the corner of his eye. He wasn't supposed to strike first. Jon was taught how to avoid violence. He was instructed about how to avoid pain whenever necessary. Therefore, Jon never opted to attack first. Then, in this situation realized, he had no other choice. And, while Jon was ready to react, he didn't have to.

Addison's first punch was a straight jab. It was hard and hit Sam directly in the chin. Producing a clean pop, until now, Jon didn't know what Addison was capable of.

Now, he did, and he liked it.

"Don't let them get into the room," said Addison.

"Right," said Jon, obeying his boss's order. Now in a severe throwdown with Sam and Frankie Castellani, it was a no-holds-barred fight to the finish. And it was on!

Let's fucking go.

CHAPTER 34
A PLAN WITHIN A PLAN

A FIGHT IN THE CLUB'S FORBIDDEN WING COULDN'T possibly be a good idea. There was so little to see here other than the doors along this narrow stretch. For this fight, Jon had only his hands and his prosthetic, and that was it. He also had Addison, and he had his enemy.

There were two enemies now.

According to Addison, whatever was hidden inside this room was something worth protecting. Jon didn't know what it was, and he didn't care. His orders were clear. He trusted Addison. Even when Addison seemed like he was lying, Jon still gave him the benefit of the doubt. Jon planned to do the same here. If Jon turned out to be wrong, then he didn't care.

So far, it was Jon fighting Frankie and Sam fighting Addison.

This was not an ideal match. Jon felt Addison could use an extra set of hands when facing Sam. Addison was skilled, yes, but he also wasn't one for getting his hands dirty either. He could fight, yet Sam was a bruiser. He was a real motherfucking scrapper. Sam aimed low and he hit clean. Addison definitely had skill, but toughness and endurance were qualities that remained to be seen.

"I'm gonna break your fucking..." As Frankie delivered this pitiful threat to Jon, the Marine kept a solid stance.

Jon's fists were up and his back was tight. He was ready to block and strike simultaneously and Jon was jacked up enough to deliver each one. But this was not part of what Jon had initially planned. Certainly, Jon could throw Frankie a beating, however, this was not his purpose.

Beating Frankie would not be enough. If Jon knew anything about Sam, he knew he had planned a fist-fight. At the very least, he was a lot smarter than Frankie. Therefore, by him being here now, it was an act of protection.

Sam wanted to stop Frankie from revealing the truth about their plan. While Frankie was sure to spill secrets, Addison was here to protect theirs. He was here to do this, but not Sam. No, Sam had come only for himself. While Frankie sank deeper into his tantrum, he responded by delivering a straight kick right into Jon's midsection. Still, the kick was weak. All Jon had to do was block down and Frankie was instantly off balance.

Suddenly, Jon recalled everything he learned from his training. Whenever a bad guy won't back down, it's up to you to use what you know to bring him down. Jon looked at the door behind Frankie. It was the same door Jon was ordered to protect.

"You don't want this club," Jon said to Frankie

Castellani. He dodged another sloppy attempt at hitting him in the face. "You never did."

"Oh yeah?" Frankie snapped back. He cocked back his fist and was set for another swing, but Jon pivoted. "You don't know me."

"No," said Jon. He dodged the punch by veering off to the side. Frankie was officially a poor-ass fighter. "I do."

Frankie tried to punch again but the Marine circled. "I know exactly who you are."

"Fuck you," said Frankie.

All Frankie's punches were pitiful. He was nothing more than a wannabe fighter. Jon watched as another hit was tried. Frankie kicked and Jon did the same as before. He motioned around the blow, and then he inserted his hand underneath. Jon pushed with his elbow, and the hit delivered was subtle but spot on.

Jon knocked Frankie Castellani to send a clear message.

Frankie was way out of his league. He had nowhere to go and nothing to do. Jon knew this. He also understood how to get Frankie so pissed off he would make countless bad moves.

"Yeah, fuck me," said Jon.

Jon held Frankie's leg under his arm. Now flexing, Jon slid his own foot forward and he reached for Frankie's shoulder. With careful ease, Jon knocked the son of the mobster down like he was a child. "Fuck me and everyone who works here, right? We're not good security. We just get in everyone's way, huh?" Jon asked with a sharp tongue. "We throw our weight around and we interfere too much, yeah? We're all just a bunch of assholes, aren't we? We're just a bunch of jerks."

"Whatever you say, and whatever you want," said Frankie. "I know how this story ends."

"Oh yeah?" Jon stood over Frankie as he lay on his back. "You want to tell me how it does?"

This was the moment Jon had been waiting for. It was the same moment whereby Frankie was going to reveal his plans and mention the many crimes he wanted to commit. Frankie would speak about how he was going to move something he called *product*. Now was the time where he was going to say it out loud and Jon could catch him.

He was going to hear every word, and Addison was too.

All Jon had to do was make sure he was set up for the recording. And he was.

Beneath Jon's shirt *was* a microphone.

And although the fight with Sam was brutal and knuckle-drivingly intense, the second microphone still stayed stuck to Jon's sweaty chest. When Jon turned his head to check on Addison, he took his eyes off Frankie. He broke the first rule of bouncing and security.

Never take your eyes off anyone ever.

Jon turned to Addison.

The cooler's suit was ripped. He now appeared disheveled and torn. Sam bobbed side to side while bleeding from his nose. No doubt, the fight had taken a lot out of both of these men.

Still, Addison looked like he'd been hit the hardest.

"Addison!"

Why Jon insisted on calling out to his friend, the cooler, was an impulsive decision. It was unwise and pointless. When Jon called to Addison, his eyes shifted back and to the side. Frankie Castellani knew where the Marine's eyes were going to go.

They were out of sight. And so Jon was compromised.

Frankie heaved the bouncer in the groin and ran. He went exactly where he shouldn't. Frankie blitzed toward the door. It was the same door Addison ordered Jon to protect. Again, he didn't know the significance of said door or what was behind it.

Jon was on his knees.

His hand was out. He was trying to grab Frankie before he escaped. Grazing the right arm of the wannabe gangster, Frankie fought and barreled toward the opened passage. In what seemed like an act of desperation, Frankie fell inside.

While in this new space, Jon sighed.

He watched as Addison and Sam returned to trading blows. Addison finished with a solid cross-block, and Sam countered with a flying elbow. Sam delivered this strike after pushing off the wall and he pounced on Addison like a panther.

"He's going through that door!" Jon screamed as he leaned onto his prosthetic.

It gave him a lot of bounce and additional movement. As a result, Jon was propelled forward. He chased Frankie across the room. While Jon was sure to follow orders, he was adamant about pursuing the one who got away.

Still, Jon was nervous.

He had turned his back on Addison as well as the fight. Although Jon didn't doubt Addison's abilities, he didn't know if he could go head-to-head with someone like Sam. Everything Jon saw from Sam demonstrated a certain rawness and skillset. Jon could see Addison didn't have the same prowess or power.

It wasn't that his boss lacked the skill, no. It was his age and just being passed his prime. Such always presents difficulties. Sam, however, was younger, and this made him more formidable, even though he wasn't.

"Go!" Addison yelled at Jon.

He was encouraging Jon to run when, in fact, the Marine was preoccupied with where he was going and why. Nonetheless, Jon heard Addison loud and clear.

He dipped his shoulder and rammed the door.

CHAPTER 35
NEW MOVEMENTS

AFTER EXPLODING INTO THIS OTHER ROOM, JON imagined what it might look like. Upon bursting inside, Jon realized how it was different than he had expected. What Jon had fallen into now was an abyss. At first, he couldn't quite describe it. To say it was dark was an understatement. To say he was among the shadows was also wrong. What Jon saw now were *not* shadows. No, Jon was now in a room so terribly black he could see nothing other than an infinite spread of endless darkness. Surrounded by this unbreakable shade, the door slammed behind Jon and he disappeared further into the black.

"Goddamn it," Jon muttered. He shook like he did whenever things got too big, too fast, or too loud too quickly. Jon waited until it passed. Faster than usual, it did. Jon steadied. He collected and calmed.

If this was the room Addison wanted Frankie to stay out of, Jon couldn't understand why.

Once he was in this unknown room, he reached for

his phone. It was drained. Without any light, how could he navigate or stop Frankie from getting away?

At this point, Jon couldn't understand why this room was a secret?

Why was it here? What was it protecting?

Jon spotted a light switch and flicked it casually. It wasn't working, not in the way Jon intended. It was still dark. He would not know the significance or the purpose of this space. When Jon stood in the darkened room, he closed his eyes and exhaled. Completing a calming technique, Jon tried to regain his faculties while deciding his next course of action.

The Conquistador was almost always a dark space.

Where Jon worked was in the shadows. The shadows were all Jon knew.

When he crept into the blackened space, he stayed sharp. He stayed frosty. Jon controlled his breathing and opened and closed his eyes. Adjusting his vision, Jon slid his foot along the gleaming floor. He was balanced as he stared at the shadows.

Jon questioned Frankie's location. How could he navigate through this room?

Where the hell was Frankie?

Jon's first instinct was to scream Frankie's name. Jon believed by doing this he might have a better idea about where he was positioned. Given his environment, this would be quite ineffective and also dangerous. Nevertheless, Jon crept in further. The room was deathly silent. It was so quiet Jon could hear his own breath drawing out of his throat.

While venturing into this space, Jon squinted. A new memory emerged in his booming consciousness.

Jon was suddenly back in the war. He was where things were more than just dark, they were pitch black. Jon and the other Marines were usually given goggles and other tech to assist them in such a perilous environment.

Sometimes, these tools helped, but on other occasions, they were unnecessary.

Jon rarely used them. His eyesight was incredible. So often, there was little Jon could not see or make out. He could read signs from miles away and read print so small that all the letters looked the same. Here, Jon's eyesight adjusted well to the darkness. He lifted the shadows just by taking a harder look around.

In war, when things get dark, things get dangerous.

When things go quiet, often it foreshadows a terrible outcome.

In this case, both were happening. Jon's ability to try and keep calm was all he had to guide him. He gawked while ahead Jon could see a slight alteration in the shadows' formation. While it was still dark, Jon was starting to see more than what he had before. Here, he could see a square divider, like sheets of glass cutting across the room in organized rows. Jon steadily approached this shape. Getting closer, Jon could use it to mark certain parts of the room.

From here, he could get a better understanding of where Frankie was.

As he stepped in, Jon realized that's where the glass sheet was, in a place brighter compared to other places. What was so secretive about this room? Jon wouldn't know until the darkness was gone.

Right now, it was the same.

Jon crept. Approximately five feet ahead of him, a cacophony emerged.

Jon tilted his head after hearing the racket. The sounds were slight but still present. They could be heard beyond the glass. Realizing this, Jon eased closer. Jon couldn't see what lay ahead completely but there was definitely something there, beyond.

Outside *this* room was another room.

Like the last one, it was occupied and it did serve a purpose. As of now, Jon didn't know what that purpose was. So, he reached out and put his hand on the glass. He still didn't know if it was a window, but Jon couldn't imagine it being anything else. He leaned in to listen closely to the sounds heard on the other side. It was vague, but still very much present. When Jon pulled his head away, he heard a faint rustling—a commotion that stirred from beyond this place.

Jon flinched as a vicious scream bellowed from behind his left ear. Not only was he not alone, but the feral roar foreshadowed an impending attack. Jon backed away. After a rapid pivot, Jon found himself face-to-face with the assailant himself.

"Yah!" The son of the mob boss was a drunken mule.

Frankie stampeded after Jon. Jon leaped back so far so quickly, he almost tripped. Though Jon managed to stay balanced, he jolted to attention and readied for any attacks. Frankie was sheathed in shadow and was barely visible.

All Jon could make out in the room was his silhouette. It was a small outline of a fool who was only barely a man. Frankie raised his hand and readied for the hard chop to Jon's head.

But Frankie could also barely see.

Though almost blind, there was still *some* light in

the space. Varying yellow spots appeared across the floor and brightened a few corners and crevasses. Therefore, Jon could make Frankie out in *some* capacity.

Nevertheless, what Jon wanted to know was what the hell he was doing here, in this room. Also, Jon wasn't sure if Frankie knew where he was or if he had just randomly entered this section. So much needed to be explained. None of this mattered now. Jon found himself in a new fight. It was a fight in the dark. The Marine could see only a little, but to combat Frankie, all Jon had to do was hold his ground and stand tall.

Frankie Castellani was no fighter. His skills were absolute trash. He didn't stand a chance against someone like Jon. Yet, besting him in a fight was not the goal. The goal was to provoke Frankie into admitting what he was up to, stop him, and then leave the rest for the police to handle.

Engaged in combat, Jon didn't rely on his fighting skills so much. His skills with another tool served him better. No, what he needed was to have command over his language and his words. Only then would Frankie fall, would he fail and lose.

"Was this your plan?" Jon asked the mobster's son. "To run and hide?"

Frankie gasped. He was winded. "Do I look like I'm running?" Frankie replied.

"No," Jon uttered. Another fist began to make its way toward his face. "It just looks like you're way out of your league." Jon decided to poke fun at Frankie Castellani's frail ego.

"You have no idea about what is or what's not in my league," Frankie said, and he turned up the volume.

Before, he was acting only on impulse and not skill. He was kicking and punching and trying to deliver on something. In order to avoid the hits, all Jon had to do was keep his hand up and block. So far, that's exactly what he was doing. And so far, it was working.

"Oh yeah?" asked Jon. "Is that what you think?"

"You don't know anything about me," said Frankie.

"Oh, I do," said Jon. Rolling along his shoulder, Jon raised his hand and blocked again. "I know what it feels like to try and leave certain things behind, to not be able to escape the things you want to. I know what it's like to want to start over again and to feel like you can't."

Jon was down on one knee. Keeping his body open, he came ready for the next strike.

"I know what it feels like to lose something you can never get back. I know that's what this is all about, Frankie. You're trying to be something you're not— because what you are is not a gangster."

Jon's words were obvious horse shit. They were easy to see through and even easier to defend. Of course, Frankie Castellani was a gangster!

It was also true Frankie was a tool.

He was someone who was ill-equipped to face what was to come.

He couldn't be a gangster, but then that's why Jon said he wasn't one. He was purposefully winding Frankie Castellani up like a toy. He was playing into his frustration, his anger. Jon wanted Frankie to implode so he could finally admit his plan. Jon wanted to catch Frankie red-handed and, at last, fall into the Marine's cunning and carefully orchestrated trap.

Jon was a decent trapper. Then again, the setting felt too familiar.

The room reminded Jon of another room. Suddenly, he was back in the tower with the cratered walls. Jon was back to fighting an opponent who could not see. Jon remembered the building coming down and taking his last breath. And, as he baited Frankie Castellani, Jon was still burdened by all the frustration. Striking frantically, Jon stayed on one knee while Frankie continued to writhe in frustration.

"Oh, you're going to see the kind of gangster I can be," Frankie assured. "Soon...you will. I'm going to take this club down!"

In that moment, Frankie began his confession. He fell into the exact trap that Jon and the other Doormen had set. It was there, and just as he was about to admit the truth, a fat arm slid along Jon's shoulder.

The Marine flinched as he tried to break away.

But it was too late.

Frankie was caught, red-handed. Busted clean.

CHAPTER 36
THE DEMON SPEEDING

Now inside the hidden room, Sam had managed to get in from the hallway and was now in the last place Jon wanted him to be.

"Not so fast there, Frankie boy." Sam grabbed Jon by the chest and kept his hand open. "Close your mouth and say nothing else," Sam now addressed Frankie.

"What? What are you talking about?"

Jon felt Sam's fortified grip seize even more. Why would another Doorman insist on pushing his hands so hard into Jon? In the end, the only one who knew the answer to that was Jon himself.

He wasn't wearing the standard "bust" tech that police wore or were accustomed to.

All Jon had to record was a tiny mic. The mic was concealed underneath. While secured, Jon could feel more of Sam's grip. Then, with a hard yank, Sam pulled the mic clean off Jon's body. Sam kneed Jon in the kidney and dropped the Marine.

Jon felt crippled. When he fell, he did so without a recording device.

"He's got you nailed," said Sam. "He's got your every word."

"Fuck you," said Jon.

When Sam released his hand, Jon tossed the mic aside. The device was pinned to his shirt. Only the other Doormen knew of these devices, so only some of them knew their purpose.

Jon didn't expect Sam to get a grip. At least, Jon hoped he wouldn't. The other half wasn't at all surprised. Mostly, he was just shocked.

"Don't say another word. Someone else is listening. They're always listening."

"Fuck," said Frankie. "Who?"

Jon watched as Sam looked around.

"I don't know," said Sam. "Somewhere we shouldn't be."

"You mean you don't know?" Frankie said to Sam. At the moment, Sam was out of breath. Still winded from his fight with Addison, his words were barely audible.

"No one is allowed here. It's *forbidden*," said Sam.

"Forbidden?" exclaimed Frankie. "What is this, Beauty and the fucking Beast?"

"No," replied Sam. His hand was tight on Jon's wrist. "We don't have time to explain. We need to get out of here now, before anyone sees."

"Right," said Frankie. "When my dad finds out what's going on here, he's going to milk this place for all it's fucking worth. The Conquistador is done for. You said it yourself."

"Yeah, well," said Sam. "We can talk about all that later. For now, let's just go. We need to go, come on."

"Okay." Still on his back, Jon used whatever strength was still in his arms to hoist himself up. Doing this, Jon staggered until he was balanced.

"You're not going anywhere," Jon said, his arm twitching.

"You just won't quit, will you?" Sam asked Jon.

Jon's prosthetic was hurting so much he could barely hold on. Jon's ribs burned like acid was poured on each bone. His face was bruised and battered. The room was still dark and Jon's eyesight, though impressive, was compromised.

Jon cracked his knuckles and regurgitated blood. He glared at Sam and Frankie. The two criminals looked promptly at Jon. The fight now approaching was far from fair but Jon didn't care. He did what he always did. He stood in his fighting stance and glowered at the men he needed to handle.

"No," said Jon. "I could go all night."

"Sure you could," said Sam. "Sure you could."

Jon spat while Sam crept closer. Sam's fists were up. Jon gazed with a look of sheer disdain. He wanted Sam to hit first. Usually, this was how Jon protected himself. He was always careful about when he hit and when he blocked. In this case, Jon knew precisely what he was going to do. He charged.

With the help of his prosthetic, Jon shot down and hugged Sam's fat legs. Frankie was close but not close enough to be in the fight. Jon and Sam rolled like two jiu-jitsu fighters scrapping on a slippery floor. The ground was so clean it was like the two were scrapping on ice.

Jon wrapped his hands around Sam's wrist while the other bouncer grimaced and grunted.

"You're not gonna armbar me, bud," Sam said. "It just ain't gonna happen."

Sam was on his knees. Fortunately, Jon had Sam in a triangle choke. Jon pulled Sam's wrist as much as he could and tried to get as much of the arm as possible. From this low, it was a struggle. Nevertheless, Jon fought to get more.

"We'll see." Truthfully, Jon had no idea how this fight would end.

Sam did have more fighting experience. At this moment, Jon struggled with his floor game. To get back, Jon squeezed and he clenched. Jon was accessing parts of his body he didn't know existed. Frankie watched from the sidelines while the two bouncers wrestled. Sam squirmed and throttled Jon's shoulders and put him on his back.

Jon thought his prosthetic might be better for kicking. But he was wrong. In the scrap, Jon was getting a considerable brace from this tool. Jon didn't think he would have this leverage, this kind of fortification, but he did. And it was awesome.

"Fuck you," grunted Sam. Although bigger than Jon, Sam was using all of his strength poorly.

Against an enemy of such size, Jon gained knowledge from Danix about how to combat this kind of opponent. In war, Jon learned how to fight from his back when he's pushed against the wall. With little resources at your disposal and with far less strength, one can only rely on what they have.

In this case, Jon knew how to fight from the ground. It wasn't perfect, but it was good.

"You can't armbar worth shit," barked Sam. Oddly, he said this while Jon was about to get him in this exact lock.

"Like I said to you before, asshole," said Jon. "Let's see!"

Returning to Danix's gym, Jon heard his friend and teacher's voice in his ear. He was telling Jon to be careful. He was telling Jon to know his limits. Right now, Jon didn't want to push himself any more than he had. He wanted to remember that the most important part of this job wasn't the fighting or the danger. He accepted this job to forget about his past. Jon did it so he could move into a new and better future.

He could do this, but to fight—to break people down—it's not what he did.

No, it's what Jon Haze *used* to do. It was his life before now, but that time was over. It was dead and gone. Now, Jon was a better grappler than Sam but he was *not* a better fighter. Jon wanted Sam to tap. And, should Jon release Sam, he might retaliate and get the upper hand.

Then, where else was Jon supposed to go?

He was confined to this one room and it was a room as dark as it was mysterious. Still, Jon seized Sam's arm and prepared for the armbar. Before he could do this, Jon was booted at the side of the head.

"Gra!" After Sam was hit, Jon let go.

He released more than just Sam, he let himself go too.

So much of Jon's body felt worn down and broken. Jon had spent all his energy and was now approaching territory he could barely endure. He was there once before, in the tower, in the desert, and then he knew he should have left. He knew this and still, he didn't do it. He didn't because he was too afraid.

But Jon refused to make the same mistake again. His mother needed him.

With Sam out and Frankie back in, Jon flipped the son of the mobster over. His plan was to simply go toward the door. Jon was to go back the way he came in. He had enough energy to do this, but it was a hope to sprint now. It would be Jon's last attempt. In many ways, it was going to be his final bow.

He was ready to take it.

"We have to get out of here," said Frankie. "We can't be seen together, or else they're going to know more about what it is we're doing."

"What *we're* doing..." said Sam. When Jon heard him speak now, he wasn't sure if Sam was asking a question. Jon didn't know anything about Sam, only that he had gained more knowledge of words and tone.

This was—and always had been—the primary tool in the world of bouncing.

Jon could read a person's intentions based on their tone and body language. He could infer from this as well as from a person's choice of words. In this case, Sam's selection was undeniable.

It *was* a question.

"What we're up to is..." Frankie said, "we're finally going to expose The Conquistador, show everyone what it *really* holds." Frankie made this statement like a point of pride. He was making a clear declaration and explaining everything right here, right now. "We're going to set up our own op. We're going to move in and start taking over."

"Even if it means breaking the law?" asked Jon. His

question was completely impulsive. After he asked it, Jon was looking past Frankie and Sam. He was staring at a clear sheet that now appeared inside the room. Jon was starting to make out certain shapes. In fact, that's exactly what he was seeing now.

He could see *shapes*. More shapes.

"Fuck the law," said Frankie. "The laws are changing, and it's time for us to start breaking the ones that won't. And, whether that means fucking killing people or stealing, which we've already done...then so fucking be it."

"So be it," confirmed Sam.

Saying what Sam and Frankie did, Jon stood, but his hand stayed on his knee. He was solid. He was balanced. In that moment, Jon had something that he did not have before. He had closure and intent. He had clarity, and he had a confession!

It was all there. It was all perfect!

CHAPTER 37
ENLIGHTENED

In a flash, the room brightened and the hardened glow burned Jon's eyes. Lifting his hand to cover himself from the harsh light, Jon observed his surroundings. The space was illuminated and he could now see beyond the glass walls.

The walls were windows, just as Jon had assumed.

Yet, what they looked out *onto* was unclear.

Now, it was.

Beyond the glass were faces. Some were familiar, and others were totally unfamiliar. But what Jon could see were men, women, and other Doormen like Danix, Li, and Jamal. Jon could see women like Kya, Divine, and other staff at The Conquistador.

They were all there too. In fact, everyone was there. The entire club was watching!

"Holy shit," Frankie could barely comprehend the sight, and neither could Jon. Actually, the sight was incomprehensible.

Jon gulped and stepped back.

How Frankie managed to sneak into a room that

bordered the entire nightclub was baffling to the rookie bouncer. Also, why this room was connected to the dance floor also floored Doorman Jon Haze. But, what was most shocking of all was Addison Krowe.

In the end, Addison was the reason why everyone was present.

He knew where Jon, Frankie, and Sam were inside this secret section of the club. Addison knew what the room was and what it could be turned into. Although both shocking and incredible, Jon was able to see the whole picture now. He wasn't the one planning a damn thing. He was just doing his job. He was confronting a bad situation, and he was doing his best to stop it.

Addison was the cooler and that meant something different. He oversaw all operations and also took care of his own. He was watching out for Jon, his fellow Doorman, and was doing all he could to protect him. He was doing this, and it worked.

"Sam Vaughn and Frankie Castellani..."

A man in a policeman's uniform marched toward the window. Seeing the two officers, Jon stepped back and didn't say a word. Now seeing looks of devastation and shame, Sam and Frankie glanced at each other. They both knew what was about to happen, and there was nothing they could do to stop it.

"You're under arrest."

CHAPTER 38
THE AFTERWARD

WHAT HAPPENED AFTER FRANKIE AND SAM WERE both caught was expected.

The police read them their rights and told them how the entire club had heard their confessions. Both were to be arrested for conspiracy to commit extortion. The cops searched Frankie as well as his friends for any contraband. Like Jon assumed, all of them were carrying. On their person, the cops found cocaine and ecstasy.

One of them was even holding meth.

Now, Jon didn't expect these narcotics to be trafficked, but then he didn't know for sure.

Again, Jon was no detective. He was just a bouncer and a damn good one at that. He was good enough to orchestrate the perfect plan, and it came together in perfect harmony. Whatever the reason, the club was almost closed. The time of their confession was just when the DJ was on his final playlist. So, it actually was really convenient when the sting did occur. Jon didn't like thinking of it as a bust, but there was no other way of seeing it. Frankie Castellani was stopped. The entire time, he was dragged to a patrol car, where he shouted the same phrase over and over.

"Wait until my father hears about this! Wait until he finds out what you did!"

Frankie's statement was loud, but it was ignored by everyone. Honestly, Jon didn't care. He had heard it all before. Now Frankie was just another spoiled rich punk who was being shown the way out. Now that Frankie Castellani was done for, Jon stopped and glared at the boy. There was nothing more to be said. What happened happened, and now it was time to move on.

Though Frankie was the first one loaded into the police cruiser, he was not the last. Due to Sam being an accomplice, he was just as liable as Frankie. He too was guided to a police patrol car, where he was set to be charged with drug suspicion and aggravated assault. The charges wouldn't do much, not for someone like Frankie.

For Sam, however, he'd never bounce again.

Jon watched Sam being taken away.

There was one last task that needed to be completed.

"You all right?" Addison asked, inexplicably arriving on the scene.

He hadn't spoken to Jon since he was pulled from that hidden room inside that hidden hallway. Addison wasn't standing alone. Danix, Li, Jamal, and Kya all stepped out to see one of their own being taken away.

"I'm fine," Jon said to Addison.

"Are you sure? It was pretty rough, and I know I should have told you what I was doing, but I really had no time to explain."

"I get it," said Jon. Truthfully, he did. Jon could grasp Addison's plan and his logic. However, Jon did this mostly as an employee—but as a friend, he was struggling.

There was a lot Addison needed to explain.

Right now, Sam was halfway to the police car. He was so close and that was the point. Jon shuffled to Sam. Just before Sam was brought into the car, Jon stopped and called the police. "Wait," he said. "Hold up a minute."

The cops stopped and looked back. Jon didn't tell them why they were asked to stop. The Doormen all eyed Jon as he moved. His prosthetic felt solid. After the fight, he was slumping somewhat. Still, he managed to get to Sam before he disappeared.

"What?" Sam barked, his face all bruised and scratched. "Did you come here to fucking gloat because you finally got the upper hand on me or some shit?"

"Nope," said Jon. "Didn't come to gloat."

"Right."

"Just here for this," Jon replied.

"For what?" Sam bit back at the Marine.

Jon ignored Sam, reached out, and grabbed the crest on his shirt.

The crest was the symbol for all Doormen. It was worn by every bouncer who served. It was a symbol meant to be honored and upheld. The crest was a red fist inside a hexagon. A line was drawn straight down the crest, and the fist symbolized power and strength. The hexagon represented how power was owned and controlled. Every Doorman respected his crest. It was their mark. Everyone did, everyone except for one.

Jon didn't expect the crest to be removed so easily.

He gripped it as tight as he could and yanked it from Sam's shirt. In a second, Sam was stripped of his right to wear the symbol and he was no longer welcomed as a Doorman in The Conquistador. Upon removing the rest, Jon raised his hand and showed Sam what he would never have.

"You don't deserve to wear this."

Sam observed Jon's gesture but said nothing. Jon nodded as the police carried his former colleague away. The cars drove down the crowded street, and Jon watched them take Sam away. Jon supposed this brought an end to the fight he was once a part of. And yet, Jon was happy to know he'd made it, that he was now safe.

———

"Good work you did today." At first, Jon didn't know who was speaking to him or why.

He thought it was Addison, but when Jon peered over his shoulder, he looked at who was speaking and it wasn't his boss. Kya stood behind Jon with her hair tied in a ponytail. She looked just as good as she did when she started work. Although this was all unexpected, in the end, Jon wasn't surprised. In fact, he was relieved.

Kya was exactly who Jon wanted to see.

"Thanks, I, uh...oh!" Jon exclaimed like a schoolboy at a dance.

He could feel his heart beating hard but not so fast. Suddenly, Jon was under control and he was no longer flushed or broken, like he was when he first began working here. Kya was now walking up to Jon, still the woman of his dreams.

At last, Jon had found himself thinking of something else.

He liked her, yes, but she was not the only one on his mind now. And Jon liked that she wasn't.

"It's you," said Jon.

Kya looked at the Marine with her eyebrows wrinkled, appearing confused. "Who else did you expect?"

Jon considered Kya's question. Who else did Jon expect was a swell question. For the first time, Jon wanted it to be someone else.

"No one," said Jon. "No one." He looked down and took a moment. He reflected on everything that happened, everything he did, and had thought about.

"Are you alright?" Jon asked Kya.

"Me?" Kya said.

Jon nodded. "Yeah."

"Yeah," said Kya. "I'm fine."

"I thought what you did was pretty cool, actually," said Jon. "I mean, in case you were wondering, you know, how it is I felt about it."

Jon was referring to how Kya responded to the Doormen's plan for bringing Frankie down. Jon recalled perfectly how Kya had purposefully poured a drink on a guest. Jon then remembered how she provoked one of Frankie's bastard friends into acting out. Kya made him move too soon and respond without thinking. In effect, she was just as responsible for what happened here as the other bouncers.

"When you spilled the drink," Jon explained. "I mean, if you didn't do that, they wouldn't have moved away, and Frankie wouldn't have run. It worked out really well is all I'm saying."

"Oh yeah?" asked Kya. "An old trick I learned while working here."

"Figured as much," said Jon.

"Yeah," replied Kya. "You work here long enough, you'll pick up a few of your own too."

"Right," said Jon. He didn't quite know what to make of Kya's comment. It all sounded so ominous and strange. "I guess."

Thus far, the only tricks Jon knew were how to follow and how to listen. But these weren't really tricks at all. However, after what happened tonight, Jon was starting to see what Kya meant. The Conquistador was a place filled with tricks. Which one would Jon learn next, only time would tell.

"Look, Addison wants everyone back inside," said Kya. "Police want statements, and Addison wants everyone in for a debriefing. Get people up to his office soon as possible."

"Debrief?" asked Jon. "Funny, I thought when I came home," he said, "I'd stop being a soldier. Weird that I just became a different one."

"The club industry isn't war," said Kya, "but you'll see it's going to be just as unpredictable with enemies who are always changing. They exist in the dark, see? They hide where you can't see 'em. Takes a strong mind to know exactly what it is you're doing and an even stronger one to know how to get it done."

"Yeah," said Jon. He couldn't agree more.

Everything Kya said to Jon made perfect sense. It was everything Jon was feeling and everything he had come to know. Jon reviewed the scenario again in his own mind, reflected and considered everything he had observed and learned. It was now all so shockingly clear.

"I guess you're a soldier too then," Jon said to Kya. "You're a Doorman, just like the rest of us."

"A Doorman?" Kya asked. "Right." She smirked and chortled. Jon could see the name appealed to her. Based on her sly grin, Jon believed she liked it a lot.

"Let's go inside," Jon said to Kya. "It's been a really long night."

Kya waited for Jon to walk alongside her. Why Kya wanted Jon to walk with her, he couldn't quite figure. Then Jon remembered her smile. He remembered how Kya touched him on the arm and how she stood closer to Jon now than she ever had before. Obviously, this didn't *prove* Kya had feelings for Jon. All it proved was she did not walk quickly. She chose to look back because she wanted to see if Jon was okay.

Maybe Kya was looking back because she thought Jon might too.

There was no doubt in Jon's mind his feelings for Kya were real.

His infatuation and his deathly attraction to her were immensely intense. There was no denying it. And yet, Jon decided to let the attraction simmer and felt it was best to wait. Jon needed time to think about Kya and what he really wanted.

Thankfully, Jon had time.

So long as he was home, he would have all the time he wanted.

"Yeah," Kya said to Jon. "I'll go with you."

———

It wasn't until hours later that all the Doormen were called into Addison's office.

There, Addison and Larry Thomas were joined by two detectives. They were the same detectives Jon encountered before. They were Officer Merchant and Officer Clanistan of the NYPD.

There were also three uniformed cops standing with Danix, Li, and Jamal.

They were taking statements while the employees of The Conquistador gave measly, textbook responses. Jon told them exactly what happened. He explained his reasoning as well as his justification. He told the cops precisely why he did what he did. He thoroughly outlined his choices and why it was a wise decision for him to intervene.

To be honest, Jon was less concerned by these responses. Instead, he focused on what Larry and Addison were saying to each other. There were a lot of questions that went unanswered. These questions pertained to what was in that hallway, what would happen to Sam, and how did both Sam and Frankie end up in that one room?

What were these secrets The Conquistador was hiding?

The detectives spoke to Addison and Larry, and they did so quietly in the corner.

"We'll deal with our rogue employee ourselves," Addison said to the police. Jon could hear some of this, but only vaguely. It was clear, however, Addison and Larry didn't want anyone else to know the details.

When Larry spoke to the detective, he was cordial, almost tactful. He touched the cop on the arm as he spoke and showed little emotion. Part of Jon thought he wasn't entirely present. Maybe he was and maybe he wasn't. Jon was the first to give his statement. The reason for this was because he was the one who was most involved in the conflict.

But this was *not* new.

And, while Jon didn't have much more to add, he watched Larry and Addison interact more with the police. Part of Jon thought they were talking legal jargon. Jon had to remember Addison was a lawyer. Maybe Larry knew the police too. Maybe they were all friends.

Yet, everything about the interaction suggested the police were more than just friends. The police touched Larry's shoulder and acted tender and respectful. They were turning back to make sure it was just them talking and no one else. Jon knew he was staring for too long. He was looking for things that weren't there—at least they weren't as present as he thought. Jon understood he needed to stop looking. And, just as he was about to turn away, he felt Danix grasping his arm.

"Hey," he said to Jon. Jon turned to Danix.

"Hey," Jon said back. At the time, he was unsure why he was there. Danix's presence could be felt even from far away. Jon was close with Danix. As he was beginning to understand now too, he was close with all Doormen.

They were all Jon's brothers.

"Pretty ballsy shit you did back there," said Danix. "Sam was quite the heavy hitter, but you got 'em good. Well done."

Jon nodded. "I did." By admitting this, Jon finally gave himself the credit he deserved. "And he was.

But..." Jon looked at Danix. "Your training helped, obviously. Those lessons at your gym were well spent."

"I hope so," said Danix.

"Right. Where is Sam?" Jon asked. Now staring at Danix, the big man shrugged and peered over his shoulder.

"Somewhere not here, but he'll be dealt with. Don't worry. Real question is Castellani."

"Yeah," replied Jon. "So...he's...what, charged?"

"Probably," said Danix. He crossed his arms. "But will it stick?" Danix shook his head and rubbed his hand around his chin. "Probably not."

"It never does, does it?"

"Not always," said Danix. "But then again, that ain't the point."

Before Jon could ask about what the point was, Danix explained.

"The point is he's no longer allowed here, and the cops are on our side. They'll back us up when keeping his ass out."

"Is that what Addison and Larry were talking to the cops about?" When Jon asked this primary question, Danix showed a slight smirk. His head moved like he wanted to nod, but then he stopped before he could complete the gesture.

Instead, Danix grinned at Jon in the same way he did before.

"Yeah," Danix said glibly. He didn't actually know what Addison and Larry were talking about. Saying what he did, Danix was giving Jon a general response that didn't have much meaning. "Sure."

"Are you okay?" Jon asked Danix.

"Me?" the big man replied.

Jon nodded. "Yeah."

"I'm fine."

"Guy was pretty tough," said Jon. "And looked pretty rough too. Actually, he was rougher than expected."

"Yeah, he was," said Danix. "He was pretty big too, no doubt. But, then again, this game is unexpected and that ain't how fights are usually won."

"Yeah, I know. It's not always about strength," said Jon.

"No, it is." Danix's reply was quick and to the point, but what he said was unexpected.

"It's just about who's strong in a different way," Danix explained. "You think the people who work here all know how to fight, yes? But, as it turns out, they know a whole lot more than just that."

Jon thought back to when he was first hired to work at The Conquistador. He remembered the club's policy about what was said when he was tested by Danix in the Green Room, which was its tactical training center.

"We hire people who aren't afraid to get hit or lose a fight, but they're also the same people who keep coming back," Danix said. "You didn't know what you were dropping into, but you went in anyway. You took a dive head first and made no apologies. You did what needed to be done, and that's what this is about, Jon. That's being a real bouncer, a real Doorman."

A surge of gratification emerged inside Jon that gifted the Marine with a sensation he hadn't felt since the war. Suddenly, he was comfortable. He was relaxed. He was oddly satisfied and completely inspired. Jon thought he always knew what it meant to be a bouncer, but hearing it spoken only confirmed Jon's previous thoughts and feelings.

"Yeah." Jon's head bowed. "I think I know what you mean."

While successful, Jon's plan did work. However, Jon didn't do it alone. Jon knew this. He just wanted to know if the other Doormen did too.

"Hey, bro!" The loud voice belonged to Jamal. Jon didn't need to turn to see who it was.

"Hey." Jon was joyous and pleased to see Jamal as well.

Jon didn't just respect Jamal, he also liked him and enjoyed his company. Throughout the entire attack on Frankie and Sam, and even during the great reveal, Jon had no idea where Jamal was. He didn't know if he was inside or by the door. Judging by the pleasantness in Jamal's voice, he knew everything, and he was happy. Jon was too.

"Jamal, what's going on?" Jon asked his friend.

"Not much. Just enjoying the little stunt you pulled off in there. You know, I never liked Sam, by the way. Glad he's out."

"So...you did see it?" asked Jon, although he already knew.

"Of course, I saw it!" Jamal exclaimed. "Man, you did good. Real good."

"Maybe," said Jon, "or did I just put a huge target on my back and this club's back? I mean, I did mess with the son of a mobster, didn't I?"

"Yeah," said Jamal, "but, man, this is bouncing," he said. "This is *elite* bouncing. If you don't have a target on your back, then you sure as hell ain't doing your job right. Besides, Addison and Larry got your back. The

Castellanis will have bigger fish to fry now that their own son put them in the hot seat again. And as far as this club...don't worry about that. We got that part handled. The Conquistador...it's our fucking castle."

"Right," said Jon. He didn't quite believe Jamal. At the same time, what he said *did* sound okay.

Jon played by the rules. He played his hand, and Frankie and Sam both played theirs. He won, they lost, and Jon was victorious because he was smarter. He had more skills and more knowledge. He exacted the right moves and the right tactics, and fortunately, all of them paid off.

Jon was pleased with this, but he was also scared. His actions were admirable, but they were also dangerous. Jon had acted out against someone who was more powerful than he was. He fought against a person with more reach and more resources. And, by defeating Frankie Castellani and Sam, Jon was no longer just another Doorman. He was now the Doorman who disrupted a corrupt system. Jon's fame would garner much attention. His status would increase, and this would create immense risk. Jon gulped as he considered the possibility that he may never be safe again. While this fear festered, Jon's hand quaked harder and chills crept down his spine and his bowels constricted. He struggled to breathe, because right now, Jon was anticipating all kinds of new scenarios and possibilities— things that could happen to him and likely would happen to him, to Kya, and to his mom.

Jon weighed his life, and consequently, his options.

Would he always have to look over his shoulder or would The Conquistador provide him a level of safety crucial to his survival? Jon considered this and trembled. He began to assimilate all the long reasons why he should be afraid and why he should not return to his club.

Jon thought about everything and he thought about nothing at all either.

When considering the consequences of his actions, Jon looked at the doorway where the rest of the Doormen now stood. Jon looked at Danix, Li, Jamal, Addison, and all the other employees of The Conquistador. Jon could see Kya and some of the other waitresses too. He thought of them and he thought of the crest he now held in his hands.

This was also Jon's mark. It was the mark of his brothers as well as his new army.

The Doormen were Jon's new Corp now. They were his guardians and they were his friends. And, so long as Jon was still standing, he would always have their backs and they would always have his. Jon would never be alone again. Jon understood this now more than ever. The Conquistador was more than just a nightclub. It was consecrated ground to be protected and adorned at all times. It was built on honor, rules, protection, and some secrets. None could cross its line without facing the full force that waited on the other side.

Jon was part of this force. And, so long as he served this cause, Jon would win. He would stand tall and he would fight. He would have friends and friends watch out for the person next to them, the same as soldiers.

And Jon was a soldier. Always and forever...*a soldier.*

CHAPTER 39
A NEW DAY

ADDISON'S DEBRIEFING DIDN'T TAKE LONG. IN FACT, Jon didn't have much to say to Addison or to Mr. Larry Thomas. In the end, Jon's story was told and all its details provided. For now, Jon only had one thought on his mind: he just wanted to go home.

"So, now that you're done talking to the police," said Addison as he stood behind his desk, "I want you to talk to me next."

Jon was so tired he could barely stand. He was also sore. He was so sore he couldn't stop thinking about how he was going to feel the next day and the day after that. Nonetheless, there was little Jon could do. He was here, and Addison did want to talk. He wanted to speak to Jon and Jon alone. Jon pretended like he wanted to speak despite not wanting to.

"Okay. What is it?" asked Jon.

"I know you heard some things from Sam, back in that hallway, about this club, about this place."

Jon said nothing.

He remembered every word and memorized every

detail. Each one was peculiar and dark. It suggested things about The Conquistador Jon tried piecing together now. He thought he might try to do this, but then Addison called Jon. Therefore, the Marine had no time to consider. All he could do was stand back and listen.

"Right," said Jon. "I remember."

"And I imagine you probably have some questions."

Jon didn't nod. He didn't do anything to indicate he had any questions at all. Although Jon did, he wanted to be crystal clear because now his goal was only to hear Addison out. It was about him and no one else. As confrontational as Addison was being right now, it was made even worse by his refusal to see any of the other bouncers.

What were the other the Doormen aware of that Jon wasn't?

What did Kya allude to that day in the coffee shop?

She had asked Jon how much he really knew about the place he worked. Jon thought about this all the time now, and yet, he didn't ask. He was silent—silent but also aware.

"Look, whatever Frankie and Sam were spewing behind the scenes," said Addison, "they don't really know what they're talking about, all right? Don't listen to them."

"Okay," Jon said. His answer was reflexive. He was being aggregable because he was done trying to be anything else. Also, he was thinking about the words Addison mentioned. He said that Sam and Frankie didn't *really* know what they were talking about. The inclusion of this one word was an important distinction. It indicated uncertainty and inconsistency. It also meant that there was some truth to what Frankie and Sam had claimed. They weren't simply making blanket statements without any evidence.

No, there was indeed something hidden in this club.

Something deep, something important, something *buried*.

"I just want you to know that this club is a good one, understand?" said Addison. "It's complicated, and it's dangerous, but just remember...you're on the right side, *okay*? And whatever happens because of what you did," Addison explained, "you'll always be protected, and you'll be safe so long as you keep working. You don't have to worry. Just...just trust me."

"I do trust you," said Jon. He wasn't sure he believed this himself but he said it like he did. "But it seems like you're trying to convince me of something here, Addison. Is that what this is, maybe?"

What Jon said, he didn't plan on saying. He had surprised even himself when he spoke to Addison using such a harsh tone. After speaking, the cooler glared at the Marine. Clearly, Jon's boldness offended his boss, but only somewhat. Clearly, Jon's position was to challenge. However, despite overstepping, his reasons behind his claim did make sense. It was a strange statement to say, especially at this time. So, when Jon looked back at Addison, he didn't break eye contact.

"I just want you to understand," Addison said again to Jon.

"I..." In Jon's mind, he was already responding. "*I understand. I get it. I believe you.*"

These words and phrases weren't spoken. They were just felt. Jon couldn't say these words because they weren't genuine. He didn't actually understand or believe anything. His mind was racing and Jon thought about all the secrets linked to The Conquistador.

Jon thought about the rules the club lived by.

Then he asked himself, where? Where did all of them come from?

Who made these rules? Who decided on them? Who were they for, and why did they exist?

Jon looked again at the photos behind Addison's desk. He had seen them all before, back when he first entered the room. Now, Jon could see that they weren't just pictures. No, they were collections. They were snapshots showing the club's history. And, when Jon continued to ask how deep this history went, he remembered what was said about Frankie Castellani's old man. Granted, Mr. Castellani was someone Jon had never crossed paths with. But still, Jon recalled Addison and Larry talking to the detectives. Again, Jon's curiosity enhanced.

Did people here know Frankie's father, Giuliani?

Was that why Frankie's demands for vengeance might never come to fruition? Did Giuliani's path intersect with Larry's? Maybe it intersected with Addison's too. If there were rules at The Conquistador that ensured the club's protection, then did they go beyond the club itself?

Jon perused the photos one at a time.

Each one contained a different face, and in each one lay another story that might be told someday. Jon didn't have time to hear any of these stories now. All he had at this moment was Addison, standing behind his desk and looking at Jon with a grim expression.

"Understand."

"Good," said Addison. "Very good."

Jon looked at his shoes. There was a time when Addison's words meant everything to Jon. Now, they counted for a lot less. Although a day might come whereby Addison returned to his former glory, for now, Jon had to keep a close watch on him, the guests, and the club.

It was exactly as Kya said. It was all one giant, uncontainable mystery.

"Given what's happened, I think you should take the next few days off," Addison said to Jon. "I think that might be a good idea."

"Oh," said Jon. He raised his hand and waved. "I don't think that's necessary."

"Wasn't a request," said Addison. "Take the next few days off. That's...an order."

"All right," agreed Jon.

"Good," said Addison.

Jon stepped toward the door because he felt it was a good time to conclude his meeting with Addison. Jon had heard enough and didn't want to hear more.

"Maybe spend it with someone important, someone close," Addison said to Jon.

His head dipped toward his window that looked out onto the dance floor. Jon followed Addison's gaze. Below, Jon could see only Kya. She was working behind the bar and was completely by herself. She didn't know Jon was watching her, but then few notice when someone else is watching.

Jon was. He always was.

The first time Jon saw Kya was exactly as she was at this moment. She looked just as pretty and just as alluring as she did at the beginning. Not much had changed. Jon was still very much attracted to her and he still very much wanted to be with her. He began to consider what his chances were that they would end up together. He accepted how he felt about her would never change. Jon believed he had made a good impression. He wanted so badly to tell Kya how he longed to be with her. And yet, the time was not right. Jon accepted this now.

He just wasn't ready.

Right now, there was only one person Jon wanted to be with. There was only one woman Jon couldn't stop thinking about, one who was the one most deserving of his attention.

"Don't let a good thing slip away," Addison advised Jon. "Make the most of your time here. Trust me, it'll be worth it."

Jon nodded.

Addison meant well, but this area was far from his jurisdiction. The comment made was invasive and bold. Then again, that's who Addison was and always would be.

"Maybe," Jon said to Addison. "But I think there's only one place I want to be right now."

Jon declined to tell Addison what this place was. No one needed to know except for Jon and this one other person. When Jon left Addison's office, he was sure to close the door behind him. He hurried to vacate the setting but on his way out, heard Kya finishing up behind the bar. Jon stopped and stared at her once again. Kya saw Jon and Jon saw Kya. The only gesture Jon gave was the same one given to anyone before saying goodbye.

Jon raised his hand and waved. He smiled and kept

smiling. It said only that he was happy to see her. Jon was even happier to grant such a simple gift. Kya made the conscious decision to wave back and Jon answered with the same blushing hue but, again, reminded himself of where he was going.

Right now, he had someplace better to be.

———

Jon hopped on the bus and checked his phone. There were a dozen messages from other Doormen, like Danix, Li, and Jamal. All had texted Jon despite having spoken to him earlier. It would seem they had more to say to the Marine.

Jon skimmed and read through a few of these messages.

He sent emojis and abbreviations back while also waiting for his bus to stop.

When it reached its spot, Jon breathed in the chilled morning air. No matter where he was or what he'd done, the smell of the air reminded Jon about what it felt like to be home. When he stepped off the plane after arriving from war, he could smell it then too. When he left his mother's car after spending a few days in the hospital after losing his leg, he smelled it there as well. The smell was something so constant Jon could smell it even when he wasn't home.

Until now, Jon didn't realize what he was smelling, at least not exactly. What Jon was a blend of roasted tomatoes, fresh garlic, bread, and freshly brewed coffee, Jon could smell his mother's homemade cookies and her deadly marshmallow squares. Jon could smell his mom's perfume, the soap she used, and the candles she lit on a dreary, rainy day.

Jon could smell all of this as he proceeded along the sidewalk and trotted up to his front door. Jon smelled all of this and so much more. And then he knew what he had all along.

Jon was home.

When Jon stepped in, his mother jumped to attention. Her reaction was not because of fear or shock, but because of joy and relief.

"You're home?"

"Yeah," Jon said to his mom. He smiled. "I'm home and you're awake."

Jon's mom nodded. "I am."

Rather than telling her what he had experienced tonight and what he had survived, Jon walked to the table and pulled out a chair. His dangerous situation was a story best saved for another day. Jon didn't want to tell it, not now, not while he had some time left with his mother.

Jon's mother walked to Jon with a pot in hand. She was just as smiley as she was when Jon first stepped through the door.

"Are you—"

"I'm fine," said Jon. He didn't want his mom to say more. No, Jon was here. He was here with her, and no matter what he did to get here, he made it. Nothing else mattered.

"How was—"

"It was fine." Before Jon's mother could go on, he decided to speak for her.

"It was perfect." While Jon was lying right through

his teeth, the truth didn't need to be said. As he learned now, some things in life just don't need to be.

"So...you're home?" Jon's mom said to her son.

She was glib as she filled Jon's mug with coffee. She filled hers as well. And, during a moment of sincere and contemplative silence, she looked at her boy and a slight tear seeped out from under her eye. Whenever he returned home, his mom would cry. Sometimes, she would sob. Jon knew his life didn't make things easier, nor did it change the profession he had selected. No, now he understood why his mother cried and why she would continue to cry whenever he walked through the door. Coming home was all part of Jon's validation. It was Jon's way of letting his mom know he would see her again. Jon relished in this concept. He hadn't observed it in its entirety, but now he did, and it was spectacular. He was right. His day was perfect.

Jon drank more coffee, leaned back, and lifted his leg onto another chair. He was so tired he could fall asleep right now but chose to stay awake.

"Are you sure you don't have any other place to be?" Jon's mom asked her son.

Jon grinned as he lifted his mug. He spoke to his mom like she was the only person in this room and now, as the only person on Earth.

She was and always would be.

"No," said Jon, still smiling and feeling the risen sun against his face. "I'm home. I'm exactly where I need to be."

ACKNOWLEDGMENTS

There are many people I need to thank for helping to publish this novel, and I think the best way to do this is to start at the beginning. First, I would like to extend my warmest and most sincere gratitude to Jake Bray, Mike Bray, Patience Bramlett, Rachel Del Grosso, and everyone else at Wolfpack and Rough Edges who has worked hard to bring this book to life. It has been a long road, but you took a chance on me as well as on this story, and I am immensely grateful for everyone's patience and understanding. You have allowed me to improve upon this book in ways I never thought possible. Long have I wanted to share stories about the enigmatic club, The Conquistador, as well as former Marine turned bouncer Jon Haze. And, because of your courage, these stories can now be told. I am also thankful to my fellow Goddardites, my Heebie Jeebie pals from Goddard College, for providing community and sanctity to a writer who was rejected by other MFA programs, and yet, you gave me a path and a voice when I thought I had none.

I would also like to thank my writing teachers: John McManus, Douglas Martin, Jan Clausen, Melodie Campbell, and David Bergen, who—though they did not assist in the creation of this novel—still, nonetheless, sculpted me into the creative artist I am today. Next, I would like to thank writers Brian Drake, Mark Allen, and Michael Black—gentlemen who have generously donated their time and their knowledge and who provided feedback to someone who was once a complete stranger. If not for your wondrous input and generosity, this book would not be where it is today and I would not be welcomed into such a glorious family of talented men and women. I also thank local writer friends, including Brent Van Staalduinen, who gave time and encouragement, and my great friend and confidant, Mark Jordan Manner. Mark, you guided me through this vast literary landscape, and without your help, I could not have navigated, conquered, or, for that matter, endured the many changes and challenges of this industry. I would also like to thank a man who is more than a friend but a mentor, Mr. John Corr. Candid and kind, receptive and lethal, you throw me on the mats, and still, you also help me both in and outside the dojo. I am thankful I met you when I did. I hope I might continue to train and learn alongside you in the years to come. I thank Naben Ruthnum, Lucy S. Snyder, Andrew F. Sullivan, and Amy Jones—writers who have taken time out of their busy schedules to look at my work and who have given me strength during tough and difficult times. I offer my gratitude to all my family and friends, including my teacher friends—good and decent colleagues. I thank my alma mater buds, Greg Zavitz, Brent Duguid, and Andrew Francella, someone who spends more time respecting my opinion than he does his own. I thank Dave Franciosa, Steve Legge, Christopher Barrett, and other like-minded geeks, and finally, to all the Mazza-Anthonys. However, I owe an extreme debt of gratitude to Sharmaine Gobind, not just a reader but a guardian angel. Sharmaine, you came to my aid when I was at such a low point and you quite literally brought me and my stories back from the dead. I could not have done this without you, and because you were there for me, I will always be there for you.

I thank the people on both sides of my splendid family:

My brother, Cody, my bud and coolest cat going. My best friend and sister, Jenna, a relentless voice of concern. My father, a decent man. My Bentley, my whole world. And above all else, my mother, Sheila. You are an amalgamation of encouragement, power, strength, and truth, which is often inconvenient, but most importantly...of love. Thank you for being my greatest fan, a great friend, and everything else in between. I thank you for following me on my many journeys. I always know where I'm going, and because of you, I am never lost.

A LOOK AT BOOK TWO:
REVENGE OF THE FALLEN SONS

In the aftermath of an unprecedented attack on New York's iconic nightclub, The Conquistador, Jon Haze, a former Marine turned elite bouncer, stands at the forefront of the club's defense. Bearing the title of "Doorman," Jon is dedicated to safeguarding those within. But the veneer of normalcy shatters when Jon encounters a nemesis whose prowess eclipses anything he's faced before—a ghost from the club's past, armed with deadly skills and a vendetta against The Conquistador. The fallen Doorman, expelled for transgressions unknown, returns with intimate knowledge of the club's defenses, targeting Jon and his fellow Doormen with a precision that hints at an insider's acumen.

As Jon grapples with this relentless enemy, he is forced to delve deeper into the murky waters of The Conquistador's legacy, unearthing truths that threaten to unravel the very fabric of his existence. Each revelation brings Jon closer to understanding the full scope of the battle he's been thrust into, a conflict steeped in betrayal, hidden agendas, and an insidious plot that extends far beyond the club's luxurious facade.

Faced with challenges that dwarf those of his military past, Jon must forge alliances with unlikely heroes, each with their own motives and secrets. Together, they stand against the Fallen Sons, whose plans for revenge could destabilize not just The Conquistador, but the entire city. Will Jon and the Doormen triumph over the specters of their past, or will the legacy of the Fallen Sons consume everything they've fought to protect?

AVAILABLE AUGUST 2024

ABOUT THE AUTHOR

Jarrett Mazza is a graduate of Goddard College's MFA in Creative Writing Program in Plainfield, Vermont as well as The Humber School For Writers.

Before completing his terminal degree, he studied writing at the University of Toronto School of Continuing Studies and comic book writing under Ty Templeton and Andy Schmidt. He has had stories published online in the GNU Journal, Bewildering Stories, Trembling With Fear, Aphelion, The Scarlet Leaf Review, and Toronto Prose Mill, The Fictional Cafe. His work is featured in anthologies by Silver Empire Publishing, a best seller, Zimbell House Publishing,NBH Publishing, MuseWrite Press, twice by Dragon Soul Press, Gypsum Sound Tales, Hellbound Books and The Ginosko Literary Journal. All are available on Amazon for purchase. He was also an Honorable Mention for the Freda Waldon Award for Fiction, nominated for an Indie Book award, and was featured as a visiting author for the nationwide We Read Canadian event in 2020. His mystery short story was published in an anthology under the editorial supervision of Michael Bracken and was published by Down and Out Books. He is currently a pulp fiction writer for the companies Airship 27 and Stormgate Press and Rough Edges Press.

He lives in Hamilton, Ontario.
You can follow him on Twitter @JarrettMazza